THE PARADISE KEY

THE PARADISE KEY
A HARVEY BENNETT THRILLER

NICK THACKER

The Paradise Key: Harvey Bennett Thrillers, Book #5
Copyright © 2022 by Nick Thacker
Published by Conundrum Publishing

PROLOGUE

THE CHILD SAT between the two trees, waiting for death. He knew it would come — his caretaker had told him as much. The two trees were supposed to provide comfort, the feeling of protection.

But they couldn't provide safety.

He would die, just as they all would. It was not a thought that plagued the boy as much as concerned him. He knew about death, as any child of his age did. He understood it, agreed with it. *Everything must die.* The jungle around him, the trees and plants and animals, all of it must go. It was told to him through the stories shared around the fire, and sometimes directly from the older children when they brought him out with the men to hunt.

He was not allowed to speak in those times, but that did not mean he misunderstood. He knew what death was, and he knew it was coming. The two trees offered solace, but not hope. They, too, would die. Not today, maybe many years from now, but they would shrivel up and disappear just like his ancestors — the mothers and fathers of his own mother and father, just as they had. His caretaker, too, would die.

But death was an easy thing to understand when you looked at it from a distance. When it was a story told by an elder around a fire, or a memory described by a hunter after a kill. The child remembered these stories, and they flooded his mind as they came back to him.

He remembered his parents' death, one after the other, struck down by a blow from a neighboring tribe, one even more ruthless than his own. They were gathering food, their only son between them. He was crouching in the brush when they came, not even slowing to search the area. So he had survived, and he had simultaneously learned of death firsthand.

He remembered the feeling. The quick snap of life taken away, not fully recognizing that he would never speak to them again. They were gone, taken brutally and quickly, yet all he could remember was the way his mother had dropped the food she was carrying, spilling it all over the forest floor. The waste of it; he hadn't even reached out to grab it.

He had returned to the village to find it had not been changed in any way. His family and friends worked, played, and slept, as if nothing had happened. No one had known about the attack until he had told them. There was a ceremony, as there always was, and then he was given to a caretaker and life had resumed as normal.

Death was here, and it was coming for him.

He felt it, stronger than he had felt it when it had taken his parents.

Stronger even than the feeling he had when listening to the stories. The forest took everyone, they said, but the taking was always far more brutal when it wasn't the forest doing the work.

He heard the screams. They'd found the village. His home, his caretaker. All of them were there. There were no hunts today, and there were no scouting groups. Everyone would be at the village, preparing the food and clothing. There were three women carrying children, and they would need preparations for their young. Everyone was there, everyone screaming. The men howled with sporadic war chants, not together and organized but scared, knowing.

He crouched closer to the forest floor. He touched the ground, feeling the forest crying out in complaint at the attack. It was all a part of them, a part of *him*. He was old enough to know that now. They were connected, the forest and the trees and the animals and the tribes. Even the tribes they fought, they were connected.

His caretaker had explained it once, in terms of a story that he had forgotten the details of. But he knew the premise: they were all part of the *same* story, part of the *same* world here. Life was far more important than bringing upon the death of others.

So he had run, without thinking and without looking back, when he had first heard the heavy trudging of the feet, crashing through the forest. They were not another tribe, they couldn't be. They were too loud, too big. He was scared, but he was able to push it away and focus on running toward the trees. The trees where the ceremony had taken place, the trees that towered over their small village. He had climbed them once, only to discover that the trees were hardly the tallest around. They poked at the canopy and even scraped it some places, but the inside roof of the canopy itself, he was surprised to learn, was formed by the bottom of even taller trees.

The world was a large place, he had learned that day. It was large, and he was a small part of it. He didn't know how large — his people didn't worry about things like that — but he was always fascinated by the thought of it. The trees he had come to trust loomed over him, reminding him that even when he thought the biggest thing around was staring down at him, there was something even bigger out there, somewhere.

Those bigger things were crashing around, causing the screams and subsequent silencing of his people back in the village. He didn't dare look, for fear of what he might see. Maybe it would be over soon, but what then? Where would he go? The nearest tribe was hostile, and they would jump at the chance to bring death upon him just as the bigger people were bringing now.

So what to do? He waited, crouched and small and shivering in the forest, the two trees offering what little they could — solace and sympathy, which he could feel through the ground. They were telling him that they were there, but that they were sorry they couldn't do more. They were sorry they couldn't help, that they —

One of the bigger people crashed around and came to his spot by the tree. He thought for a moment, hoped, that they wouldn't see him. That he had somehow become a tree, or a bush, or something that didn't seem like it needed death brought upon it.

But they saw him. He knew it when the feet of the thing turned toward him, the shadow of it creeping out and over and around him, consuming him like its owner didn't even need to move to know it had captured him. He sobbed, once, then told himself to be strong. *Death comes upon us all*, he told himself. *Death is not the enemy.*

The feet stepped forward, and he smelled the person. This was certainly not another tribe. The legs were covered, as well as the feet. Some sort of cloth or skin, bunched in places but sturdy, stained with the dirt and mud of trekking through the jungle for days. Splashes of silt on the things covering the feet. Not sandals, but something bigger. Stronger.

The feet moved again, but not toward him. They simply shifted, moving slightly, leaving an ugly streak in the mud. He felt a hand grasping at his hair, which he had kept just long enough to cover his ears. It was black, oily and nice, some of the nicest hair of any of the children his age. He was proud of it.

The person's hand ripped his hair upward, and he yelped in pain. His hair stayed attached to his head, and he stood up with the force of the person's hand. He fought against the hand, but the hand was wrenched around his hair and yanking him up, up.

He cried now, openly. He was a child, and he knew children were allowed to cry. They were encouraged to think about their tears with wisdom, as reactions to a particular feeling. If one could understand the feeling, one could fight against the tears, it was said.

He knew the feeling — pain. Loss. He wanted his caretaker.

He wanted his mother. His father.

He wanted *anyone*.

He looked up, forced to by the hand that was wrapped tightly into his hair. The face was of a man's, but the man's skin was light, not bronzed by the sun but browned by the mud. His eyes sparkled, a light-greenish blue that the boy had never seen before.

He was suddenly scared. The fear gripped him tighter than the hand in his hair, and he sobbed once again. The man stood, frozen. Examining him. Questioning him.

He wanted to speak, to ask why. To understand. The tears kept coming. The man kept staring.

Finally the man released his hand from the boy's hair and reached into a bag he was wearing. It was also made of skin, some sort of leather that the boy hadn't seen before. The man watched the boy with those sparkling eyes as he fumbled through his bag.

He retrieved something from inside the bag, held it tight in his hand. It was sharp, pointed and clear, like water that had been hardened into a tube shape and placed around a shiny, bright point. He pointed it at the boy, near his left arm.

The boy shook, sobbing.

The man looked down at the boy, smiled. He opened his mouth and spoke words the boy didn't know, didn't understand.

"You will do just fine, boy," the man said. "Just fine, indeed."

CHAPTER 1

THE MAN WATCHED him through the glass, his hands and arms pressed up against the pane, like an animal anxiously awaiting for his captor to feed him. The man cocked his head sideways, watching Dr. Joseph Lin as he fumbled around with the gray, metal box in his hands.

Dr. Lin knew what the man wanted. It was what they all wanted. *Freedom.*

The man was docile, tamed through hundreds of cocktails of medications and sedatives, but Dr. Lin couldn't help but feel like the subjects were always watching for a mistake, for an opening. Something they might be able to take advantage of.

He wouldn't fail today. He hadn't failed yet, and he wouldn't now. The task was simple, mindless even, but then again that was why it was easy to fail when performing it. The mundane tasks were the ones to be worried about — a person could go through the motions much more easily with these types of tasks and assignments, and that's where mistakes were made.

It wasn't the large-scale, complicated things he needed to worry about. The multi-layered tasks that required a nuanced understanding of something or a delicate hand were, in a way, easier to perform flawlessly. He was the best in the world at those types of things, which was why he was here in the first place.

It was the *easy* things, the simple and repetitive that he needed to be most careful with. That was how he — a world-renowned scientist — had ended up doing the job of one of the lab assistants; the girl had been careless, she had lapsed and allowed a small oversight to become a large mistake.

And here in the lab, mistakes were unacceptable. The assistant had learned that the hard way, but in this environment there were no second chances. There were no lessons — it was perform or be removed.

Dr. Lin was disappointed with the girl's removal, as she had been a good assistant. But he also understood the reasons behind it. He was calm, centered, not allowing the assistant's removal to affect his work, and for that he was proud. He could do the work of a lowly assistant. He could stoop to that level and get the job done. It would mean a later night for him — his own work sat by idly awaiting his return — but he would finish.

The man brushed up against the glass, an inquisitive look on his face. Dr. Lin watched him for a moment. The man turned his head again, his eyes searching the doctor's face. There would be nothing there for him to read, Dr. Lin knew. Even if Dr. Lin had been the type of man to allow the weakness of emotion to show on his face, this man on the other side of the glass was incapable of recognizing and acknowledging it. That function of his neural programming had been stifled to the point of being useless. The 'empathy gene,' or 'emotional resonance,' the marketing suits upstairs called it. The ability for a human to recognize, acknowledge, and respond to a particular micro-expression.

Dr. Lin opened the metal box. The lid snapped up abruptly, as if it had been fitted for a slightly smaller box, and Dr. Lin peered inside. He reached in and grabbed the first tube that lay on top of the pile. He closed the box, then set it down on the cart that sat next to him.

He reached for the syringe on the cart and placed the tube inside the back of the syringe.

The man inside watched him. Waiting. Knowing what was coming but unable to react in any overt way.

Dr. Lin pressed the tube down into the syringe until he felt and heard the slight popping sound that told him the medication's seal had been opened and was ready for injection. He turned to the man behind the glass and held up the medication.

"Time for your medicine, 31-3," he said. His voice was quiet, softened from exhaustion. He'd already been awake for twenty-four hours and he knew his job would continue for at least another ten. He was glad there were no meetings scheduled, no reason to use his voice much.

The man eyed him, not nodding or shaking his head. He stared. Waited. Knowing. Patient yet unaware of his own patience. Hungry, yet sated. Just... *there*.

Dr. Lin slid open the fist-sized door in the center of the glass, revealing a rectangular hole. The scent from the other side wafted out, a mixture of sweat and feces. He made a face, then recovered. The man did not move. Dr. Lin moved back toward the hole, involuntarily holding his breath. The man nudged toward the rectangular hole, then stopped about three inches from it. He looked up at Dr. Lin, waited for him to nod to continue, then he pushed himself against the glass. The skin of his right arm, just below the shoulder, was pushing through the rectangular hole in the glass now, and Dr. Lin reached down and aimed the point of the needle at the open area of skin.

He leaned forward. Pushed the needle onto the man's skin. The man watched, interested, yet unaware of what was happening. Dr. Lin held his breath, an old habit. *Helps to calm the shaking,* his residency supervisor used to say. *Everyone shakes, even when we don't realize we're shaking.* He poked the skin, watched the man for any reaction. There was none. He drove the needle down, farther into the layer beneath the skin, right before it hit bone.

Dr. Lin continued to watch the man's face with his peripheral vision, another habit yet knowing what he would see. *Nothing.* The man was completely unfazed by the needle, just as he had been every other time. Dr. Lin waited a beat, then began pushing the medication down through the syringe, out the hole in the end of the needle, and into the man's bloodstream.

If there was pain, the man didn't register it. He stared up at Dr. Lin, both men nearly eye to eye, and Dr. Lin moved his gaze to focus directly on the man's face. Still no change. Still no registration of emotion. No registration of anything, really.

But Dr. Lin felt something. He felt the wave of surprise, the bizarre realization of what was happening. Or rather, what *wasn't* happening. The scientific reasons behind it, still unknown to him or anyone else, the hundreds of studies and research papers he'd read and pored over, the talks and presentations he'd heard and seen over twenty years of practicing medicine. His mind raced through these resources but every time it came up blank. Every time there was a disconnect, as if there were something out there he was forgetting that would explain everything.

But there *was* nothing out there. He had checked. They all had. For years, they'd checked and re-checked. They had done the research, the tests, analyzed the results. None of it lined up with what they were seeing here. Dr. Lin was the best in the world at this very thing, and he had been stumped for going on three years. It was a professional slight, and he intended to fix it. He would find the answer, and he would publish it. He would prevail, as he had with every other challenge throughout his distinguished career.

He finished administering the dosage of medication and looked back down to the syringe. He extracted it from the man's upper arm slowly and carefully, just as he had a thousand times with a thousand patients, back when he was merely a practicing physician. It was a learned habit, one he could do in his sleep. But he *didn't* approach the task lightly. Something simple like this, the extraction of an empty syringe following the medicating procedure, seemed like such an easy, simple thing.

But that was how mistakes were made. By assuming one was better than the task they were performing. By taking their expertise for granted. That had happened to his assistant, and now she was no longer with him. So he did not take the task lightly. He extracted the syringe purposefully, rolling it slightly between his thumb and forefinger to ensure none of the serum would drip. It would also prevent any blood from pooling around the tiny wound.

He focused on the syringe, taking his time. Ensuring there were no mistakes.

That was why he didn't see the man's face. Dr. Lin was focusing on the wrong thing, looking at the wrong area behind the glass. He was gazing intently at the man's shoulder and the syringe he was carefully extracting from it, so he didn't notice at first.

Then something in his subconscious called his attention to it. Screamed at him, as if begging him to look up and take note of the man's face once again. He felt the syringe shake in his grip, faltering a bit. He blinked. Once, twice. Then he looked up and saw the man.

31-3. *Thirty-one dash three* was how they said it. The thirty-first group of subjects they'd been testing, and the first male in the group. Related to all of the other subjects in some way.

Dr. Lin took a step backward, then another. Steady at first, then nearly stumbling. He felt the rolling cart behind him as he backed into it, still unable to take his eyes off the man behind the glass. He stared, knowing the man was staring back at him and within seconds the cameras mounted around the room would analyze the situation and automatically send in an alert. They would see Lin staring, record the infraction, and log it in the security manifest.

But he didn't care.

How could he? What he was seeing right now was simply... unexplainable.

And yet his entire job here was to find just this very thing, and then explain it. It had always been a tall order, but then again no one seemed to believe that this was even possible.

He continued to stare, even as he heard the beeping warning sound alerting him to his mistake. Dr. Lin held his pose, staring straight into the eyes of the man on the other side of the glass, his mouth opening and shutting slowly as he tried to comprehend.

Why? Why now? And how?

The man stared back, his eyes as expressionless and as stoic as ever, but it wasn't his *eyes* Dr. Lin was focusing on.

It was the man's mouth, upturned slightly at the sides.

The man behind the glass was smiling.

CHAPTER 2

"ANY IDEA WHERE IT'S FROM?" Reggie asked. He was standing near the television, where Mr. E and his wife were onscreen, staring back at him.

Mrs. E shook her head. *'Unfortunately, no. We will get the lab scans back next week, if not sooner. But — and we are no scientists — our initial investigation leads us to believe that the skull is from Central or South America.'*

Mr. E leaned in, his characteristically stoic expression tightening just a bit. He moved as though he had no neck, no ability to shift his head from its fixed spot on his upper body. *'My wife is correct,'* he said, *'but she downplays her knowledge of anthropology.'*

"Well, I'll take her word for it then," Reggie said. "Somewhere in Central or South America. How can you tell?"

Mrs. E looked at something offscreen for a moment. *'Human anatomy, and differences in cranial structure among known regions of the world. I just ran a simple search, really. The results are promising, but, as I said, we are not scientists.'*

Reggie nodded. He was sitting in the makeshift office space he'd added to the corner of a small apartment living room in Anchorage, Alaska. The organization he worked for — Civilian Special Operations — had furnished a one-bedroom apartment in the nearby city while they finished their additions to the full-time operations headquarters. He was excited to see what the cabin-turned-headquarters would look like, and he was even more excited to see the reaction of the cabin's owner.

Harvey Bennett was a close friend of his, but he couldn't imagine a person more resistant to the massive renovation taking place at his home. He'd purchased the cabin a couple years ago, but the CSO had recruited Ben and Reggie, offered Ben enough money that it was stupid to refuse them, and began turning his beloved two-room log home into a modern communications oasis. There would be an entire wing added, with a second story, and enough square footage inside to fit three more of Ben's cabins.

Reggie smiled as he thought about it. Ben would pretend to be upset, complain to him and his fiancee, Julie, about it, but secretly love the new, upgraded space. He would enjoy working there with his friends, and he would enjoy the company.

"So if the lab comes back with the same results, will we be able to narrow it down from there?"

Mr. E nodded. *'Yes, but the lab should be able to do that for us. They have the ability to isolate the specific ancestral geography of the specimen, assuming they have matching samples in their database.'*

"I see," Reggie said. "So it's a waiting game."

They were waiting on the results of laboratory testing on a human skull they discovered two months ago in the Rocky Mountains, near Glacier National Park in Montana. The skull had been found with a map, silver and gold coins, and had been stored in a chest inside a cave. All of it had been very exciting, and Reggie's interest in history and longing for adventure had immediately been piqued.

But from the moment they'd brought the skull in to the lab, Reggie knew it was going to be a 'waiting game.' Wait for the skull to be admitted, wait for a team to begin the analysis, wait for results. He would have been surprised with the slow pace of work if he hadn't been in the Army for years. Government work *always* took forever. The lab itself wasn't a government lab, but it was funded with government money.

He had been anxiously awaiting an update for over a month, and his weekly check-ins with Mr. E hadn't been enough to keep him sated. Now, to hear that they were so close to an answer, yet still without a definitive direction to explore, he was growing more impatient.

'Unfortunately yes,' Mr. E said. *'But we are optimistic the laboratory will be able to point us in the right direction.'*

Reggie pushed the chair away from the glass desk. It was a corner desk, two simple slabs of tempered glass on a cheap aluminum frame that he'd picked up used, but he liked the simplicity of it. It didn't interfere with the rest of the room, gently falling into the background of the space unless he wanted to see it. Aside from the desk, the chair, and a couch, there wasn't much else in the room for decor. He had a television, but it was currently being used as his computer monitor, so the couch sat in the center of the living room and stared at the blank off-white wall.

He stood up and stretched. He felt cooped up in here, in his temporary home. He had nowhere to go, and he wasn't one for walking around aimlessly in search of something to do. He hated boredom, feared it like the plague, and sitting in an Anchorage apartment with no one but a computer screen to talk to was starting to wear him down. He had books, but he'd already read them. He had food, and while he liked to cook, he didn't like the temptation — anything he cooked he would eat.

So he was frustrated. He wanted out, wanted something to do. He wanted a mission.

"Come on, E," he said, talking to the opposite wall, knowing the microphone was more than capable of picking up his voice in the otherwise quiet room. "I need to *do* something. Can't I at least get a jump on it? Take a flight to Mexico City or somewhere south of the border?”

There was no response. He waited. Still nothing. He whirled around, expecting to see that the video had temporarily seized. The internet connectivity in the apartment was fast, technically within the realm of what the marketers at the telecommunications companies called 'high-speed,' but compared to what he was used to it was no better than dialup.

Mr. E owned a telecommunications company, a small one in terms of market cap, but through a brilliant career of networking and hobnobbing with the DC crowd, he had built an empire with very little overhead and the cash flow to rival the slickest of Silicon Valley startups.

He looked again at the screen, pulling the two-dimensional people on it into focus. Mr. and Mrs. E stared back at him in stark contrast to one another. Mr. E was thin, graying, almost frail in build and leaning into the camera. Mrs. E. was wider in the shoulders, taller, built like a Russian tank, and smiling a wide, unnatural grin.

He almost laughed. He had seen the woman smile — they had spent some time together in Antarctica and shared pleasantries on numerous occasions after that, but the wide, sheepish grin was *his* trademark, not hers. She didn't wear it well, either — it came across as an odd, forced rhythm, like something she knew she needed to do but not something she really knew *how* to do.

“Wh — why are you smiling?” Reggie asked. He was genuinely confused.

'We are *sending you somewhere,'* Mrs. E said. *'So pack your bags.'*

“I never got a chance to *un*pack,” he replied.

'Perfect. Your flight leaves tomorrow morning, first thing. Can you get a ride to the airport?'

He nodded, pulling out his cellphone and holding it up to the camera. “Kids are using these little computer thingies for all sorts of things, including scheduling rides to the airport and calling people.”

If Mr. E got the joke, it wasn't apparent on his face. He sat, motionless, onscreen. Mrs. E somehow found a way to widen her smile. It stretched her cheeks out, making her face look gaunt, like a skeleton that had been forced through the business end of a steamroller.

"Okay," he said. "What's the ruse? Where are you sending me?"

Mrs. E flashed a glance at her husband, who revealed nothing. *Man, that guy can act,* he thought. Mrs. E, gleaning nothing from the man sitting next to her, turned back to the camera and faced Reggie.

'*Cozumel, Mexico,*' she said.

"Cozumel? That's an island, right?"

'*It is. And you need to be there by 3:30pm, local time, tomorrow.*'

He frowned. "Why? I thought we didn't have conclusive data from the lab yet?"

'*We do not,*' she said. '*There has been a development elsewhere, and we would like you to follow up on it.*'

"A development?"

'*A situation, if you will.*'

He walked back to the television screen and computer monitor, pushing the chair out of the way. "What kind of *situation?* And what am I supposed to do in Cozumel?"

Mrs. E told him, all while her husband sat silent next to her.

No way, he thought. *There's no way I can do that.*

He'll kill me.

CHAPTER 3

"DR. LIN," the man said again, calling his attention back. "Would you please explain to us your infraction?"

Dr. Lin swallowed. He wasn't good with confrontation. He was a scientist, a doctor, ready to analyze and prescribe and confident in his abilities, but he had never been comfortable with this sort of thing. The board sat around him, three of them in person and four of them digitally filling the screens that curved around one edge of the room.

He watched their expressions, tried to read them. The people on the screens — all calling in from their locations around the world — were most difficult. They seemed to feel his scrutiny, and were working to mask their emotion by staring straight into their cameras. He looked at the man who had spoken, then swallowed again. *This man was incapable of hiding his emotion.*

And right now, the man's emotion was especially easy to read: he was livid.

"*Dr. Lin,*" he said a third time. "Do I need to remind you of the gravity of this —"

"N — no," Dr. Lin stammered. "I apologize, I — I was just collecting my thoughts."

The man's eyebrow rose, but he still looked as though he were frowning. "Well I do hope you've *collected* them all." He made a point of checking his watch, a large flourish of spinning it out and around his wrist while bringing his forearm out in front of his torso. If Dr. Lin hadn't been so terrified, he would have been annoyed.

"Yes," he said. "I have. Again, I am sorry. My deviation was remedied, and it is one that will not be repeated, under any circum —"

"There were to be no deviations under any circumstances *in the first place*, Dr. Lin," the man said. The woman on the screen behind him was nodding.

"Yes, I — that was clear, yes. I apologize."

The man stared.

"It was a surprise to me as well. I was unaware of the applied effect of patient 31-3's latest dosage, and —"

One of the board members listening in on one of the screens, a man Dr. Lin had never met in person, interrupted. "Dr. Lin, would you kindly speak as though you are addressing a group of *non-medical* professionals?" the man's voice was thick with a southern American accent, and he smiled a bit as he said it. Dr. Lin didn't for a moment believe the smile.

"Sorry. Yes, I only meant that I was not aware that the dosage *had* an immediate effect."

"Is it your job to be aware of these things?"

Lin swallowed again. "Yes."

"And why were you not aware?"

"I — I was attempting to ensure..." he stopped, looked at the southern gentleman, then continued. "I was trying to make sure there were no mistakes with the medication."

"So you weren't looking at the subject."

"I was not, no. But the reaction would have taken me by surprise nonetheless, whether or not I was watching the patient's face."

"Subject," the man said, correcting him.

"Yes."

"So you were surprised by the *subject's* reaction? Why?"

Dr. Lin frowned. *Do I really need to spell it out for them?* These were the men and women who had *built* this company. Surely they didn't have time for this.

"It will all be detailed in my report, which I will prepare and —"

"I'm most certain it will," the man said. "But since we were already having a board meeting, and I'm sure we are all most interested in what you discovered, I would ask that you indulge us."

Dr. Lin nodded. "Very well. I was administering a dosage of the medication we have designed specifically for 31-3. It was the fifty-third dosage in a nearly two-year timespan, and it was a routine operation."

"For 'routine operations' such as these, do we not have laboratory assistants?"

"We do," Lin responded. "The woman on duty was recently removed."

The man watched Lin's face. He knew everything already, so this was a game. Cat and mouse, and Lin felt the trap closing around him. "And for what reason was she removed?"

He felt the tension in the room shift, tightening up. The woman and man on the screen to his left leaned in toward their computers. The man to his right, sitting next to Dr. Lin's boss, the man conducting the interrogation, looked up at him anxiously. They didn't know the full story, and Dr. Lin was hoping they would have found out some other way than this.

Any other way than this.

"She — there was a deviating incident."

"Also involving 31-3?"

"Also involving 31-3."

"And what was the outcome of that incident?"

"She was relieved of her duty."

"She was *removed*," the man corrected.

"Yes."

The man looked down. There was a manila folder on the tabletop in front of him, but it was closed. He placed his hands on it, felt its surface, then jerked his head back up and stared at Dr. Lin. His bright, large eyes bored into Lin's, and he could almost feel the pressure, pushing him backwards. This man got high from encounters such as this. He *longed* for them. The dimple on his cheek grew, punctuating the man's thoughts.

"So, Dr. Lin, there was an infraction involving your laboratory assistant, and she was removed. A day later you were administering a dosage of the subject's medication and *you* were found to have instigated a infraction. What, may I ask, was the nature of this deviation?"

Dr. Lin sighed. He knew there was no sense hiding behind it now. They would all find out, so he might as well attempt to control what was said. He shifted on his feet.

"The man smiled."

"The *subject* smiled?"

Dr. Lin nodded. "He did. Just after I had finished. He smiled, directly at me."

"You provoked him."

"I did no such thing," Dr. Lin said. "I administered the dosage, extracted the needle, and I saw him smiling."

The woman onscreen sniffed, moving around in her chair to vie for attention without coming across as rude. The man addressing Dr. Lin stopped and turned, waiting. "Dr. Lin," the woman said. "Is it not *impossible* for these subjects to be able to experience what you are describing?"

"We believed that to be the case, yes," Dr. Lin said. "The dosage has always had the unintended side effect of removing the ability for our subjects to respond to emotional stimuli. Smiling, waving, arching of eyebrows — these are all impossible tasks."

"Yet, 31-3 *smiled* at you."

"Indeed."

The man took over the interrogation once again by clearing his throat. "Dr. Lin, the interest of this meeting with you today is not to discuss the nature of the subject's response — that will come at a later time. Rather, we would like to discuss the nature of the deviation itself."

"I understand, and I will ensure that no more such deviation will —"

"Dr. Lin," the man said. "You are our best researcher. Hired away from one of the world's most premier health institutions. We cannot afford to waste a valuable asset such as yourself."

Dr. Lin bowed his head. "Thank you."

"That said," the man continued, "we cannot afford *any more infractions*. Provoking the subjects, as you wrote early on, will only lead to wildly unpredictable outcomes."

"But I didn't *provoke* —"

The man held up a hand. "We must inform you that any more deviations or infractions by anyone on your team will result in your immediate removal from this facility."

Now he was angry. He had *never* been 'removed.' He had never even been let go. He was the best, the one in demand. He waited for offers to come to *him*, not the other way around. How dare these people stomp on his reputation and his career solely out of retribution for an event they couldn't even *understand*? How dare they assume something had happened one way, when he had specifically told them —

"Dr. Lin? Do you understand?"

Lin's face darkened. He couldn't help it any longer. He was a pawn to these people. A tool to use, abuse, and discard. Like his assistant had been. She had made a mistake, and she knew the consequences. But he wasn't an *assistant*. He was an esteemed practitioner. He wasn't one to make mistakes. He hadn't *made* a mistake when he'd stared back at the man behind the glass. He *knew* what he was doing, and he was *observing* the subject. His patient. They didn't understand that.

And he knew that now. They *couldn't* understand that.

"Yes," he said. "I understand perfectly."

CHAPTER 4

07:34 AM. BBC WORLD NEWS.
FOR IMMEDIATE RELEASE.
LIMA, PERU.

INITIAL REPORTS SEEM *to indicate the discovery and subsequent disappearance of a previously uncontacted tribe of natives in the Peruvian highlands. Located 300 kilometers north of Cusco, Peru, near the dense Parque Nacional Alto Purus and the closest city of Alerta, the last known location of the mysterious city of natives is known only to those who have traveled to visit it.*

Dr. Rodney Barrett, esteemed archeologist and professor emeritus of Classical Archeology at King's College, reported in an unpublished journal article that 'there have been signs of habitation in the town, though recent investigation has turned up nary a thing. Quite a puzzling instance, indeed.'

Barrett declined to be interviewed, citing jet lag due to his recent jaunt to the jungled region bordering Brazil and the Amazon Rainforest, but the journal article he plans to publish next month indicates evidence that Barrett believes the tribe to have been a docile, localized group of native peoples.

'The town is really much more like a small group of huts, still well-maintained, with a few larger structures intended for the larger requirements of civilised life. As an example, the structure we are calling Main No. 1, situated in the central area of the 'town,' is a large, rectangular building crafted from reeds and wood poles, and we believe it to be the central gathering place for ritualistic medical practices as well as meal gatherings.'

While this reads typical of many such Amazonian settlements both in the Basin and in neighboring countries, Barrett went on in the article to describe a conversation with one of his colleagues at King's College regarding the most unique feature of this find:

'The town itself has been abandoned, and from what we can gather, it was abandoned quite recently. It really is a curious thing; the town seems to have simply disappeared. There was smoke from an earlier fire, there were canoes filled with lines and tools and even the recent catch of the day. The main hall was found to have a working smoking pit, filled with the meat of fish and game and well past the point of being done.'

Dr. Barrett's archeological team, consisting of eight Peruvian- and Brazilian-born porters, three undergraduate work-study students, and three graduate-level archeology students, have all corroborated Barrett's theory.

Said one student of the expedition's final destination: 'It truly is quite strange. There was a town, and every indication that this town had been — quite recently — inhabited insofar as a working town should be, but there was no one around. No human interaction with us, and none on our return trip. Very spooky indeed.'

Barrett will make a statement to the department chair and attending guests in a week, though no specific date has been set; further information will be posted online as it is received.

CHAPTER 5

HARVEY 'BEN' Bennett looked out at the cerulean waters of the Caribbean. The points of the waves lanced up and down, miniature pinpricks of lighter blue against the deep blue backdrop of the ocean. It was never-ending, and yet it was full, loaded with life and creatures and an entire world he didn't understand.

He'd never been drawn to the ocean. He didn't dislike it, per se, but it was something he'd never felt a deep desire to be near. He preferred the woods, the deep scent of pines and earth, the moist air and cold winters. Ben had thought long and hard about this, about why a person would be more drawn to the warm, maritime climate of a beachfront umbrella than a secluded, cold cabin, but he hadn't been able to reach a believable conclusion. He had to chalk it up to a simple difference in personality — some people preferred one, while some people preferred the exact opposite.

And this was the exact opposite of what he preferred. Again, he didn't necessarily *dislike* it, but he would never have chosen it as a retreat. He never would have sprung for the multi-thousand-dollar vacation he currently found himself enjoying.

This all was Julie's idea, something she'd been pushing him toward for nearly a year. Juliette Richardson was the only person on the planet he'd ever met who was as stubborn as him, and for some unbelievably annoying reason, it made him love her even more. She wasn't going to take no for an answer when she'd made her mind up, and this vacation was no exception.

She'd begged, pleaded, and argued, and finally had simply started planning the trip on her own, fully aware of the power she had over him. She set the dates, knowing he was otherwise unoccupied and completely free, and she set the schedule, knowing his preferences, tastes, and expectations.

For that reason, he had little to complain about. He was watching the ocean of the southern Caribbean pass him by while sitting on a deck chair on something called a 'Lido Deck.' The railing in front of him blocked the view of the water directly below the port side of the ship, but there was enough water in the immediate vicinity that there was plenty to go around in his vision, all the way up to the point where the setting sun met the flat, horizontal line of the horizon.

He was wearing a tight-fitting bathing suit that Julie had picked out for him. Flowers that didn't look like any flowers he'd ever seen in real life, white on a blue background. The blue was a good color, but he was constantly feeling like the suit was too tight, revealing more than it had been designed to cover. His shirt was lying next to the chair, and whenever a person walked near the chair he felt as though he needed to reach down and grab it, cover himself, and apologize for exposing his upper body. Julie seemed to be able to read directly into his struggle and know exactly what he was going through, which she used to her advantage by poking fun and making jokes at his expense.

The worst of it for Ben, however, was the footwear. She'd purchased matching sets of flip-flops, which she'd claimed were a popular type of sandal worn by many people, but he had never in his life of thirty-three years felt like he'd had less on his feet. He would have been more comfortable in socks. At least socks stayed on his feet. She told him the flip-flops would take practice to get used to, and his argument against that line of reasoning had been that any type of footwear that required 'practice to get used to' was better off staying in the suitcase.

The flip-flops were currently hanging loosely off his feet, the space between his first and second toes the only thing holding them onto his body. They had started to form to his feet, and he was trying desperately to change his mind about how comfortable they had become.

"What are you thinking about?" Julie asked from the lounge chair next to him.

He looked over, taking an extra few seconds to enjoy the *other* view. He had been enjoying himself on the trip so far, contrary to what he'd initially expected. The food was amazing, the entertainment had lived up to expectations, and the overall feeling of relaxation had somehow snuck up on him and set in, against his desire to push it away. But the best part of the trip, hands down, was the view.

Not the view of the ocean, but the view on deck.

Specifically of his fiancee, and her choice of garments for this trip.

Julie was currently wearing a bikini emblazoned with the Australian flag, the blues and reds and whites all working together to form an image less enticing than the image of the person it was intended to cover.

He shifted in his chair, not taking his eyes off her.

"Ben," she said, "I'm up here."

He smiled, a goofy open-mouthed grin. "Sorry. I — I really like that swimsuit."

"You like *all* of my swimsuits."

He nodded. *Nothing I can say to that.*

"Did you hear me?" she asked.

"About your swimsuits?"

"About what you're thinking," she said.

He laughed. "I was thinking about your swimsuits," he said.

She smiled back from behind large, oval-shaped sunglasses. "Well, *besides* that. What's on your mind?"

He shrugged, looking once again at the endless expanse of blue. "I don't know. Nothing, really. Just enjoying it all."

"Are you?"

He rolled to his side. "What do you mean? Do I not seem like I'm enjoying it here?"

Julie nodded. "You do, but you're also... contemplative. You're not usually lost in your own thoughts."

He stopped and thought for a moment. She was right. *But what am I thinking?* He was confused about it as well. He was sitting on the deck of a massive cruise ship, luxurious and designed exclusively for his comfort and entertainment, with the woman of his dreams, and he wasn't able to feel completely satisfied.

"I... I just feel like there's something else."

"Something else?"

He frowned. "I mean like there's something missing."

It was Julie's turn to laugh. "Ben, you're in the middle of an ocean on a floating 5-star hotel with free food. What else could there be?"

"I know, I know," he said. "It's not that. This — all of this — is amazing. And you're here. It's not the trip, I guess."

"What is it?"

He looked over at her. "Life?"

"Life?"

"Yeah, I guess."

"Sorry Ben, I'm not sure I understand your meaning."

He sensed a bit of hostility in her voice — a warning shot. *Say what I think you're saying and we're going to have a fight.*

He tried to backpedal. "No, it's not about you at all."

She raised an eyebrow.

"Seriously," he said. "I love you. That hasn't changed. But think about where I was two years ago. We had never met, and I was living in a cabin and chasing bears out of campsites."

Ben had spent the entirety of his adult life as a ranger at Yellowstone National Park. It had been a perfect fit for him, a naturally reclusive and isolated individual. When a terrorist threat forced his hand, he and Juliette Richardson had been pushed together to find out what had happened and clean up the mess.

They had grown close and then fallen in love, and their adventures together had taken them from Yellowstone to the Amazon rainforest, then to Antarctica and a quick tour of United States Midwest. It wasn't a life Ben could have ever imagined, and while he felt proud of his accomplishments over the past year and a half, there was still... something.

"You want to go back to Yellowstone? Keep chasing bears?"

He shrugged. "Sometimes it seems to have some appeal."

"I get that, Ben," Julie said, still laying back while the sun bathed her body. Her head was leaned over, facing Ben, and he could see the outline of her large eyes through the dark ovals of her sunglasses. "But everyone has to grow up."

"Grow up?" he asked. He raised an eyebrow, squinted with his other eye. It was a look she would know well.

"Sorry," she said. "I didn't mean it like that. But still, everyone changes," she said.

"Maybe I don't change."

She smiled. "You certainly change less than anyone I've ever met. And that's what I love about you. But still — don't you agree that it's time to move on from the 'strong silent type?'"

He sat up, looked out at the water, then turned to his fiancee. "I'm sorry," he said. "What's wrong with the 'strong silent type?' and more importantly, why do I *need* to change?"

She shook her head. "You're not getting the point. You don't *need* to change, but that doesn't mean you *won't*. Everyone does, Ben, it's the natural order of things."

"Well what am I supposed to change *into*, then?" he asked.

"I don't know, Ben. But you can't just keep moping all the time. We're supposed to be relaxing. Enjoying ourselves. We're getting married in two months, Ben, and you haven't even thought to ask me how the wedding planning is going."

He was beginning to get a little frustrated. After all, he had been the one to bring this all up in the first place, and now she was making their little spat about something else entirely. He didn't ask about the wedding plans because he didn't *care* — he just wanted to marry her, and he didn't care how it all happened. And besides, she was enjoying it. She loved this sort of thing, so he stayed out of her way.

He sighed, reaching down for his drink. It was something with rum in it, a large cornucopia of at least two different liquors, three different fruit juices, and a lot of ice.

A *lot* of ice.

He stared at the melting pot of booze and fruit juice and mostly ice and sighed again. He felt the frustration growing again as he thought back to his earlier conversation with Julie, which had led to an argument about money. She had wanted these fancy cocktails, but he hadn't been enthused about the nearly twenty-dollar price tag for a bucket of ice with some flavor thrown in. She had argued that they weren't really paying for them anyway, that the drinks — like everything else — were on the company's tab, and that he should forget about it and focus on just relaxing.

"I can't relax," he finally said.

"Yeah, we all know that," she said. "Anyone who's ever met you. We know."

"Well, I wish I could. That's all," he said. He was still sitting up, still rotating the slush around in his drink, waiting for a cruise employee to walk by and ask him for a refill.

"I wish you could, too," Julie said. She laid back down on the lounge chair and stared straight up into the sun. It was just past noon, and the deck was hopping with just about every passenger on the boat. Kids splashed and yelled in one of the three pools, while adults and teens vied for a spot in one of the four hot tubs situated around the perimeter of the deck.

And there were two more decks similar to this one, one at the front of the ship and one near the stern, both up one level. He had been amazed at the size of the place when they'd first embarked, and the novelty hadn't yet worn off. Julie had caught him more than once staring up at light fixtures and the elaborate ceiling decorations with his mouth hanging open.

"This isn't about you, is it?" Julie asked.

He looked over at her. She wasn't looking back at him, but he shook his head anyway. "No, I guess it's not."

"Well you'd better figure out what you're going to do about it, Ben," she said. "We're on a boat in the middle of the ocean. You can't change anything here."

He stood up, stretched, and left his fiancée basking in the sun as he went to find a drink refill.

CHAPTER 6

HE BALANCED the drink on the edge of the counter with one hand as he waited for the bartender to give him the check. The thing was inside of a real pineapple, full of rum and juice and all sorts of sweet things. An extra-long toothpick poked through two slices of orange, a banana, and a maraschino cherry before plunging into the wide, open top of the pineapple.

Ridiculous, he thought.

Ben had only wanted a Rum Runner, a tiki drink made with rum and banana and usually a type of liqueur like blackberry. It was sweet, fruity, and felt summery, and he liked them. But the drink he was holding now seemed more like the centerpiece at a tropical wedding than a drink. The straw even spun a loop once, and he knew he would be throwing away the cute purple umbrella lodged into the side of the thing long before he brought the drink up to his mouth.

He signed for the drink, turned back to the side of the ship he and Julie had been lounging on, and stopped.

What the...

Julie was talking to a man. Her head was thrown back, her knees touching one another as she laughed at whatever it was the man had said.

The man was out of sight, his head blocked by the floor of the deck right above them, so Ben took a few larger strides and came out from underneath the balcony. He felt a pang of jealousy as Julie laughed, wondering who in the world she was —

No.

He shook his head, still holding his pineapple.

It can't be.

"Reggie?" he asked.

Reggie turned around and beamed. "Ben, welcome back! How are you?" He walked over and extended his hand. "Nice pineapple, by the way."

Ben nodded. "Thanks."

They shook hands, but Ben wasn't trying to hide his emotion. His expression was one of confusion and annoyance, and Reggie apparently could tell. He brought his hands up, backing up a step. "Easy there, buddy," Reggie said. "I didn't come to crash your little date. E sent me."

"So you *did* come to crash my date," Ben said. "Reggie, why are you here?"

Reggie's smile grew. "We have a job."

Ben looked down at Julie, who hadn't moved from the lounge chair. Her laugh had shrunk to a smile, small and light on her petite face. She shrugged.

"What job?"

"We can talk about it — "

"We can talk about it *now*, Reggie," Ben said. "Because we're on *vacation*. And we're not leaving until I've had about forty of these ridiculous pineapple things." He held up the cocktail and swirled it around in his hand. He caught Julie's eye as he stood face-to-face with his friend and coworker. Only right now, at this moment, he didn't feel friendly *or* interested in working.

Reggie just smiled, the gigantic grin on his face almost contradicting the man's eyes. If Ben didn't know him any better he would have assumed that Reggie was faking it, wearing the smile for his sake.

"How did you get here?" Ben asked.

Reggie shrugged. "I walked on. Just went right through the security wall like it wasn't there."

"Really?" Julie asked.

"They're looking for booze, really," he said. "Let's be honest. They're rent-a-cops at best, working minimum wage for the cruise line. They don't care who comes aboard."

Ben squinted into the light, directly at Reggie. "How'd you *really* get here?"

Reggie's smile waned a few notches. "Fine. Got me. I had Mrs. E arrange it. Through the transit authority, couple calls in to the Mexican tourism board, I'm sure. Still though, wasn't really that difficult."

"You just get here?"

Reggie shook his head. "No, I stayed in Cozumel while you were coming in, then I got on the ship that evening. Been holed up belowdecks with a nice crew member named Suarez. Doesn't really speak much English, or at least he wasn't interested in speaking with me."

"Why'd you wait to come find us?" Julie asked.

"You're enjoying yourselves. I didn't want to ruin that."

"Thanks," Ben said, his face belying the sarcasm. "Definitely haven't ruined our vacation."

"What am I supposed to do?" Reggie asked. "Mr. E said it was urgent."

Ben sighed. He took another glance out at the water, at the receding sunlight as the orange orb floated downward, casting its glow out to the far reaches of their world. He wanted to sit here and watch it, like he'd done every other night of their trip, but he knew that was all over. Even though there was no chance he'd agree to whatever scheme Reggie and Mr. E had cooked up, he wouldn't be able to shake it from his mind. It would affect him, and Julie would pick up on that. She could read him like a book, so there was no sense trying to hide his feelings. He was curious, concerned, interested, angry. All of those things, all at once. Reggie had crashed their almost perfect vacation and given it a death sentence, and there was nothing he could do about that now.

"Okay, Reggie," Julie said. "Ben's not going to drop it, and neither am I. Want to grab a drink."

Reggie's mouth grew by another two inches. His smile was contagious, but Ben's internal monologue fought against the charisma of his friend. *One drink,* he told himself. *One drink, hear him out, then back to cruising. Back to my vacation.*

He deserved it, and Julie deserved it as well.

One drink.

CHAPTER 7

THREE DRINKS later and Ben was starting to feel it. Rum, then whiskey, then some sort of cocktail Reggie had explained was Brazilian in nature, complete with a type of liquor called cachaca, a sort of Brazilian rum.

Reggie had lived in Brazil for a few years, running a survival training camp for corporate executives who really just needed a way to feel important once again. He'd explained to Ben and Julie that he'd enjoyed the information, the practice, but hated the clientele. They were all soft, mentally and physically. When Ben's and Reggie's paths had crossed under unfortunate circumstances, they had struck up a fantastic friendship and had been nearly inseparable ever since.

But now, in the dingy, smoky lounge Reggie had chosen for their 'one drink,' Ben felt as though he wished he and Reggie had never met. Here was a man so focused on his job, so aligned with his mission, that he would stow away on a cruise ship to interrupt the vacation of his so-called friends. Ben was frustrated that he had to waste the time hearing his pitch, but he was also frustrated that he *wanted* to hear it.

"Whatever it is," Ben started, "we're not doing it."

"Easy, Ben," Reggie said. "We just got our drinks."

Julie rolled her eyes. "We just got our *third* drink."

They had spent the last hour catching up — while it was difficult to admit that Ben was glad to see his friend, he *was* glad to catch up with him. He liked Reggie. He just knew there was more going on under the surface. There was a *reason* he'd crashed their vacation.

Reggie held up his hands in mock surrender. "Fine, fine. You got me. Drinks are on me, by the way."

"We know," Ben said. "Why are you here?"

Reggie looked at his watch, a ridiculously oversized military-issue thing that Ben had seen him use as a weapon before. "Right now," Reggie said, "we're heading north-ish. Right? Toward Florida?"

"That's where the cruise ends, yeah."

"Mr. E wants us to take a look at something down there."

"Florida?"

"Off the coast of Florida."

"So the Keys?"

Reggie shook his head. "Other side. East of Florida."

Julie frowned. "Like The Bahamas?"

"Farther north, actually."

"Out in the middle of the ocean?" Julie asked. "Seems like that's a bad place to put anything, right out there where it's prone to get hit with hurricanes."

"It is, in my opinion. But that's where we're heading."

"That's where *you're* heading."

Reggie grinned. "I know you're not wanting to get involved, Ben," Reggie said. "But we need your help. *Both* of you."

"We're on vacation. We already covered this."

"We did. But you haven't heard what it *is,* yet."

Ben crossed his arms. The bartender, a man who looked to be about ninety years old, took it as a slight and backed away slowly from the edge of the bar. "Don't need to know what it is. I'm here with my *wife,* Reggie."

"Fiancée," Reggie said. "You got another two months."

Ben glared at the man sitting next to him. "Make your case, and make it quick. We have dinner at eight o'clock." Reggie's eyes widened, but before he could say anything, Ben jumped in. "And *no*, you're not invited."

"Okay, okay. Here's the deal. Mr. E wants us to check up on something in the area. Like I said, off the coast of Florida, about forty miles east of Palm Beach, and twenty north of The Bahamas."

"What sort of thing are we 'checking up on?'"

"It's a park."

"A *park*?"

"Yeah, like a nature park or something."

"A *nature park* in the middle of the ocean?" Julie asked. She grabbed at her glass, a vodka cranberry made with vanilla vodka, a new concoction she'd recently discovered.

"A nature park off the coast of Florida, yes," Reggie said. "I don't really know much more about it than that. But we've got a week-long pass."

"If you don't know any more about it, why does E need us there?"

Reggie shrugged. "I never asked." Ben eyed him, not believing his friend.

"If you had to guess?" Julie asked.

"If I had to guess, I would guess that he needs us there because he's our *boss*, and he *told us to*."

Ben motioned to stand up, gripping the leather arms of the chair and pushing himself upward. Julie's and Reggie's heads snapped over at him. "Ben..." Julie said.

"No. I'm done here," Ben said. He sniffed. The bartender looked over and Ben gave the man a quick nod.

Reggie stood up next, reaching for Ben's shoulder.

"Listen, buddy," he said. "I don't know what this is about. But I know it wouldn't even be on the radar unless Mr. E thought it was important. Crucial, even."

Ben crossed his arms over his chest as Julie rose to her feet. "Don't lie to me, Reggie."

"Ben," Julie said again.

Ben waited. Watched Reggie's face. It hardened, softened again, then he looked down and grinned. "Okay, fine. I know *a little* about what this is about. Not the end game, not even the real 'why' behind it, but I know the motive of sending us there."

"And what's that?" he asked.

"The security team at the park. They were just hired, contracted by the park's employment department."

"And?"

"And it's a company called Ravenshadow."

CHAPTER 8

JULIE WATCHED her fiancé's body language. She was no master of reading the subtle clues of movement and facial expression, but she was better than average. To make things easier, Ben was nearly incapable of hiding his feelings from her. She used to assume that he was doing it on purpose, letting her in, allowing her to know him better, but it turned out that she was able to read Ben easier than anyone else she'd ever met.

And it drove him crazy.

He would try to conceal his emotions from her, which only made them more obvious. If he was angry, he would pout and furrow his brow, then turn away from her so she couldn't see his face.

Now, standing in the smoky atmosphere in the depths of the cruise ship, surrounded by old men puffing on cigars and their unfortunate wives, she was amazed with what she saw in his reaction to Reggie's words.

A complete reversal. A one-eighty, from the reluctant, frustrated friend to the eager, overenthusiastic man raring to go. He was doing his best to hide it, but she could see it all over his person: his arms, relaxing and tightening over and over, his palms squeezing shut and open again and his forehead wrinkling. He was thinking, trying to figure out how to keep his thoughts to himself, all the while knowing Julie was reading every word of his inner monologue.

"Ben," she said a third time. Finally he looked at her. Saw her, as if for the first time that day. "Ben, we're not —"

"Julie," he said softly. "It's..."

"I know. But *no*. We're *not going*. Ben, think about it. We're on *vacation*. The first one we've had since, hell, since we met."

"We stayed at The Broadmoor that one time," he said.

"We stayed at The Broadmoor before we left *for Antarctica*. For a *mission*, Ben. It wasn't vacation."

He flashed his eyes at Reggie, then at Julie. Stopped on Julie. "I — I want to find him, Jules."

She gritted her teeth. Looked down, felt her face flush. *I didn't want to think about this. Of all the things we were supposed to do on this trip, all of it was so I wouldn't have to think about* this. *About* him.

About Joshua Jefferson.

Their friend and de facto leader of their small group, the newly formed Civilian Special Operations, had been murdered in Philadelphia at the hand of a man who had kidnapped Julie, chased the rest of her team around the nation, and finally escaped without answering for his crimes.

The man was the founder and CEO of the private security firm, Ravenshadow.

The same security firm that this park had hired.

"We will find him, Ben. But there's no reason to —"

"Jules, we're *there*. We're already at the park. We're in the Caribbean, closer than we'll ever be to him. Reggie, how long will it take —"

"Mr. E has a helicopter waiting on the mainland, dispatching from Miami tomorrow afternoon. It'll be an hour flight from there."

"How will it get to the ship? There's no helipad."

Reggie nodded. "My understanding is that Mr. E arranged a small dinghy that we'll take out of the range of the ship, then the chopper will grab us from there. That was the compromise, since the cruise company was *very* adamantly against this whole thing. If I understand correctly, Mr. E's company runs communications for this entire region of the ship's operating area."

Julie couldn't believe what she was hearing. "No, Ben. Stop. Think about it. We're not taking a *blowup boat* off of a cruise ship and then getting picked up by a *helicopter in the middle of the ocean.* It's insane."

"It's the only way."

She felt her entire body heat up. "Listen to yourself. You're already scheming. You're already on board."

"I've already decided."

Reggie took a step back, probably without realizing it. He scratched the back of his head.

Julie balled her fists. "Have you? Really? Fine. Enjoy your trip, Ben."

She turned to Reggie and nodded once, the only thing she could think of doing that wasn't going to get her kicked out of the lounge. She was leaving anyway, so she should have hit him. It couldn't have made things worse. She wanted to smack him for coming here, for crashing their vacation and wasting their time.

And she wanted to *kill* Ben. She loved him for a lot of reasons, not the least of which was his constant fight for justice. He was the first to rush into a dangerous situation, and he was the last to leave. That was how they met, in fact, back at Yellowstone, racing after the terrorists who'd planted and detonated a bomb beneath the world's largest active volcano. He was bold, resilient, and even a bit reckless, and what he lacked in professional training he more than made up for in sheer willpower and determination.

There was a lot to love about the man, but those same characteristics were easy to hate. He wouldn't give up, and she knew it. He'd set his mind on finding the man who'd killed Joshua Jefferson, and he was going to relentlessly pursue that goal until it was done. He had been thinking about it constantly since they'd started this vacation, and while he'd done his best to hide it from her and enjoy his time away, she read it on him as clearly as if he'd just come right out and told her.

She was angry with him, and angry with herself for being surprised. She *knew* he would react this way — as soon as Reggie had said the words she'd known. He would be obsessed, focused on nothing else. Reggie had sold him with a single word.

Ravenshadow.

Like Ben, she wanted to catch the leader of the organization as well. She wanted vengeance for the death of their friend and coworker, and she certainly wanted to see justice served. But she wasn't a fighter — she was scrappy when she needed to be, but she tried to stay *out* of fights. Ben, on the other hand, was foolhardy. He put his head down and rushed forward, like a bull, into whatever mess lay on the other side.

She reached the set of open double doors at the end of the long, low-ceilinged lounge before Ben called to her. He'd waited until she made it here, as a test. To see if she was *really* going to leave him here with Reggie. She was seething, the anger surging through her, feeling betrayed and blindsided and disappointed and let down all at once.

"Julie," Ben said again, louder. "Julie, wait."

Reggie didn't say anything — he knew better. Ben would try to salvage this, to make her feel okay about it, but he wouldn't try to *change* it. He'd already made up his mind, and now he would try to make up hers as well.

She checked her watch. *7:54.* She would be late for dinner. It was a formal night, and she'd brought the perfect dress for the occasion. She wouldn't have time to change now, and she hated being late. It was a table for six, and there were two other couples sharing their space. She'd be embarrassed for showing up after their scheduled appointment, and even more so for showing up without her date.

She ignored the pleading calls of Ben and left him standing in the center of the lounge. She marched toward the elevators and waited impatiently for the car to arrive.

Screw it, she thought. *I'm hungry.*

CHAPTER 9

"WELCOME TO *OCEANTECH INSTITUTE,*" Adrian Crawford said. "And welcome to the new era of science and entertainment."

He forced his smile wider, knowing the large dimple on his left cheek would add to the effect. It had caused more than one woman in his past to swoon, and ever since he'd reached adulthood he'd banked on his good looks as a secret weapon, a final card to play after he'd used his intelligence and business acumen to make the sale.

"*OceanTech* is an innovative new company, and a cutting-edge idea, funded by the best in the venture capital and angel business, as well as a firm vote of support from the leading nonprofit educational and scientific organizations the world over."

He chuckled a bit under his breath, both underlying and enhancing his charisma and delivery and simultaneously enjoying the fancy non-speak. 'A firm vote of support' really just came down to different organizations agreeing with his vision, and 'leading nonprofit educational and scientific organizations' really just meant he'd received a positive response to the question, 'should I build this?'

It was all marketing, all the time. That's what his job came down to. He was qualified, a gifted scientist in his own right, but this phase of the process was purely superficial — bringing in the deep-pocketed philanthropists and business gurus who saw the potential of a first-to-market investment opportunity.

He needed their money, even though they had been fully funded a year ago. But funding was fickle. It was there when you needed it, until it wasn't. No projections, data analysis, or budgeting could change the reality of a growing startup with big plans. Things changed, and he needed to be prepared.

He didn't mind. He was good at it, after all. The board had unanimously agreed to put him in charge of fundraising, which gave him even more power than his declared 'President and CEO' status already bestowed upon him.

The people in the room smiled back at him, their backs straight as they jostled around one another, trying to make themselves the most noticeable one in the room. To the men in the room it was a competition, to the women an information-gathering session for later gossip and scheming.

Crawford watched it all with mild amusement. These people were fabulously wealthy, each of them in their own right, having accomplished everything in their lives they desired, yet when reduced to their simplest natures they were no different than a set of schoolyard cliques.

"If you'll please direct your attention to the screens behind me," he continued, "we will begin the presentation shortly. If you need a drink refill, one of the girls will be around to offer a champagne."

The group milled around, looking for the screens he'd mentioned. His amusement grew as he watched them squint and frown, trying to understand what he was talking about. He had anticipated their confusion, built it into his presentation. He'd rehearsed it four times, just this morning, and he knew it was a world-class performance. His excitement grew as he awaited the next big reveal.

From behind him, the entire curved back wall of the low-ceilinged room lit up in brilliant 4K color, and the recessed speakers hidden throughout the room swelled to life with the sound of a low, deep rumble. The lights dimmed automatically, and he heard audible gasps and sighs from the group assembled before him. The room was electric, and he almost expected a burst of applause.

That will come later, he knew. *All in good time.*

He squeezed his smile over to enhance his dimple, widening his eyes and clenching his jaw as he stared at the woman standing in the front row of people, a champagne glass in her hand. She was the daughter of an oil man, and the wife of a Wall Street exec, but he knew she was *also* a sucker for a good show. A good, *expensive* show. She also had a reputation in some wealthy circles that he was hoping to exploit a bit, hence his earlier invitation to her to continue a tour of his facility in a more *private* nature.

She grinned back at him, her lips pushed out like a tiny pout, her eyes narrow but still smiling. He had her, and it was just a matter of time before she threw herself on him. He shifted, feeling the excitement rising inside himself.

He cleared his throat right as the deep rumble subsided and was replaced by a pleasant, gentle string triad, building slowly and rolling over note-by-note in a cascading wave of music. It was programmed to blanket the room in sound from all angles, yet not overwhelm his own voice.

"*OceanTech* began as a small research firm, of which I was the founding member and lead scientist. We were making progress studying the phenomenal properties of some of the world's most mysterious creatures. By analyzing and synthesizing some of the chemical and even genetic makeups of some of these specimens, *OceanTech* was able to bring the world fantastic new treatments for ailments that have continued to plague the human race for centuries."

The screen behind Crawford wrapped around the room and displayed well-designed graphical representations of everything he was describing. A strand of DNA, exploded, spun around, and then blown up to see the individual chains of amino acids. The amino acids bonded with other materials and chemicals, then morphed into a common pill. On the opposite wall a simple graph detailed the growth and success rates of *Ocean Tech's* medical products and pharmaceuticals.

"Our line of focused chemotherapy has shown a radical increase in the rate of recovery and remission of leukemia patients, for example. And the secret? We found it in the mitochondrial attributes of the common Mako shark."

The group clapped, a quiet, awkward clap as they realized they were all holding champagne glasses. Adrian Crawford beamed, stretching his arms out in a dramatic flourish of attention, then continued. "But we knew we could do *so much more...*"

The curved screen fell blank, perfectly timed with Crawford's speech. The entire room disappeared into darkness, and he waited. *Three... two... one...*

A tiny pinpoint of light grew in a swirling, spinning orb at the center of the giant curved screen. He had stepped to the side to ensure he wouldn't block their view, all the while staring straight ahead at the group. He could see the whites of their eyes, the sparkled reflection of the orb in their glasses, but they were otherwise ghosts at the other side of the room.

The orb grew, spinning faster and taking on a blueish hue as it expanded to fill half of the center of the screen. The music picked up, a low cello ostinato with a tremolo violin run over slow, ascending whole notes. It was dramatic, possibly over the top, but Adrian Crawford knew what he was doing.

Selling.

"What you are seeing is a dramatization of the growth of the synthetic cell structures we've been working with." He paused, looking around as the faces came back into view. "A *dramatization* because there's usually no music when it happens."

A spattering of laughter spread throughout the room.

"We are exploring the possibilities of these synthetic cells, now that we have the technology to create them. Think of it as a combination of stem cell research and nanotechnology — a perfect marriage between two cutting-edge — and, I might add — somewhat controversial fields of research. But as we all know, there's a difference between *politically* driven controversy and *real, tangible*, scientific research."

He watched the man near the back, a wide, pockmarked senator from Illinois. The man was grinning, taking the joke in stride with no sign of offense on his face. These people were all on Crawford's side — he'd made sure of it long before he'd invited them here to ask for money — and he knew a few jabs toward the media's side of the fence on the issue would be well-received here.

The video continued, the cell splitting into a pair of blinding-white lights that grew and swelled and throbbed with life. It was masterfully done, and he made a mental note to send a fruit basket to the company they'd hired to put it together. "These synthetic cells will provide the missing link in medicine," he said. "We hope they will bridge the gap between sections of dormant DNA found in droves inside the nucleus of human cells and modern advances in science."

The video concluded with cellular mitosis, the tiny orbs splitting and splitting again, until they filled the screen and pressed against one another, causing a bright-white light that completely consumed the curved television display. It lit the room from behind, and Crawford knew he was a silhouette, just the outline of a man.

"But the best part of it all is that we are bridging the gap between *science* and *humanity*. For millennia, science has been relegated to the realm of the brilliant, the geniuses and intellectually superior. The general public has been able to benefit from their efforts, but they have not been able to actively *take part* in those efforts.

"*OceanTech Institute* is the first of its kind — a park, focused on education through entertainment, a concept that's been tried before but has always fallen short. The *Institute* will be a premium, state-of-the-art laboratory, but it will be transparent in every way. The research that happens here will be observable at every level. Families can enjoy the luxurious atmosphere and phenomenal cuisine, and take part in a number of science-based activities that stretch the imagination, foster the childlike wonder we've all felt, and, most importantly, introduce questions that *must* be answered.

"*OceanTech* is almost complete, and we are almost operating at full capacity. We're a bit short-staffed, but for that reason you will be our only guests for the next week."

Adrian Crawford stepped forward, into the down lighting from above and the side-lit alcove lighting that brought him back into focus. His smile waned, a practiced expression of seriousness and intensity. "I want you to enjoy yourselves here. I want you to experience what we've *truly* built — a floating five-star luxury resort hotel, designed to capture your minds and introduce new ideas that you thought were only dreams.

"Any questions?"

The room exploded in applause.

CHAPTER 10

DINNER WAS BLAND, surprisingly. Julie had a spread in front of her — lobster tail, sirloin, shallot aioli, and steamed summer vegetables. There were two glasses of wine, as she wasn't sure if she should go with white or red for the surf and turf dinner, but she hadn't had a drink of either.

The couples around her had begun to ignore her, intuitively understanding that she was struggling. It was funny to her how people got *more* awkward by trying not to be awkward. It would have been better for them to simply pretend like she was fine, ask her questions about her day, and be done with it.

But *she* couldn't pretend like she was fine. She was mad at Ben, and she was upset that Reggie had thought it wise to find them and approach them about this mission. Mr. E would have understood, and even if he didn't Mrs. E would have convinced him that it was a bad idea to commandeer a couples' vacation for work purposes.

She understood the pressure — they were close to Ravenshadow, and their leader. The Hawk, or Vicente Garza, was a ruthless criminal successfully hiding behind the facade of a private mercenary force, operating fully within the bounds of United States law. But he had committed atrocious acts before, and Reggie, who knew the man long before their encounter a couple months ago, had filled them in on his specific grievances against the man.

But that didn't excuse either Reggie or Ben. It didn't excuse Mr. and Mrs. E from sending him here.

And it didn't excuse any of them from forcing Julie to care about it.

She sat at dinner silent, reflecting. They'd played her, all of them, knowing she was almost as stubborn as Ben. She'd spent a month working side-by-side with her fiancé trying to track down The Hawk and his twisted team of killers to no avail, and they'd finally decided to give up until they had a lead. They'd gone on vacation, tried to forget about it, to forget about Joshua Jefferson and his brutal murder, about Julie's kidnapping and torture, and about their miserable failure back in Philadelphia.

But she still cared. She couldn't hide it from herself, even if she had effectively hidden it from Ben.

She knew she wanted to find The Hawk, and she knew she would follow Ben wherever he decided to go. He needed her, even if he didn't realize it. They all needed her, and she needed them. They were a team now, and she was no good to anyone sitting at a dining room table in a massive restaurant at the stern of a cruise liner, facing down a smorgasbord of food.

Julie shook her head. Smiled a little, out of spite. She wasn't happy about it. Not at all. But it was the truth, and she'd always been one to focus on the truth and what it meant rather than the emotional desire that could successfully fool her into making the wrong decision. The truth was that she *wanted* to find him, she *wanted* to be with the team again, and she *wanted* to stay on the cruise ship and enjoy her vacation.

But that ship had sailed. Neither of them would be able to enjoy anything if they stayed here. Neither of them would be any closer to tracking down Ravenshadow and serving justice to The Hawk, and they would forever regret not taking the opportunity when they had it.

Damn you, Reggie, she thought.

She cleared her throat. The others at the table looked up at her. A couple from Iowa on one side of her, a farmer of some sort and his wife, both thick and muscular and wearing fancy clothes that barely fit over their matching barrel chests. Two men to her right, a couple on their honeymoon from Miami, one an investor and the other a self-declared 'trophy husband.' They smiled, the awkward anticipation evident on all four sets of eyes.

"S — sorry," she said. "I've had a rough day. I apologize for not being much a part of the conversation. I'm afraid I need to go."

The trophy husband smiled at her and placed his hand on hers. "Honey, it's okay. You go get that hunk of a man back. He's worth every —"

The man's husband grunted and cut him off. "We're with you, Julie. Don't worry about it — relax and enjoy your trip. We'll be here tomorrow night, same time. No need to apologize." He smiled at her, genuine and rich.

She smiled back as she stood up. The barrel-chested farmer stood as well, but was far too late to help her with her chair, so she gave him a polite nod and tucked it back in under the tablecloth. The group watched her collect her clutch and the couple on her right waved as she turned to leave.

Nice people, she thought. *Too bad I won't be joining them tomorrow night.*

CHAPTER 11

"WE'RE STOPPING off in the Bahamas first," Reggie yelled into the headset. The beating of the rotor wash filled every pore, vibrated every bone in his body. "Nassau. It's not on the way, but that was the cheapest flight, I guess."

"Cheapest flight for who?" Ben asked. He was seated in the chopper next to Julie, facing forward, directly across from Reggie. The three of them had reached the GPS coordinates after being lowered to the ocean from the top deck of the cruise ship in the inflatable dinghy. Reggie wasn't afraid of flying, but he would do his best to never have to take a ride on a cruise ship pulley system in a blowup boat ever again.

"We're meeting up with a doctor. She's coming along for support."

"What's her specialty?"

Reggie shrugged. "Probably doctoring? I didn't set it up; I'm not sure."

Julie smiled. "So four of us, total. What's the mission?"

"Recon, mainly. The park is called *Ocean Tech Institute*. Trying to exploit a niche market of nerdy families interested in and rich enough for a luxury vacation of learning and science."

Ben scrunched his nose. "Sounds awful. Like camping in a children's museum."

"I'm not really anticipating much either," Reggie said. "But E told me they've solidified an unbelievable amount of early angel investment, and they've got a few venture capital firms standing by for a B-round. Besides that, their CEO and President, Adrian Crawford, has done pretty well for himself in the past. His board is made up of the wealthy elite in the scientific and medical communities as well."

"So they've got money."

"They've got enough. The park itself is a semi-floating structure off the coast of Florida, and its website describes it as an 'all-inclusive, luxury resort with all the amenities one family could want.'"

"Sounds fancy," Julie said. Her headset was larger than her head, and she was constantly struggling to keep it balanced between her ears. "Maybe it'll be as nice as the cruise ship."

Reggie knew what she was implying. *Maybe our vacation* won't *be over so soon. Maybe this place will be just as relaxing.*

He could only hope.

"We're supposed to find Ravenshadow, see if we can locate Garza in the park, and take him in."

"Take him in? We're not cops, Reggie."

"We're also not exactly civilians. I mean we *are*, but we've got backing from military heads. So we're it — we go in, try to find him, and *discreetly* get him back out."

"How?"

"How do we get him?"

"How do we get back out?"

Reggie nodded. "Our chopper is coming back in three days. We'll get a feel for the layout, enjoy ourselves the first two days, keep our eyes open, and make our move on day three."

"And if we miss our ride?"

He smiled. "You two know how to swim?"

Julie smirked. "Right. Seriously, our plan hinges on timing? We have to get to Garza at the perfect time to take him down, arrest him, and then get him to the helicopter at the right time? What about his men? What about the fact that Garza himself is a *trained killer*?"

"It's — it's not the most thorough plan, I'll admit," Reggie said.

Ben's eyes widened.

"But we can work it out once we land. Once we get a feel for the park we can make a more solid plan. Maybe they've got a skeleton crew, you know? Mr. E said they're not at full capacity with staffing and employees just yet, and the only other guests in the park will be a handful of investors, on an extended tour."

Ben sighed. "There are other civilians there? Reggie, this is already a mess."

Reggie smiled. "What have we ever done together that *hasn't* been a mess? Look, guys, it's not that big a deal. We try to get The Hawk, or we don't. This isn't a long-term planned op, it's an *opportunity*. Mr. E wanted to capitalize on our situation. You two were close, I was a flight away, and we can take advantage of timing."

Ben frowned. "Does that mean they don't know we're coming?"

Reggie shook his head. "Not really. The guy running the place, Adrian Crawford, was more than happy to have us — he's actually planned a bit of a welcoming party, from what I hear. Benefits of being CSO, I guess."

It was true — they had been in most of the major newspapers across the country lately, on account of their travels and adventures. Most of the reports had been tamed and watered down to give them the plausibility they needed as well as to ensure no explicit details would be revealed, but the effect was the same. They were considered minor-league celebrities at this point. The public loved the idea that 'normal people' like them were taking on some of the nation's challenges. The military was too large, too fragmented, and too disorganized to worry about the smaller issues, and local and regional law enforcement often ran up against budget constraints, resources, and priority conflicts to care.

The CSO had carte blanche to meddle in domestic affairs, as long as it was not a currently active military operation or a state-level operation. The board members of the CSO were from all branches of the military and approved the team's operations or denied them, giving only enough information to justify their decision.

It was a good arrangement, and Reggie had no doubt the reason it had been so successful so far was in no small part due to Mr. E's wide-reaching influence and network, as well as the size of his wallet. For Reggie, an ex-Army sniper, the increased freedom was enough of a draw to the group without even considering the phenomenal pay.

"But Ravenshadow *doesn't* know," Julie said. "Is that what you're saying?"

"That's what I think. I'm not sure if Crawford is tight with Garza, but I can't imagine he's going to be telling his security the names of every single person who comes into his park."

"Probably not," Ben said. "But there isn't really anyone *at* the park yet, remember? Just a handful of investors and us. We're going to stick out like sore thumbs."

"Maybe," Reggie said. "But I'd bet Garza will be busy setting up his systems and getting everything ready for the park's soft launch in a month. We'll be under the radar because we'll just be tourists. In and out, hopefully with The Hawk in tow."

"Hopefully."

CHAPTER 12

THERE WAS a sudden realization that came over Ben as they waited on the tarmac of the airport in Nassau. The chopper hadn't spun down, as they were only there to refuel and pick up their fourth passenger. He sat with Julie leaning against his side, asleep. Reggie was grinning about something he was looking at on his phone, which left Ben to his own thoughts, a somewhat dangerous proposition.

The realization that he'd had was that he had *decided*. It was a single word, a simple word. He had *decided*, and now he was *here*.

It was sort of like a brief, one word story of his life. He had *decided* to run away from home at eighteen years old and work to become a ranger, eventually ending up at Yellowstone. He'd *decided* to stay there, to live life as a recluse and somewhat withdrawn from the rest of the staff and team there, up until he'd met Julie. She'd raced into his life like a whirlwind, snapping him up and taking him away to help solve a crime, but he realized now that he'd *decided* it. It had been a conscious, active decision. Something he'd had a choice over, and he'd chosen to follow her.

He had chosen to get involved with the CSO as it had been formed, and he had chosen to accept the role they'd given him.

None of his life had been an accident, when viewed through that lens. Sure, things had happened that he had no control over, but at every step of the way when he'd been given a choice to make, he'd made a *decision.*

It was sobering, really. To know that his life *was* his own, that it was something he was in nearly full control of. He wasn't sure if he liked that or not. He wasn't sure if he liked it because he wasn't sure what he truly *wanted.* He loved Julie with all his heart, of that much he was sure. But he had ridden along with her during their courtship, allowing her to take the lead on things like wedding planning, vacation planning, and just about every other big decision.

But that, in itself, was a *decision.*

He'd *decided* to take the backseat. He'd *decided* to not care about those things. And he was realizing it now.

What would be different if I'd decided something different all those times? Where would I be?

He couldn't be sure of anything, but he was almost positive he wouldn't be anywhere near *here.* He wouldn't be anywhere remotely close to The Bahamas, stopping over on their way to examine a 'science park,' and he wouldn't be with Julie or Reggie.

He wouldn't be fighting a war against a man who'd killed a man he'd hardly known a year ago.

He yawned, feeling the weight of the thoughts that circled his mind and the fatigue of travel hit him all at once. He wished for a moment he was Julie, small enough she could tuck her feet up underneath her and curl into Ben's side and actually be comfortable. He was far too large for that. Tall, wide-shouldered, and — thanks to Reggie's help over the past half-year — in very good shape. But that made it even harder to get comfortable. He couldn't rest on any particular limb because his bodyweight would put it to sleep in minutes, and he couldn't just curl up and rest because there were not very many chairs or seats in the world large enough for that to be useful.

He watched the tarmac, focused on the wavy lines of heat

streaming up off the concrete. It was hot outside, but the inside of the chopper was a crisp 65 degrees. It was humid, which made it feel cooler, but he wasn't complaining. He liked the feeling of the cold snapping against his skin.

A door opened on the side of a building nearby, and he saw a man step out, lugging a suitcase in one hand. It was the kind that had wheels, but the man must have felt the need to prove himself, as he carried it in a way that made him lean almost 45 degrees to the side in order to balance it properly.

Behind the man and the suitcase a woman stepped over the threshold and out onto the baking tarmac. Ben felt himself straighten, then relax so as not to wake Julie. But his eyes were riveted on the woman. Tall, thin, sun-darkened skin and curly black hair, the woman looked like she had spent her entire life on the island. She wore tight, short cargo shorts, folded up at the very bottom, hiking boots, and low ankle socks, allowing just about all of her perfectly formed legs to show. They shined in the sunlight, the deep brown color of them contradicting the white of the concrete beneath her.

She slid forward more than walked, and he watched the entire time. Her face was long and thin as well, with small features and eyes that seemed to be peeking out from beneath her skin.

Her sky-blue blouse was buttoned up to the second button, and he could see a large bead necklace hanging around her neck. She wore a matching anklet.

Reggie whistled. "Wow," he said. "Looks like this trip just got a whole lot more fun."

Ben glared at his friend. "You're disgusting. What, are you going to ask her to dinner?"

Reggie grinned. "We're all eating together, I believe. So yeah, maybe. Unless you're going to ask her first, in which case I'll see what Julie's up to —"

"Save it, pal," Ben said. "Better keep your sights set on the doctor here."

The doctor approached the side of the chopper and put her hand over her head to protect her hair. The man struggled against the weight of the suitcase and finally set it down when she had reached the open door. Reggie leaned out to grab the luggage and he hoisted it up and inside, effortlessly. The man scowled at him, but Reggie just widened his grin.

"Reggie," he yelled to the woman.

"What?" she yelled in reply.

She stepped up onto the ladder and into the chopper's bay, then looked around for a seat. Julie awoke, stretched, looked at the woman, and nodded toward her.

"I said, name's Reggie!"

"Hey bud," Ben said into his headset mic. "We can all hear you loud and clear. Stop blowing my eardrums out."

He laughed, then reached for the fourth set of ear protection headphones dangling behind the seat and offered them to the doctor. He waited for her to put them on, then he started up again. "Name's Reggie," he said.

She smiled, nodding. "Pleasure to meet you. Dr. Sarah Lindgren."

"Lindgren," Julie said. "Swedish?"

She nodded. "I'm Swedish-American." She laughed, an easy, warm chuckle. "I don't look very Swedish, I know. I grew up in the Cayman Islands, but my father, Graham Lindgren, is Swedish. My mother's Jamaican, and I got her looks."

Julie shifted in her seat to address Sarah. "*Professor* Graham Lindgren?"

Sarah smiled, impressed. "Yes — you've heard of him?"

"I did a semester at Cambridge. Didn't he teach there?"

She nodded. "Yes, I believe he did. Visiting professor for a few years. Did you study archeology?"

Julie laughed. "I have a Master's in Computer Science, and an undergrad in Information Systems. But I *dated* a guy who studied anthropology, and he dragged me along to your dad's lecture once. His idea of a date."

Ben watched the exchange with amusement, reading Julie's facial cues as she explained this part of her past. A part, he noticed, she had never explained to *him*.

"And just who was this knight in shining armor?" Ben asked.

Julie seemed surprised for a moment, as if she'd forgotten that everyone else in the chopper could hear her conversation with the newcomer, but Sarah Lindgren leaned forward easily and stretched out her hand. "You must be Ben," she said.

He nodded. "Pleasure."

"All mine," she said. They locked eyes for a moment, then she turned back to Julie. "And yes," she said. "I'm interested in hearing all about this 'knight in shining armor' as well."

Julie blushed. "Well, he was a fling. Just a year, maybe. The point is that I remember your father's lecture *far* more than I remember the boy I went with."

"Oh?"

"He gave a phenomenal presentation. All about this idea that there could have been a 'master race' that seeded different areas of the world after a cataclysmic event knocked their civilization off the map."

Sarah's head fell back as she grinned. "Ah, yes. The old 'ancient aliens' theory. I got loads of that growing up. He dragged us all over the world actually, trying to find proof of it."

"Aliens?" Reggie asked.

"Well he didn't believe that, necessarily. But that was the common criticism of his peers. Everyone seemed to think that humans just sort of stood up one day and started walking, eventually getting to all corners of the globe. Even though no one really knows *what* exactly happened, it's a pretty commonly held belief that they spread out *first,* then developed in pockets of civilization *after.*"

"And your father believed there was some civilization *before* all that, right?" Julie asked.

"Precisely. He looked at similarities between ancient societies, as well as creation myths from all over the world, analyzing similarities. Ultimately he believed that there was a race of people who spread out after their home was destroyed, reaching these primitive societies and teaching them things like farming, medicine, and architecture."

The chopper began to rise, and Ben involuntarily gripped the seatbelt tighter. Their pilot was a pro, and he hardly felt the jostle of lifting off the skids, but it was the acceleration, against the direction of the pull of gravity, that shook him. He hated flying. Always had, though he was never sure when he'd developed the phobia.

Reggie and Julie loved to tease him for it, especially since they spent a lot of their time in the CSO flying to one place or another. Reggie was a trained pilot, quite capable, and on trips from the cabin to Anchorage in the tiny Cessna the CSO owned, he often took the opportunity to give Ben a hair-raising experience by tossing them into a quick dive or throwing the plane one direction in a sharp spin. 'Dodging a bird,' he would say. Ben never laughed.

The helicopter continued to rise, and he tried his best to listen in on the rest of Sarah's conversation with Julie. She was an interesting woman, growing up with the archeological wisdom of her father's obsession, and no doubt picking up quite a few tidbits along the way. But her own career was impressive as well: an undergraduate degree in Evolutionary Biology and a graduate degree in Archeology and Social Anthropology from the University of Edinburgh, and a PhD in Anthropology from Australian National University.

On top of that, she was humble. Charismatic, kind, and quick to follow up an answer to their questions with a question of her own, Ben immediately took a liking to her.

He noticed that Reggie did, as well.

His friend had slid over in the chopper's seat as far as his belt would allow, and his arm was perched precariously close to her hand.

He was riveted to her face, watching and taking in every word she spoke as if she were a prophet. If she noticed, she didn't show it.

Ben was amused, knowing that the behavior was typical of Reggie. He was divorced, currently single, and thought quite highly of himself. He was a good-looking man, tall, fit, and carried himself the way an Army man would, with strong, broad shoulders and a chiseled jaw that would have looked at home on a GI Joe toy.

But Sarah seemed much more interested in chatting with Julie. The talk went from her background to Julie's, then to how she'd met Ben, and finally it had devolved into girl talk, discussing the latest reality shows that neither of them had time to watch.

Ben and Reggie stared at them as they talked, waiting for a lull in the conversation, but one never came. An hour passed quickly, and Ben found himself just starting to fall asleep against the humming and vibrating hull of the chopper when the pilot's voice cut into his headset.

"We're here," he said. "Two minutes out, but you should be able to see the outer ring of the park out your window, Ben."

Ben looked out at the water, the sun's reflection bright and straining his eyes. It took a moment for his eyes to adjust, but then, out on the horizon, he saw it.

CHAPTER 13

LIKE THE PILOT HAD SAID, the first thing Ben saw was a circle, stretching out east to west nearly as far as he could see. At first it appeared to be nothing more than a line on the horizon, like a whitish jetty jutting out from the shoreline, but there was no shoreline anywhere in sight.

As they drew near in the helicopter he could see the edges, how they bent back around itself to form the 'ring' the pilot had described. If he had to guess, he would have said the park was a mile in diameter, but there was little to go off other than raw intuition. The ocean sprawled outward on all sides, dominating the landscape and dwarfing the park itself.

The line that came into focus eventually gave way to its true shape: an 'outer ring,' in that there were more rings inside it he could see, concentric circles stacked one inside the other, three in total. They had the appearance of floating on the surface of the water, though he knew they had to be anchored in some way to the ocean floor. He knew little about oil rigs, but the structure in front of them now seemed to be designed with an oil rig in mind. Semi-submersible, round rather than squared, and about ten times the size.

The circle that made up the center ring supported a building that stretched upward, probably five or eight stories tall, rounded to match the circumference of the ring it sat on. The other, larger rings had smaller buildings sprouting out from the surface, most only two or three stories tall.

The second ring was the sparsest, with only a few buildings dotting the perimeter. They were short, squat, and unassuming, and most looked like cabana beach houses, complete with palm-frond roofs and wooden sides. The outer, largest ring featured more buildings, all dressed in the similar cabana style and of differing heights, but Ben could see that this ring had been designed to emulate a beach. The inner circumference of the ring had been filled with sand, giving the water between the first and second rings a greener, lighter appearance. The helicopter flew over the southern edge and turned east, heading toward the helipad on the far side of the largest ring, and Ben got a view of the artificial 'beach' that the park boasted.

Dots became individual lounge chairs, much like the ones he had just left behind on the cruise ship, and bright splashes of color became umbrellas and the smaller circles of drink tables. The cabana-style houses came into closer view, and he could see that many of them were in fact three-sided structures with bar tops installed, bar chairs sunk into the sand beneath them.

"Looks like the top deck of the cruise ship," Julie said into her headset.

Ben nodded. "Yeah, but they've imported the sand to complete the effect."

The pilot cut in. "The park spent a lot of money on this place. They're hoping there are enough people interested in an all-inclusive 'science' vacation."

"You think there are?" Dr. Lindgren asked.

"No idea. Not really my thing, but I've got a grandson who might get a kick out of it. I'm not sure about the whole 'learning plus relaxation' idea. Seems like two mutually exclusive things, if you ask me."

Ben nodded along, though he wasn't sure he agreed. Something about the place intrigued him. It was beautiful, situated in an isolated area of ocean near The Bahamas and the Florida coast, but unlike the theme parks he'd visited as a child and the nature repositories he'd worked at as an adult, this place was trying to combine the benefits of both worlds. Learning about nature and wildlife while enjoying an all-inclusive vacation seemed like a pretty good deal.

Seems like just what I was missing from the cruise, he thought.

The cruise — at least the few days they had experienced — was more of a 'lay back and enjoy the ride' sort of trip. A circular trip that ended up right where they'd started didn't hold much appeal for him, even when considering the free food. He didn't consider himself an intellectual, but he did enjoy learning, studying, discovering. He had a hard time sitting still, something his friend Reggie could relate to.

Julie, on the other hand, was a *phenomenal* relaxer. She was one of the hardest workers he'd ever met, finagling the insides of computers and their programs and bending them to her will however she wanted, but when it was time to detach and relax, she was *done.* She could binge an entire Netflix series in a night, whereas Ben started getting cabin fever after a single episode.

The cruise was a compromise — Julie had convinced him to take the trip by showing him how massive the ship was, all the amenities, including a gym and training facility, and a sample food menu. He did like the idea of being able to eat whatever he wanted at whatever hour of the day, but what sealed the deal for him was when she'd showed him a sample of her *swimsuit* menu.

He'd agreed, and they'd disembarked less than a week ago from the Port of Miami. He'd enjoyed the experience, but he'd also found it difficult to get out of his own head about the reason they were here.

It wasn't as much a *vacation* as it was a *way of forgetting.* Joshua Jefferson, their friend and coworker, had been brutally murdered.

They were supposed to get married in two months' time, but all he could think about during their cruise was their earlier mission in Philadelphia and their failure to bring in the leader of the Ravenshadow security organization.

The problem was that his mind wasn't occupied by a cruise — it was just drinking, eating, and... fun — nothing to give him a challenge, nothing to keep him thinking about the solution to a problem.

And that *was* his problem — he had to constantly be thinking about the answer to some problem or another, trying to figure out the solution to an issue he had. A cruise offered plenty of time to think, but without a specific problem to think about, it was just constant, mindless emptiness.

A place like this, a 'science park,' bringing together the best in entertainment and education — whatever that meant — seemed to him like a brilliant idea. It would be relaxing in the best way. All food and drink included, combined with a life-sized encyclopedia to walk through for inspiration.

The helicopter banked and flew over the helipad on the largest of the three circles and prepared to land. They hovered in midair as the pilot righted the craft, then he throttled down and Ben felt the chopper sliding downward. Their pilot performed a perfect landing, the skids dusting the ground and bouncing only once before finally settling on the asphalt pad, and Ben looked over at Julie.

She strained through a smile. There was tension in her eyes, but she wasn't as mad at him as she had been when they'd left. She wasn't exactly *content* with him, either. "Here goes nothing," she said.

He nodded. "I sure do hope it's nothing," he said.

CHAPTER 14

THE MAN who came to greet them at the helipad could have passed for a politician. Perfectly coifed hair, dark but not too black, the beginnings of some salted coloring on the sides, just above the ears. He wore glasses that were obviously more for show than anything else, black thick-rimmed frames. He had a dimple on his left cheek, and it seemed as though he knew how to use it.

Reggie watched him carefully, assessing the man as he approached the open door of the chopper. Reggie was the first one out, and he extended a hand. The man gripped it between both of his, unsurprisingly squeezing it just the right amount but continuing to look Reggie in the eye.

"Welcome, friend," the man said. "I'm Adrian Crawford."

"CEO and President of *Ocean Tech*," Reggie said.

If Reggie wasn't mistaken, it seemed to him as though Crawford's smile was sheepish, as if he were playing the role of the humble praised.

"Well, yes," Crawford replied, waving away his statement. "But *more* importantly, I will be your personal concierge and representative during your stay."

Reggie grinned in reply. "An honor, in that case. And what prestige have we been bestowed with that lends us this recognition?"

Crawford didn't even flinch. "You are here as the Civilian Special Operations. Your own reputation bestows upon you that honor."

Reggie nodded. "A couple of news reports and magazine editorials, nothing to write home about."

"And yet the *actual* truth of your accomplishments still found a way to reach my ears."

Okay, then, Reggie thought. *We're working with a pro here.* The man was a politician, of that he had no doubt. The question now was which side this man was playing, and what those sides were. *I'll crack you,* he thought.

"Still," Reggie continued, "we are grateful for your allowing us to pop in on such late notice."

Crawford again waved away the statement. "Truly, it's nothing. We have plenty of room, and aside from a group of insufferable investors and advisors, you will be the only ones in the park. Our staff, while still thin, has plenty of margin to take on a few more guests."

He turned to the side, opening up the dialogue for the others who had just disembarked from the heli. "Besides," he said, "I am anxious to show off our little slice of paradise here. I believe we're on to something quite spectacular."

Reggie nodded. "And in that regard, *your* reputation precedes you. We are looking forward to our stay."

Ben appeared next to Reggie. He waited for Crawford to notice him, extend a hand, and look him in the eyes before shaking. "Ben Bennett," Ben said.

"*Harvey* Bennett, I presume?" Crawford asked. He performed the double-handed shake and eye contact maneuver on Ben, but Ben seemed to be completely unfazed by the man's charm.

"Yes," Ben said. "Pleasure."

Crawford turned to the two women in their group. "And you

two are Dr. Sarah Lindgren — big fan of your father's — and Juliette Richardson. Soon to be Juliette *Bennett*, if I'm not mistaken?"

Julie smiled. "Yes, that's right. Two months, unless he keeps dragging me around the world like this."

Crawford threw his head back and laughed. "Well I understand the sentiment, but I do anticipate you will find the accommodations here *quite* luxurious. I take pride in the fact that *Ocean Tech*'s first foray into the world of entertainment and research attractions has been lauded as one of this century's most ambitious hospitality projects."

Reggie allowed him to finish, feeding off the man's excitement. "Well we certainly are excited to see the place, Mr. Crawford. And personally, I'm excited to see the *bar*."

Crawford smiled at an angle, pushing his dimple out toward the group that was now assembled around him. "Which one?"

"Now *that* is an answer worthy of a five-star review, friend," Reggie said.

Crawford beamed, soaking in the praise, and the others shifted uncomfortable by Reggie's side.

"Let's get on with it then, shall we?" Crawford said, waving them toward him as he began walking away from the helicopter. They had been nearly shouting at one another in order to hear over the sound of the rotors, and Reggie was grateful for the reprieve. "The first bar we'll pass is on your right," Crawford explained, and Reggie could see the cabana house situated near the outer edge of the ring they were walking on, facing inward. "It's open, but I will have to fetch a bartender for you, which could take a few minutes. I do recommend waiting until we reach the main hotel, however. I've sent for some specialties for each of you, and I feel they will all be to your liking. If you'd prefer something else, however, please don't hesitate to reach out to one of my staff and let them know."

Reggie exchanged a glance with Ben. *Seems a bit too good to be true,* he thought.

Ben nodded, and Reggie could imagine his response. *Yeah, it does.*

Reggie smiled, the large, face-wide grin plastered on his face. The grin that hid himself from the world. He'd worn it well for years. Learned how to use it.

Crawford was a nice man, practiced and perfected. He was a salesman, and in and of itself that was perfectly fine to Reggie.

It all just depended on *what* exactly this man was selling.

CHAPTER 15

"BEN," she said, "Can you believe this place?"

Julie was still mad at her fiancé, but she couldn't help but break her cold shoulder temporarily on account of the room she found herself in.

"Seriously," he said. "I think this place is even nicer than the ship."

The room they'd been led to by Crawford was one of the 'diamond' suites, part of a wing of rooms classified as the 'Great Reef Wing.' The four of them were all in this wing, separated into three rooms total: one for Ben and Julie, one for Reggie, and one for Dr. Lindgren.

And the 'diamond' label certainly appeared to be a fitting description. The room had the softest, finest carpet Julie had ever stepped onto, dark maroon and ordained with an embroidered floral pattern that was subtle but striking at the same time. The carpet faded nicely into a light hardwood floor that surrounded the immediate area next to a large glass wall that looked out over the water. The hotel was in the central ring of islands, and she could see the outer two lit by the bright mid-afternoon sun, the brilliant greenish-blue ocean resting between each of the circles, and stretching out toward the horizon.

The glass wall was curved, outlining the edge of the hotel itself. Both of the side walls in the room extended outward from the main entrance hallway at a diagonal toward the longer ocean-facing edge, giving the entire room a somewhat triangular shape.

The bed sat on the carpet against the left wall, a bathroom closed off near it, and a large flatscreen television sat on an entertainment center on the opposite wall. Two armchairs sat on either side of the television, and another poked out from beneath a desk in the corner of the room.

"Yeah," she said. "I think this place is a *little* nicer than the ship."

The centerpiece of the room was located between the end of the king-sized bed and the television. An oval-shaped piece of thick glass, about eight feet long and five feet wide, rested on the floor, providing a view directly into the ocean beneath the room. A pair of floodlights shot their beams straight downward from their mounts beneath the room, lighting up the entire oval — and reflecting off the walls and ceiling of the room — in a wonderful array of bluish-green colors.

"It's amazing," Ben said. "They even have automatic curtains. Check this out."

Julie watched as Ben reached for a remote control on the table next to the bed, poked at a button, and the curtains began to slide closed over the curved glass wall. The curtains were a mahogany brown, both matching and contradicting the carpet and lighter wood floor colors in a perfect way. The entire space had been meticulously appointed, and Julie couldn't help but wonder at the genius of it all. It had been designed as a complete package — every piece fit into the whole before it had even been constructed.

The room slid into darkness, the only light emanating from the orange glow from the two floodlights beneath the glass oval on the floor. The shadows they cast up and into the room were soft, just blurred lines and waves, matching the shimmering lines of the ocean itself underneath them.

"Ben," she whispered. "It's unbelievable." She looked up to find her fiancé holding on to the top of one of the closed curtains, his body swaying slightly. Suddenly she realized what he'd done.

She laughed. "Ben..."

"I always did look better in soft light," he said, still swaying.

"You never were one for dancing, though," she answered. "You going to put on a little show for me?"

He let go of the curtain and stalked over to the bed, kicking off his shoes on the way. "Takes two to tango, my dear," he said.

"Good lord," Julie replied. "You could at least be original."

She found herself sliding closer to the bed as well, opposite Ben. She slid out of her flats, her bare feet cold on the carpeted floor but surprised at just how soft it was. *This place isn't just for looks*, she thought. *It's the real deal.*

Ben was already tossing the twenty or so throw pillows that sat on the bed haphazardly in every direction. It was like watching an animal rip through a carcass. She shook her head, still laughing.

"Someone's going to have to clean all that up," she said.

He looked up, not stopping. "They've *definitely* got someone for that."

Ben had reached the bottom of the pile, finally finding the two pillows on his side that were intended for sleeping, and he yanked them up and away from the comforter, which he pulled down halfway.

Julie was fiddling with her earrings, small diamond studs that Ben had gotten for her before the trip, when a knock sounded at the door.

She looked at Ben, a slight frown on her face.

He groaned. "We were just about to —"

"I'll get it," she said. Julie walked over to the door and turned the handle. She cracked it open and looked out into the curved hallway.

A man, dressed in a black shirt and long black slacks, with shined black shoes, greeted her. "Your bags, miss..." the man said, ending the sentence with an upward lilt.

"Richardson."

"Miss Richardson, indeed. Welcome." The man smiled and raised an eyebrow, implying that he wanted to carry the bags inside. She opened the door further and he rolled in their suitcases, leaving them along the wall near the closet. He didn't look at Ben.

The man shuffled back out and nodded at Julie. "If you need anything, I am number 4 on your phones."

"Thank you," she said. The man nodded again and turned and started walking down the hall. She shut the door.

Ben was waiting, shirtless, next to the bed.

"Wow," she said. "You're really feeling this place, huh?"

He grinned, then shrugged. "It definitely has the right mood, wouldn't you say?"

She walked over to the bed and began working on her earrings again. She knew there was more to talk about with Ben, but she also knew he'd be more apt to *want* to talk if they'd spent some time reconnecting first.

Besides, if the goofy grin on his face told her anything, it was that he wasn't going to be willing to do *anything* until they'd 'reconnected.'

She was about to pull her side of the sheets down when another knock sounded on the door.

Ben groaned again, this time nearly running to the door. "*I'll* get it this time," he said.

She walked to the hallway and stood next to the bathroom to listen in. He opened the door, swung it open quickly, and put a hand on his waist.

It was Reggie. "Hey there, bud," he said, smiling. "Thanks for taking your shirt off for me, but I'm afraid we don't have time."

"What are you talking about?" Ben asked.

"Crawford wants us up for dinner, stat."

"Well Crawford can wait, Reg—"

"It's a seafood special tonight," Reggie said. "All-you-can-eat *anything,* from lobster to crab legs to scallops, from what I heard."

Ben paused. Julie rolled her eyes. *Unbelievable.* If there was anything the man was drawn to more than her, it was food.

As if on cue, her stomach growled. She reached up and started putting the earring back into its designated spot on her ear, and walked over to where she'd laid her shoes on the carpet.

"You hear that, Julie?" he asked. "I'd love to stay, but Reggie says we *have* to leave now to get there on time."

"Yeah, I heard. Your stomach's bigger than your —"

"We'll be out in a minute," Ben said to Reggie, cutting her off. "Sorry. Hold up for a bit?"

She heard Reggie confirm, then he heard the thick door swing shut.

CHAPTER 16

ALL OF IT IS INCRIMINATING, he told himself. *Every single piece of data. Every single file. Every single thing I've* touched *in this blasted —*

Dr. Lin stopped, thinking. *Stop it,* he thought. *You're smarter than this. That's why you're here in the first place. You're smarter than all of them.*

He forced himself to slow down, to think. He used a trick a colleague taught him once. He took a few deep breaths and focused on the walls, the floor, and the table in front of him. Noted the coolness of the metal surface, the off-white color of the paint on the walls. Sniffed, noting the stale clinical odor, almost like a hospital. By focusing on the physical characteristics in his immediate area, he forced his mind to relax and worry only about the present. *No good can come to one who worries about the future,* he thought. An old idiom his father used to repeat. *No good can come...*

It was a cheap trick, but it worked. He was a doctor, so he hated such 'hacks' that didn't rely on articulated, data-backed science. It felt gimmicky, like something a shrink would use on a patient for job security.

But again, it worked. It always had. Dr. Lin struggled with

anxiety when he allowed his mind to race forward into the future, extrapolating a problem to its worst possible conclusion. He often went to bed dreaming of a solution to a particular problem, only to awake in the middle of the night sweating, anxious about the same problem's sudden tenfold increase.

He took a few more deep breaths, let them out. Calmed himself as best he could. He tried to focus on the positives: this was only a temporary setback, this problem, like all problems, had a solution.

But he knew the truth. Unlike his irrational mind in the middle of the night, turning a niggling nonissue into a life-sized bites of terror, this problem was *real*. This problem *was* life-sized.

Literally.

And, worst of all, Crawford knew about it.

There had been no getting around that. Dr. Lin had opted for honesty during the board meeting, and he was now second-guessing that decision.

What good has come of my telling the truth? he wondered.

He picked up his flattened palm from the top of the metal table and slid around it to the other side. The computer he'd installed and set up sat there, the blank screen waiting. He shook the mouse and the desktop — no icons or clutter to be found on it — immediately stared back at him.

All of it is incriminating.

He knew the answer.

There was research here that he could not destroy. Research that existed *outside* the realm of what a computer's hard drive could recall. Research not based on the 1s and 0s of binary computer-speak but the biological binary of DNA and molecules and amino acids.

Living, real proof.

He couldn't do a thing about that. He *wouldn't* do a thing about that.

But he could get rid of the evidence that existed in front of him.

He opened a shell prompt and typed a few commands. Unix-based, as he preferred, and his fingers flew over the keyboard with the consistency and familiarity of a professional programmer. His genius extended beyond his primary role and day job into all realms of science and mathematics, allowing Lin to explore and prosper in many areas unrelated to medicine. Computers were just one of many 'languages' he had thoroughly conquered.

The prompt dialog box stared back at him, and he read it quickly, three times, just to be sure.

When in doubt, there is no doubt.

He'd read that in a book somewhere, some time long ago. He had never really known what it meant — it seemed as though if there was doubt, there... *was* doubt. The statement reeked of untested postulation, the sort of fancy non-speak he prescribed to the type of folks who thought holistic and homeopathic medicine was real medicine.

But now, staring at the prompt, he understood.

The question he had posed to himself, unprovoked, was simple: *should I press the key?*

And the answer, if he was being honest, was filled with doubt.

When in doubt, there is no doubt.

He was doubting himself, which was a rare occurrence for Dr. Lin. Was it his arrogance? Was this for posterity, his mind making semi-rational arguments against his better nature for reasons of long-term gain? *Was* there a way he could gain in this?

No, he knew. *I've lost. It is done.*

He pressed the key, and the prompt immediately threw up the tiny hourglass graphic, followed by an empty horizontal bar, slowly filling in as the task completed.

What now? he thought. *Is there anything else?*

His assistant had already been 'removed,' so he knew she wouldn't be a problem. If they needed her to talk, she would have talked. Nothing to do about her. He moved away from the computer and looked at the bank of monitors on another table, against the wall at the far side of the room.

They were all just displaying information collected and filtered from the server, which was downstairs in Sublevel 3. The computer he had just used was the controlling CPU for the entire room, so there was nothing more he could do from here. The monitors would slowly begin to display error messages and 'not found' messages as the data was removed from the storage systems.

The backups.

He realized it then, as he was staring at the monitors. There were backups upon backups, a multi-part redundant data storage system he had done some advising on before taking the job at the laboratory. The backups were accessible only by physically walking down into the space and touching them, not remotely in any way.

He had even advised that they set up a *remote* backup facility, again that could only be accessed physically, to ensure that if a cataclysmic failure happened here in their facilities they would at least have a retrievable backup.

Okay, that's the plan, he thought. He had initiated the first phase of the process — deleting the local files and the first stack of data. That would cause a bit of panic at the top, but the board and Crawford would react quickly, working to bring the backups online. So the second phase of the plan was to remove the backups that existed locally, on Sublevel 3, then find and take down the last line of defense, the remote backups.

A tall order, especially for one man. There would be firewalls and heavy security in place, and he felt a pang of anxiety as he thought about it all. He gripped the table, looked at the wall and ceiling and floor again, forced a few breaths.

You're okay, he thought. *Nothing you can't handle.*

It was true. It was nothing he couldn't handle. Nothing he hadn't done before, technically. No task too large for a man with his brainpower. It would be difficult, and it would require some luck getting into the right places, but he was already starting to formulate a plan of action.

He liked plans. They gave him courage, and they fought off the anxiety for him.

He looked away from the monitors, already starting to glow with the lines of errors he knew would eventually fill the screens, and walked toward the end of the room.

Toward the glass cages.

Toward the *live* proof. The proof he couldn't — wouldn't — delete.

They would still be here. They had no backups, but they didn't need them. *They* were the data.

He sighed heavily, feeling weary.

CHAPTER 17

BEN'S DISAPPOINTMENT lasted only for a few minutes. He had been looking forward to some time alone with Julie, knowing that there was a lot they needed to talk about. They had left their cruise on shaky terms, and a bit of pillow talk and alone time would have been well-deserved.

But as soon as he walked out into the hallway once again and began to follow Reggie, his spirits lifted. The hallway was rather plain, not alluding much at all to the fantastic rooms found behind each door, but it was plain in a thoughtful way. Images of the Bahaman coastline stretched across gorgeous landscapes, framed subtly between thin metal frames, no glass. The carpet in the hallway, unlike the soft, luxurious stuff in their room, was harder and thinner, no doubt the industrial, easy-to-clean version of a nice style. It had some embroidered pattern on its edges, gold ribbons on a maroon backdrop, and the entire stretch of carpeting curved along to the left, following the shape the of building they were in.

"Where's the dining hall?" Ben asked.

Reggie cast a glance toward him. "Which one?" he questioned in reply. "There are three restaurants, one of them expecting four-star status by the end of the year, a buffet cafeteria, and two brunch-exclusive restaurants."

Julie whistled at Ben's side. "Which one are we going to?" she asked.

"None of them. We're at the *chef's table*, apparently attached to the four-star place but not technically *part* of it. We'll meet Crawford and his executive chef there, but the menu's special to the night."

"Sounds like *we're* special to the night."

Reggie nodded. "It does seem that way, doesn't it? He must be bored, not having anyone else here to entertain besides the investors. Apparently they're all upstairs in some of the smaller rooms, enjoying the open bar."

Ben's eyebrows jumped. "I wouldn't mind enjoying that either," he said.

Reggie laughed. "I wouldn't be surprised if we're brought up there after dinner. Crawford's apparently got a decent taste for whiskey."

Julie grabbed Reggie's arm. "By the way, *friend*," she said. "How do you know all of this? I don't seem to remember any 'welcome kit' on our bed."

Reggie smiled. "I, uh, got to know my bag lady a bit," he said.

"Your *bag lady?*" she asked. "Are you kidding?"

"Well, whatever she's called. Don't worry, Jules — I tipped her."

He winked at Ben. Ben rolled his eyes. Julie made a disgusted noise.

"There she is now," Reggie said, picking up speed as he walked past the elevators and moved toward the set of doors at the opposite end of the hall. "This is Dr. Lindgren's room."

A woman left the room, turned, and smiled at Reggie. She was wearing the same black outfit as the man who'd brought in Ben's and Julie's luggage, a blouse instead of a shirt. She offered a quick wave. "Well hello again, Mr. Red."

Gareth Red, or 'Reggie,' as his unit had dubbed him, blushed.

Ben wasn't sure he'd ever seen the man do such a thing, but he understood why as soon as he came up close enough to the open door.

Dr. Sarah Lindgren stepped out of the room, wearing a gorgeous dinner dress. Sea-blue, tight, and short. Her shoes matched, short heels that revealed much of the top of her foot. She had changed her hair, too, her curls caught up in a wispy bunch that hung off the back of her head and allowed a few strands to trickle down over her neck. Her lipstick was more gloss than color, and her makeup was subtly applied.

"H — hey, Dr.," Reggie said.

"Please," she responded. "Call me Sarah. All of you." She looked at each of them in turn and nodded. She patted the woman who'd emerged from the room first on the shoulder, but addressed Reggie. "Elia here tells me you and her have already had a chance to get acquainted."

Reggie's blush returned with a vengeance, his entire face darkening. "I — uh, yeah... we met."

Sarah smiled from behind calculating eyes. "Well, then I assume you know already our plans for dinner?"

Reggie nodded. "I did get filled in, thanks."

"*We* didn't," Julie said. "No one bothered to let us know this was a formal affair." She stared at Sarah, standing innocently in her dress, as she said it, and Ben felt the heat rising in the air.

"I apologize," Elia said, sheepishly. "Your bellhop should have informed you. We are understaffed, however, so it could be that he simply forgot —"

"It's fine," Julie said. "We'll just have to make do with what we're wearing."

Ben looked down at himself and Julie. He was wearing flip-flops and board shorts with a green t-shirt that was stained with ketchup from lunch from two days ago. Julie, on the other hand, looked as amazing as always. She was wearing a cotton coverup over her swimsuit, the same flats she'd worn here from the ship, and a matching anklet and necklace set. Her hair was pulled up into a quick bun, her dark-brownish black hair 'accidentally' perfect.

"Well," Reggie said, clapping his hands together. "We've all met, had a moment to gather ourselves, and I'm sure we're hungry." He turned to the female bellhop and extended his arm. "Would you show us the way, Elia?"

She nodded and began walking off, a bit too quickly. Ben found himself rushing to keep up. She reached the elevator and flicked at the 'up' button. The door immediately opened, and she stepped in, held the door for the rest of them.

Ben followed Julie in and took up a spot near the mirrored side wall of the elevator. He turned slowly, realizing that there were mirrors on only *three* walls of the car.

The fourth wall, opposite the door, was glass. Rounded, bubbling outward, with a metal railing bending around at waist-high level. They were essentially at sea level, the water extending outward from the outside of the elevator to the opposite shoreline of the second, larger island ring. The water was deeper than the water between the second and third rings, judging by the darker blue color.

He grabbed Julie's arm and pulled her close as they started ascending, ensuring that she had a view of the three circular rings that made up the park. They rose to the top, the fifth floor, and the view only became more astonishing the higher they went.

The ocean surrounded the park on all sides as far as he could see, giving Ben the impression that the place was far smaller than it truly was. But he could see that the largest ring was massive — stretching out in a wide arc around the two inner rings, the artificial beach situated between it and the second section. The tiny dots of lounge chairs and tables that he'd seen from the helicopter when they'd flown over were smaller now, but from this angle he could see that the cabana-style bars were fully stocked, three ascending rows of whiskeys and rums and other spirits he couldn't wait to try.

The team had never discussed an official 'drinking on the job' policy, but since Mr. E wasn't a drinker and the others were responsible about it, Ben assumed it was a nonissue, unless a situation became an issue. He and Reggie, in fact, had enjoyed plenty of whiskey while 'on the job,' since the lines between being paid and being off work were blurred.

He only hoped that this trip would allow them some relaxation time. He was growing more excited for the dinner, his expectations high for the quality of food they would be served. If the rest of the place was any indication, this park would be an amazing facility and do quite well for themselves.

The elevator dinged and the doors slid open. Ben turned back around and watched as the doors parted. The first thing he noticed was the size of this floor. It was small, and he could see the opposite side of the room. The walls were glass, curved like the rest of the building, and they provided a 360-degree bird's-eye-view of the entire park. A table sat in the middle of the room, round as well, and a lit candelabra formed from coconuts and palm fronds sat at the center of the spread.

"Welcome, again!" Crawford's enthusiastic voice reached Ben's ears before he saw the man.

Adrian Crawford was standing against the far wall, near a rolling cart piled high with prepared dishes.

"Come in," he said, waving them all toward him. "The first course is ready. And I cannot *wait* to tell you about the park! Come sit!"

CHAPTER 18

THE FOOD WAS BETTER than anything he'd imagined. Perfectly cooked scallops, wrapped in bacon and served beneath a coating of white wine garlic-basil reduction, on a bed of arugula. And that was just *one* of the main course options. Mounds of fresh king crab, piled in a towering assortment of rings around a large bowl of garlic butter, and a stack of sea bass fillets with a rosemary lemon pesto.

The vegetables looked just as appetizing. Broccoli and cauliflower, steamed, and carrots and beets nearby.

It was shocking, really. All of the food had just seemed to appear before them, even though Ben had been watching the waiters and waitress the entire time. The food was revealed from within the silver serving platters and domed lids, placed in exacting locations around the center of the table.

"I hope you all like seafood," Crawford said, taking a spot at the head of the table. "But if not, please do let one of our servers know. There is another group of guests staying with us that will be dining in about half an hour, and their meal will consist of more *terrestrial* cuisine. Steak, chicken, lamb. All cooked in a southern-Caribbean style."

Reggie had opened his mouth to respond, but Ben beat him to it. "Uh, wow. That all sounds amazing."

Julie kneed him under the table.

"Sorry, this — *here* — this is all amazing," Ben said. "I didn't mean to imply —"

"Nonsense!" Crawford said. His enthusiasm grew. "Shannon," he said, gently grabbing the elbow of the woman who was pouring ice water into his glass. "Would you mind bringing up a sampling of the dinner we're serving on 2?"

She nodded, finished pouring, then handed the pitcher to her associate and left the room.

"Let's get started, shall we?" Crawford said.

Ben nodded, excited to get started on the food sprawled out in front of him.

"*OceanTech* was a dream of mine from a very young age," Crawford began.

Oh, Ben thought. *It's a speech. I thought we were starting dinner.* He released the section of crab legs he'd picked up.

"I wanted to combine the thrill of education with the excitement and mystery of the sea," he said. "I was, admittedly, a bit of a *nerd*, but I realized then something that I've built my career on: people love to learn. The trouble is that they just don't know *how*, or *what* they'd like to learn. *OceanTech,* and this place, the Institute, is the product of that line of reasoning.

"By combining the wonders of the deep with a relaxing, intriguing, and *fun* environment, *OceanTech Institute* will hopefully rekindle the spark in all of us. The spark of *knowledge*."

Ben wanted to roll his eyes. Sure, this place was great, and the food looked amazing — he was still impatiently awaiting the moment he could dig in — but he had never been one for *learning*. School wasn't his best subject.

Reggie, on the other hand, was enjoying Crawford's monologue immensely, sitting perched at the edge of his seat, his elbows on the table. Dr. Lindgren was next to him, leaning back to see around him. Julie sat on the opposite side of the table next to Ben, and she also seemed engaged.

Isn't anyone else hungry? he wondered. *What are we waiting for?*

The food beckoned. His stomach growled. Julie kneed him again under the table.

"Enough for now," Crawford said. "I do have a bit of the performance bug in me. I apologize — let's eat."

He waved his hands around in a flourish and the two remaining waiters rushed in on opposite sides of the table and began to serve the items onto everyone's plate. Crawford, however, did not stop his presentation.

"When I first began doing research for this place, I wanted to build a place that could exist independently from its combined idea. I wanted a five-star resort, in and of itself, as well as a museum of sorts. And I wanted both to be able to stand alone as the best in the world of their kind."

"And by combining them it's the best of both worlds," Reggie said.

"Precisely," Crawford said. "The institute is perfect for everyone — come to study, learn, and grow, or come to relax, be pampered. Or, of course, both."

"Why here?" Julie asked. "This location — it's... odd. It seems like you would be more hurricane-prone out here than on the other side of the state, in the Gulf somewhere. Or at least north of The Bahamas rather than northwest."

Crawford examined Julie for a moment before answering. "An intriguing question, Ms. Richardson. The answer is quite simple, but it is one you might not expect."

Ben listened intently, suddenly interested.

"Let me answer that by giving you a very brief overview of the technology we've put into place here. I do admit I'm quite proud of this place, but I also need the practice — I'm considering this week a *soft* soft launch, if you will." He smiled, the dimple on his cheek exaggerated and seeming to stare directly at Ben.

"Are you familiar with oil rigs?" Crawford asked. Reggie and Julie nodded, Ben and Sarah stared. "Well, there are quite a few different methods for constructing a rig. Most of the oil platforms we are familiar with are fixed platforms, those types that are affixed to the ocean bed, or semi-submersible, which, as the name implies, float on the water but have enough weight in their center to keep them upright."

Ben took his first bite of crab leg after dipping it into the tiny bowl of garlic butter the server had poured. He closed his eyes, amazed at the taste, and missed the beginning of Crawford's next sentence.

"...another type of platform, called a tension-leg structure, which is sort of like anchoring — it's tightly pulled to the seabed, which eliminates most of the movement. Our outer two rings are affixed in this way, their bases constructed of floats with artificial terrain installed on them. The center tower, the one we're in now, is directly fixed, built into the seabed itself.

"There are also two special submersible vehicles that run on cables, sort of like underwater ski lifts or gondolas, that we engineered, and are working to have patented. They travel beneath the water from one side of the largest ring to the other, each making stops at the inner circle and this tower. There are bridges, of course, and ferry rafts that we use for our guests, but the Subshuttles allow our staff to travel from one side of the park to the other without needing to be seen by guests."

Ben frowned. *Interesting choice.* "That seems expensive," he said.

Crawford laughed. "We've spared *no* expense here, Mr. Bennett. Hence the luxurious dinner we've prepared for our guests this evening. Did I mention the guests downstairs are some of our investors? They are here on a similar tour, but theirs will end in another day. After that, you'll have the place to yourselves."

"Better make a good impression on them, I guess," Ben said.

"Indeed." Crawford took a sip of his water. "Anyway, the two structures — the central fixed tower and the two floating outer rings — work together to stabilize one another. It saves on energy costs, and it was actually *cheaper* to build that way."

"But why not just make both sections — the tower and the rings — float?" Reggie asked.

"Yeah," Sarah Lindgren jumped in, "seems like you could benefit by moving the entire place around like a giant cruise ship. Take your museum park anywhere in the world."

Crawford was nodding along. "Yes, yes, we did consider that. It would be quite the accomplishment as well, and — like you said — it would benefit us in terms of mobility. We could relocate in one corner of the globe during the calm season there, dodging any catastrophic weather. Or we could offer different experience packages, much like cruises. Winter in the Caribbean, summer in Alaska or the Antarctic.

"But we had no choice. The scientific branch of *OceanTech* needed to be here. The institute was built over a shallow section of land off the coast of The Bahamas purposefully, anchored in place."

Ben looked over at Reggie, watched his friend trying to work it out. Shallow section of land, anchored in place, the 'tower' they were in extending both above *and* below the water. In the middle of a storm-riddled section of the Atlantic.

They were here because *OceanTech* needed *this* location.

"What's here?" Ben asked. "What are we sitting on?"

Crawford's dimple grew and shrank as the man tried on multiple smiles, finally settling on a flattering one that Ben almost believed. "*That*, my friend, is the *perfect* question."

"*OceanTech Institute* was designed and built in this precise location because of what lies on the ocean floor directly beneath us. We surveyed and found this spot, and precisely this spot."

"Because it's shallow?"

"Because it's the spot of an old shipwreck. We're sitting on the wrecked boat right now, ten stories above it."

CHAPTER 19

"THAT WAS ENTERTAINING," Julie said, sighing heavily as she crashed onto the soft bed. She hadn't had time to test the mattress, get a feel for the room, earlier, so she was relieved to find that it was every bit as luxurious as their dinner had been, and the rest of the room.

"Crawford's a character," Ben said. "That's for sure. But I like him."

"Me too," Julie said. "Seems nice, and definitely passionate about his park."

"*Science* park," Ben corrected, smiling at her. He was removing his shoes and socks, and she knew the shirt would come next. He had little habits like this that she'd learned. Shoes, socks, shirt. Right foot, left foot, shirt. His pants or shorts would either stay on or come off, depending on how cool the room felt. She assumed that here, in a climate-controlled hotel room, they would be coming off.

She wasn't wrong. Ben stripped to his briefs and plowed down onto his side of the bed. For a fancy mattress, it didn't do well trying to spread out the impact, and Julie felt herself thrown up into the air a few inches before coming back down again.

"That dinner was *amazing,*" Ben said.

"I could tell you liked it. You still smell like crab."

He grinned, picking his teeth.

"And steak. And fish. And chicken."

"Sorry," he said. "It was all good."

"The vegetables were good too. You could've had a few bites of those."

"Why?" he shot back. "They just take up space where more *meat* could fit."

Julie shook her head and looked to her right, trying to find the remote control for the television. She wasn't particularly interested in watching TV, but she knew it was a ritualistic way of winding down at night. Ben would be out in a few minutes, and she would let the sounds of whatever channel she fell onto persuade her to sleep.

"We should talk," she suddenly said.

Ben groaned. "I thought we were —"

"*You* thought we were over it. Ben, come on. You were about to leave me behind on that ship."

"I *never* would have left you, Jules. You know that."

"That's the *point*, Ben. You *knew* I'd come with, even though it wasn't what I wanted to do."

Ben shifted up onto an elbow and looked over the bed at her. "You saying you don't want to be here?"

She rolled her eyes.

"No, seriously. This place is *amazing*, Julie. *Way* better than the cruise ship. Nicer — bigger — rooms, fewer people. And my God, the food."

"I'm not saying it's not nice, Ben."

"You're just saying it's not what you wanted to do. Got it."

She huffed, feeling the anger and resentment rush back as if it had not been temporarily calmed for the past few hours.

"What?" Ben asked. "You said you wanted to talk, so let's —"

"Just forget it, Ben. It's not worth it."

"Jules, I —"

"No. Forget it. You know what, Ben? You're so caught up in your own personal battles all the time you forget that there are *other people* around you who care about you."

He frowned at her, but she held fast. *I'm right,* she thought. *And he knows it.*

"What's that supposed to mean?"

"Exactly what I said," she said. "You don't care that we're all here, you just do what you want and hope we come along for the ride."

"Reggie invited *us*, remember?"

"Reggie didn't *invite* us, Ben. He told us it was a *mission*. But that's not the point. You *came*, and you were *going to come* whether or not I did. You didn't even stop to ask me —"

Someone knocked on their door. Light, quick tapping.

"Come *on*," Julie said, swinging her legs over the edge of the bed and onto the floor. "Can't he just leave us alone?"

She reached the door and unlocked it, not bothering to look through the peephole. She swung it open, let it hit the wall next to her, the little rubber stopper thudding with the impact.

"Julie?" Ben asked. "Who is it?"

She stared. "I — I don't know." She took a step back, slightly, allowing the man at the door to step forward. "I'm sorry," she said. "Can I help you?"

The man was Asian, short but fit. He looked up at Julie and nodded. "I hope so." His accent was perfect American. "I truly hope so. But there's not much time."

Julie frowned. *Do I invite him in?* She shook her head, talking herself out of it. *Should I go into the hall? What if he attacks me? Is there something I can use as a weapon, or —*

"I need you to help me," the man said. "Right now. *Please.* I need to get out of the park. We can take the Subshuttle to the opposite bank, and then to the helipad, if you would just call your pilot and —"

"I'm sorry," Julie said again. "I don't know... I'm not sure —"

"*Please,*" the man said, stressing the word more this time. "There's not much time. They'll be here any minute, and you were the closest occupied room to —"

"Who is it?" Ben called out again.

"Hang on!" Julie yelled. *That was stupid,* she thought. *I should have asked him to come over here.*

She didn't need to, however. She heard Ben groan again and start walking over to the door.

The man flicked his head left and right, frantically, peering down the hallway in both directions. If he heard something, Julie couldn't tell. He swallowed, then looked back up at her. There was a moment they matched expressions, both frantic, scared. Then Julie shifted back to confusion, the man to frustration. He looked both ways once more, stopping with his head bent looking to his left.

"Too late," he whispered. "Too late. They're here."

The man shifted, changing his approach. He pulled something out of his pocket and handed it to Julie.

It was a smartphone. The screen lit up as he placed the object in her hand, then shut off again.

"What?" she asked. "Who's here? And what am I supposed to do with this?" she asked.

He shook his head. "Listen to me — are you listening? Listen. Not enough time, but you'll need..." he looked again to the left, then back at Julie. "You need the number. *0-4-0-3-0-2.* Got it?"

She started to repeat it just as Ben reached the door. "What's up?" he asked. He saw the man, but the man had already turned and was heading down the hall, to his right. Julie watched him for a moment. She could hear his breaths, loud and erratic. Then the man picked up his pace and started running.

Frantically.

CHAPTER 20

REGGIE OPENED the door to his hotel room with an audible sigh. *Just when I was about to pour a glass of wine,* he thought. He let the door swing open and moved to the side to allow Julie and Ben to step through.

He wasn't much of a wine drinker, but he had found a bottle of red in the mini fridge hidden behind a cabinet door near the closet. After dinner he had found himself in an unusually wine-focused mood.

Ben nodded a quick greeting, but Julie headed straight for the glass wall at the back of the room, aiming toward the armchair there.

"Come on in, I guess," Reggie said. "Don't... call first or anything."

Ben ignored the remark, but Julie was already talking. "The guy was Asian, but sounded American. Probably grew up in the states..."

She stopped when she realized that Reggie wasn't the only other person in the room.

"H — hello," the woman said. Reggie walked back into the room just as Ben noticed the woman as well.

"Dr. Lindgren?" Julie asked.

"Sorry, Reggie and I were about to —"

"Enjoy this bottle of fine California red, a merlot and Cabernet blend," Reggie said.

"We were about to *talk*," Sarah clarified.

Julie glanced at Ben, but Ben was just looking at the woman, stretched out on Reggie's bed. She was fully clothed, but she had changed and was now wearing jean shorts and a gray sweatshirt that said 'Jamaica' across the front in multi-colored lettering.

Reggie cleared his throat. "Of course. She and I were chatting in the hall but I knew there was more to drink here in the room. Plus it was more comfortable."

"What... what were you talking about?" Julie asked.

"The mission, actually," Sarah answered abruptly. "I asked about the CSO and how you all came to be together, and about your previous missions."

Ben walked over to the other armchair and sat, leaving Reggie to pace around the room. The end of the bed was open, but he knew there was already a bit of a stigma in the air, and he didn't want to inspire any further questions from his teammates.

"And she told me how she came to be a part of this mission as well," Reggie said. He walked back over to the bottle of wine he had just opened, still sitting on the countertop.

"Mind if you repeat some of that for our sake?" Ben asked. "I'm not sure we know the details."

Julie cut in. "Well, actually, I think that needs to wait, right Ben?"

The couple looked at each other, and Ben nodded. "Right. Uh, so there was..."

"An incident," Julie finished.

"An *incident*?" Sarah asked.

Reggie walked over to the bed and handed Sarah one of the two glasses of wine. "You two want anything?"

Julie shook her head. "Is there whiskey in there?" Ben asked.

Reggie walked over to check while Julie continued their story.

"This man, the Asian guy, he was all frantic and scared. In a huge hurry. Not sure why he knocked on our door, but I answered it and he told us he didn't 'have much time,' and that we needed 'the number.'"

"The number?"

"0-4-0-3-0-2," Julie and Ben said simultaneously."

"Interesting," Reggie said.

"Weird," Sarah added.

"What is the number for?" Reggie asked.

"This, probably." Julie picked the man's phone out of her pocket and held it up. "I haven't tried it, but it's probably the lockscreen combination."

Everyone stopped and thought for a moment. Reggie walked over to Ben and handed him what he had found in the fridge. Two airline-sized bottles of Wild Turkey bourbon. *Not bad, not great.* Ben thanked him and twisted the cap off the first one.

"Let's see it, then," Reggie said. "Open it up, Jules."

Reggie watched Julie fumble with the extra-large phone for a moment, swinging it around in her hand until it sat comfortably in her palm. She held her thumb up, prepared to type in the combination.

A light tapping came from the door. Reggie walked over and looked through the hole. "Crawford," he said.

He opened the door and held it, the gap just wide enough that he could block the man from seeing inside. "Crawford, good to see you again. I'd invite you inside, but —"

Crawford cut him off by holding up a hand. "Thank you, Mr. Red, but that won't be necessary. I'm in a bit of a hurry, actually, and I just wanted to check with the four of you about something. Dr. Lindgren wasn't in her room, however, so I —"

"They all went on a walk, I believe. Or at least an elevator ride. I'm not sure, but I think they were just taking a stroll to see the premises."

"Fine, fine. Very well. I'll keep an eye out for them, and if you see them just pass this along."

"Of course. What can I help you with?"

"I'm wondering if you've seen a man, Asian-looking, a bit shorter than me?"

Reggie shook his head. "No, I apologize. I've been in my room since dinner."

"Right. Well, it is of the upmost importance that we track him down."

Reggie frowned. "Why? Is he dangerous?"

"Oh, no, no," Crawford said. "He is quite harmless, he's just... well, we're afraid he might be... you know, it's really nothing. I would just ask that you let me know immediately if you happen across him."

Reggie nodded. "Absolutely. You have my word. If I see him I'll be sure to call it in. And I'll let my group know as well, if I see them first."

Crawford looked solemn. "Thank you, Mr. Red. I hope you are enjoying your stay thus far?"

"It's amazing. Well done, Crawford. This place is truly breathtaking."

Crawford's smile came back, the dimple pressing into Reggie's vision as if it were a dimple with a face attached instead of the other way around. "Good, good. Thank you for your time, and I'm sorry again to disturb you."

Reggie thanked him and closed the door. He walked back into the center of the room.

"Okay, folks," he said, addressing the three people seated on the bed and chairs. "Time to put our heads together. Sounds like we've got ourselves a mystery here."

CHAPTER 21

"BUT WHY WOULD he come to us?" Julie asked. She was sitting on her feet in the armchair, curled up into her clothes. She was cold for some reason, even though Reggie kept his own room a few degrees warmer than theirs. Ben sat next to her, stretched out with his legs wide, his right knee nearly touching her left.

Sarah Lindgren was still on the bed, but she had bunched her bare legs up and tucked them beneath her so Reggie could sit on the bottom half of the bed.

"Yeah," Sarah said. "Why not go to the police, or whatever it is they have here?"

Ben and Reggie exchanged a glance. "We have reason to believe that wouldn't have been a smart move," Reggie said. "The, uh, security here is not exactly... aboveboard."

"Aboveboard?"

"Trustworthy."

"I know what you mean, but why? You've got experience with them?"

Ben sniffed, Reggie looked around the room. Julie decided to jump in. "Yes, we do," she said softly. "The group protecting the park is called Ravenshadow. They were the group that chased us over the Lewis and Clark trail, and in Philadelphia."

"They're the ones that killed your friend," Sarah said. It wasn't a question as much as a statement of fact.

"Yes," Reggie said. "Joshua Jefferson. They murdered him in cold blood, and they would have killed all of us. They got away, but our director, Mr. E, tracked them here. We came to find their leader, Vicente Garza."

Sarah looked half shocked and half puzzled. "Okay, makes sense, I guess. I reached out to your director as well, but, like I was telling you earlier, I'm just here to follow up on some research I've been doing."

Ben shifted in his chair and leaned forward. "We do a lot better together when all the information's on the table. I hope you don't mind repeating yourself for our sake."

"No, not at all. Reggie and I had just started, anyway. He told me a bit about the group you were trying to find here, but I didn't realize it was the contracted security force. And I told him that I was following up on a lead I found in an online article."

"An online article?" Julie asked. "Something on a blog, or Wikipedia?"

"No, a journal, actually. Peer-reviewed, usually. The type of stuff that usually makes the rounds at universities, publishing stuff the vast majority of the public doesn't care anything about."

"So a bit more trustworthy than just a blog, then," Ben said.

"Exactly. The article was pulled, though. About an hour after it was published."

"An *hour*? That seems fast. How'd you catch it?"

"I have an RSS feed that scans for keywords and pulls down anything related to my search queries."

Ben nodded as if he understood what she was talking about. Julie nodded because she *did* know what she was talking about.

"Unfortunately I wasn't keeping downloads of the articles, and I can't find any cache results with the content anywhere online."

"So it's gone," Ben said.

"Sort of," Sarah answered. "I, uh, have somewhat of an eidetic memory. It's been useful throughout my life, but I can't control what my mind decides to retain."

Reggie looked over at Dr. Lindgren with a renewed interest. "I'm guessing this article wasn't one of those things your mind decided to keep filed away?"

She shook her head. "No, not all of it. Just the first page, which I could recite to you. But it was severely limited in detail, and while I remember a bit about the second and third pages of the publication, I don't recall the specifics."

"What's the gist, Dr. — Sarah —" Ben said, "why'd you come along?"

"Well, it's why I came to talk to Reggie after dinner. I would have come to you two, first, but..."

"I was closer," Reggie said. "Right?"

Sarah smiled. "Right."

"Go on," Julie said, not a little bit of strain in her voice.

"Right, sorry. I reached out to Mr. E and asked if he had information about this park. He got back to me right away and told me he was sending a team of three, and that I was welcome to come along, all expenses paid."

"Interesting."

"That's what I thought, too. But I understand why you're here now, and I can assure you I have no knowledge about Ravenshadow or the man who killed your teammate."

"That's fine, Sarah. No need to apologize," Reggie said. Julie half-expected the man to reach out and place his hand on her leg.

"The article gave me some clues, but I'm here to figure out the rest, if possible. The article was about a shipwreck."

Julie's eyes widened. "Like Crawford said. This park is right on top of a shipwreck."

"Right," Sarah said. "It was *built* on top of the wreck, actually. And if the article is to be believed, they began dredging the wreck and draining water from it."

"Whoa," Reggie said. "That's elaborate. And overkill, especially for a park attraction."

"I don't think it's supposed to be an *attraction*," Sarah said. "At least not totally. They'll probably open it up to viewing, behind glass or something, but I think they are studying the wreck somehow."

Julie stood up and walked to Reggie's mini fridge. "You mind?" she asked, tossing the question over her shoulder toward the man on the bed.

"Not at all."

She opened it and found a two-shot bottle of Canadian Club. *That'll have to do,* she thought. She twisted it open as she walked back to her chair. "Sarah — and I truly mean this with no offense — you're an anthropologist, correct?"

Sarah smiled. "None taken. Yes, you are correct. And I know what you're all thinking — why should an *anthropologist* care about a shipwreck? That would be my father's territory. Ancient mysteries, sunken below the sea, all that jazz, right?"

Julie nodded.

"Well the article mentioned that they had *found* things in the ship. Not just artifacts, like gold and silver, which they did find, but other things."

"Things... like what?" Ben asked.

"Well, like people."

"People?"

"Skeletons. Remnants of bones. Structural samplings that seem to imply the people inside the ship were mostly of Spanish descent."

"Mostly?"

"Mostly," she said, nodding. "And the rest was on the other pages of the article, so I don't have a clear recollection of the details, how they did the testing, that sort of thing, but I do remember that the *other* major line of descent seemed to be Incan."

"Incan," Reggie said. "Hmm."

"Yes," she said. "My working hypothesis is that this ship was part of a treasure fleet, heading back to Spain, when it got caught in a storm and sank. There was treasure on board, surely, judging by the coins and artifacts that they found, but I believe the *real* treasure — the *real* reason this ship was booking it back to the motherland — was because of its *human* cargo. The skeletons."

CHAPTER 22

HUMAN CARGO. Ben wasn't sure why human cargo would have been important to the Spanish unless they planned on using the people as slaves, but he knew they didn't have the full story yet. They really had *no idea* what was going on here, but Ben was getting the impression they were about to find out.

"Julie, you should check the phone," he said.

Julie looked at him strangely for a second, then her eyes lit up. "I almost forgot about that! Yes, let's check out this guy's phone."

She held the phone up and waited for the lock screen to flash the prompt, waiting for the combination of numbers. She typed in the code the man had given her, *0-4-0-3-0-2*, and watched.

The lock screen changed to a home screen, with a row of folders and icons spread over the top three rows. There were the standard apps, like *Settings*, and *Calendar*, as well as some that she didn't understand, and she assumed they were meant for the man's work.

"Any idea what we should check first?" Julie asked.

"User information?" Reggie asked. "Maybe get a name?"

She nodded, already flicking through the folders to find the *Contacts* app. She tapped it, opened the first entry labeled, '*My*

Card,' and started reading out loud. "Dr. Joseph Lin. Employed at *Ocean Tech*. Has a phone number and email address."

"Okay, Dr. Lin," Reggie said, now strolling across the carpeted room. "What secrets do you have in store for us?"

She kept reading, but none of the information was immediately useful. "Any other ideas?"

"Pictures," Ben said. "Find the pictures."

Ben watched Julie's face as she navigated through the phone's folders and screens. She found the app, and he watched what little part of the screen he could see as she opened the first album inside the app.

Julie froze, and Ben noticed the hair on the back of her neck stand straight up. She gasped, then swallowed. She set the phone down on her knee as if it were suddenly hot, not wanting to touch it. But she didn't look away.

Ben leaned in to see, while Reggie ran toward them. Sarah, too, got off the bed and came over.

Ben put a hand over his mouth. *God, that's disgusting*. He held his hand there, not speaking.

The image on the screen in front of Julie was of an arm. A human arm, laying out on an empty, metal table. There was no body attached to the arm, but it was clear that the arm had been recently *detached*.

Clear, because the location where the arm would have met the shoulder had been wrenched free, skin and open muscle tissue bleeding and wretched over the entire open wound. A gash in the flesh showed the peeking end of bone, the head of the humerus. Ben wasn't sure what to think. It was one thing to see an image of a limb on television, or in a textbook, or even in an online article. But on a person's *phone*, an image that person took personally... that was something else entirely.

"What the *hell* is that?" Reggie asked. "Is it real?"

"Looks like it," Sarah said. "And judging by the wound, it wasn't surgically removed."

"Not unless 'surgery' to you means 'brutally ripped apart.'"

"Wow," Julie said. "I can't — I don't…"

"Jules, go to the next picture," Ben said. He could see that there were tiny icons at the bottom of the phone's screen, depicting more images in the series, though he couldn't tell what they were.

She did. The next picture was of the same arm, from another angle. This image showed more bruising, the purplish-black scarring just beneath the skin of the upper arm. It looked to Ben as if a massive creature had grabbed the person's arm and ripped it clean off the bone.

But something in the picture caught Ben's attention.

"Go to the next picture," he said. The others were gathered around Julie's chair, looking down at the phone.

She swiped to the right and the next image filled the screen. Ben's suspicions were confirmed: this image was of the area right next to the arm, which was barely visible in the last image but in-focus on the screen in this one.

It was the body the arm belonged to.

"Yuck," Reggie said. "I hate seeing dead bodies."

"You've seen a lot of them?" Sarah asked.

He glanced at her. "Just a few."

The body was white, cold-looking and stiff. It was a shot of the torso, from the angle just above the severed arm, looking at the left side of the body the arm had come off of. There was a wound where the arm had been removed, but the wound appeared to have been cleaned and stitched up, unlike the arm's open bloody gash. The shoulder on the torso looked enlarged from this angle, wider and taller than the opposite shoulder, and small bumps of bone pushed outward beneath the healing skin of the wound.

"I agree with Reggie," Ben said. "Yuck."

"What are we looking at here, doctor?" Reggie asked.

Dr. Lindgren shook her head, but she didn't take her eyes off the phone in Julie's hand. "Your guess is as good as mine, guys. It's a body, and it's an arm. They've been removed from one another."

"An *inquisitive* observation, doctor," Reggie said. No one laughed.

"Seriously," she added. "I'm an anthropologist. I don't get to look at much more than old bones most of the time. My anatomy and mortician studies classes were just core curriculum, so I'm not really able to tell what's going on here besides the obvious."

"If you had to guess?" Julie asked.

"If I had to guess," Sarah replied, "I'd say the person's arm was removed violently. You can see where the bones snapped apart, and the tendons and muscle structure imply that there was severe trauma during the operation."

Ben nodded. "So this Lin fellow is a murderer."

"We don't know that," Reggie said. "He was involved in something here, that's for sure, or he wouldn't have come running down the hall, looking for help. And there's a strong possibility that he was trying to clear his name — he did give you his phone and passcode, after all."

"Right," Ben said, "but why? If he was involved in all of this, why come to us?"

"We were the first people he saw?" Sarah asked.

"Maybe. But aren't there other people like him around? Staff, employees, something like that?"

"Probably. Could be that he was here, in the hotel, instead of the lab for some reason. Didn't Crawford say the hotel was the central ring and the second one was for the labs and staff quarters?"

Ben nodded. "Any other pictures?" he asked.

Julie flicked to the next image. This one was of another man, sitting, his back against a wall.

"I think he's still alive," Sarah said. "His head is down, but it seems like he's sleeping."

Ben realized she was right. He couldn't tell why, but the man seemed to be in a deep sleep, but not dead. He was dark-skinned, naked, his right arm at his side. His right side was facing the camera, so Ben couldn't tell for sure, but it seemed as though —

"He's missing an arm," Reggie said. "His left arm is gone."

"Can you tell from that angle?" Julie asked. "I can't see it." She pinched the screen and pulled her fingers apart, magnifying the image. The quality was good, and the image enlarged with little pixelation. Still, it was hard to tell.

"I think," Reggie said. "Go to the next one."

Julie scrolled to the next image, and this time Ben was sure. The picture was of a woman in the same type of space — three walls in view with a very low ceiling. A strangely small room, and the picture had been taken from below the woman, looking up at her. As if the cameraperson had been lying on the floor for the shot.

"Guess that answers your question," Sarah said.

The woman was not sleeping or dead but wide awake, facing at the camera from her position sitting along the back wall. There was a blank expression on her face as she stared forward. She, too, was dark-skinned, her long black hair falling around her shoulders, untreated and shiny with oil but still scratchy from wear and little attention. The hair was long enough to drape her neck but not long enough to cover her naked breasts.

And she was missing a leg.

Julie's head fell back a bit. Ben stared, trying to make sense of what he was seeing. The woman didn't seem upset, but she wasn't happy either. Her emotion was something else entirely — it seemed to be nonexistent. Just an empty shell of a woman. She wasn't trying to cover herself, nor did she seem to care that she was being photographed. She just... *was.*

"Weird," Ben said.

"*Very* weird. She's missing a leg, that guy was probably missing an arm..."

"And the first guy was missing an arm *and* his life."

"What the hell is all of this?" Julie asked. "You think this is happening *here*?"

Reggie shrugged, glancing at his watch. "No idea. I hope not. But it's getting late, and no one ever solved a mystery when they were tired. Let's get some sleep. We can check in with Mr. E first thing tomorrow morning, let him know what's going on."

He looked around. Ben didn't have any trouble with Reggie's decision, though the nagging feeling of wanting to understand what this Dr. Joseph Lin fellow had gotten himself into was growing.

It'll have to wait, he thought. *I could use some sleep. We all could.*

Julie yawned next to him, turning off the phone's screen. She looked over at him.

"Right," Ben said. "Let's relax a bit, get some sleep. Tomorrow's a new day. We can get up early, check in with Mr. E, get a good breakfast in us, then see what this place is *really* about."

CHAPTER 23

THE MORNING CAME FAST. Ben half-expected to wake up and realize he was still in a dream. He felt as though he hadn't slept at all, tossing and turning overnight until the sun's brutal intensity burned through the open shades.

He groaned, sitting up. *I'm going to have to shut those before I go to bed tonight,* he thought. He put his feet on the floor and waited, stretching his back and neck. He was in his mid-thirties, but sometimes it felt as though he was nearing sixty. His body was in the best shape of his life thanks to an oppressive workout regimen designed by Reggie that he'd been following for the past six months, but he was realizing that the older he got the harder he had to work just to keep things working the way they were supposed to.

Julie snored a quick snorting breath, then rolled over and flopped her arm over his pillow and spread to the middle of the bed. She was a selfish sleeper, taking up more than her fair share of space. Ben thought it was cute, but he never told her that. He watched her for a moment and smiled. He felt like they were still back on the cruise ship, waking up after a lazy day of sitting in the sun and in no hurry to begin all over again.

But they *weren't* on a cruise ship, nor was this a vacation. He would do his best to enjoy his time here with her, but he wanted to *work*. He wanted to find The Hawk — Vicente Garza — and the rest of his Ravenshadow goons, and he wanted to bring them in for justice. Or take care of it himself.

It was a fanciful long shot, but the CSO had been created for this sort of work. Finding answers to pressing concerns that the US government couldn't, wouldn't, or shouldn't get involved in. Things that needed more care than an untrained civilian could offer but didn't necessarily need a special forces team.

Ben, Reggie, and Julie — and previously Joshua Jefferson — had formed the backbone of the organization, becoming some sort of amalgamation between treasure hunters, detectives, and citizen cops. Mr. E and his wife provided the top-level support, including financing and communications logistics, while the three remaining members of the team became the on-the-ground task force.

So Ben wasn't entirely sure what exactly they'd be doing here, but the mission, as it had been explained to them by their leader, was simple: figure out what *OceanTech* was doing here at their new institute, see if they could find Ravenshadow and the man responsible for the deaths of many people, and then... report in.

It was the last part that Ben struggled with. He knew himself well. He wasn't rash or reckless, but he wasn't sure he'd be able to restrain from taking matters into his own hands if they *did* happen across Vicente Garza. Worse, he wasn't sure if *Julie* could restrain herself.

He stood up and continued stretching, forcing those thoughts to the back of his mind. He had more important concerns for now, and the first order of business was taking care of business. He walked into the restroom and started to close the door.

"You up?" he heard Julie say.

He opened the door again. "Yeah. Why?"

"I'm hungry," she said.

He smiled again. "Not surprised. You're a fatty in the morning."

"Hey," she said. The tiredness ruined any feigned anger she was trying to muster.

"I'll call for room service," Ben said. "I saw a menu on the desk. Looks like there's pretty much no limit to what we can order."

Julie laughed, her voice deep and full of sleep. "Well, in that case, I want pancakes *and* waffles. You never get to order that, you know? It's always one or the other."

"Yeah," he said. "I've heard the speech."

"I'm just saying."

He closed the bathroom door and decided he'd call for room service now, using the phone in the bathroom, so it would be ready for them by the time he got out of the shower.

He turned on the water, felt it, and saw that the jets were on both the wall *and* the ceiling, a significant step up from the trickle they'd had in the matchbook-sized restroom on the cruise ship. He sighed, knowing that no matter what today or tomorrow would bring, this shower would be a form of respite for him. He was a simple man, and a scalding hot shower was usually enough to calm his nerves.

Before he could step inside, however, he heard a knock on the door. He turned and grabbed the robe off of one of the hooks near the door, slipped into it, and walked to the hotel room's front door.

"Hello?" he said as he answered.

The man greeted him with a smile far too joyous for this time of day. "Room service, sir," the man said.

"Already?" Ben asked. "I was just about to get in the shower."

The man's face turned into an expression of severe disappointment, and Ben was sure he would have had the same look on his face if he'd kicked his dog. "I do apologize, sir. I can return in a few —"

"No," Ben said. "That's fine. Great, actually. My wi — fiancee is starving. Come on in."

The man did as he was told and entered, wheeling a cart full of silver platters and covers behind him. He pulled it into the room and stopped just outside the bathroom. He wouldn't look into the rest of the bedroom, and Ben assumed it was so that he didn't embarrass the other guest.

He smiled, the man turned and bowed quickly, then exited the room.

Ben looked down at the platters. There were five in total, and he began removing the lids on each to see how breakfast at this place compared to the cruise ship. He wasn't disappointed. The first two, the largest, contained the pancakes and waffles, a tower of each. The third and fourth were fruit and grains, tropical selections and what he assumed were different cereals available in the Caribbean islands. The fifth platter had a plate full of smoked salmon, pink and smelling of oakwood. A folded letter sat next to the plate.

Dear Harvey, the note began. *I remember you saying how much you enjoyed seafood last night. I hope you don't mind the small indulgence — I had some salmon flown in late last night for my own dining accommodations, and I thought of you. Enjoy — Adrian.*

"What's that?" Julie asked.

"Salmon," Ben said. "As well as a monster buffet of pancakes and waffles."

"You ordered smoked salmon?"

He shook his head. "No. Crawford sent it down, I guess."

"Wow," Julie said, not hiding the look of shock on her face. "He's really trying to impress us." She walked into the bathroom and grabbed her own robe, slung it on, and walked back out and started to poke at the pancakes without grabbing a plate.

"Yeah, he is," Ben said. "And it's working." He picked up a slab of salmon and inspected it, then popped it into his mouth. It melted, turning into a conglomeration of flavors: fish, smoke, butter. Perfect in every way. He'd never thought of fish as a breakfast food, even though to the other Alaskans he knew fish was a way of life. He closed his eyes, chewed, swallowed. *Amazing.*

Julie dug into the pancakes again, this time sliding three of the discs onto a plate. "Good?" she asked.

Ben didn't even speak. He chewed, made some noises, and kept his eyes closed.

"Okay," Julie said. "I get the point."

"So what's on the agenda for today?" Julie asked.

Ben finally opened his eyes, but he continued shoveling food into his mouth. First another salmon filet, then a half of a pancake, then a whole waffle. Julie watched and waited, impatiently judging by the look on her face.

"Well," he said, trying to chew and speak at the same time. "I guess we should try to salvage this vacation, right?"

Julie frowned. "Really? After what happened?"

"What happened?"

"Dr. Lin," Julie said. "We can't just ignore it. The man was... frantic."

"We're not ignoring anything, Jules. I'm just saying we should take our time with it, take advantage of our *extended* vacation."

"Is that what this is now?" she asked. Her voice had risen a few notes and was starting to sound shrill.

"What?"

"You — you forced us here, following Reggie, apparently so you could continue working, even though we were supposed to —"

"Be on vacation," Ben said. "I know. I was thinking about it, and I think it'd be best to take things slow. Relax a bit and enjoy the scenery."

Julie shook her head, her fists balled beside her. Neither of them had moved from the cart. Both were eating from plates that they had set on the edge of the rolling food tray, taking bites between words.

"What's the problem?" Ben asked. His own voice was starting to rise.

"The *problem*? Ben, you're kidding me, right? No one is this *dense*."

"Dense? I'm sorry, I'm not sure what you're talking —"

"Ben, come on. You and I were supposed to have a nice week-long vacation. Just me. And you. *Not* Reggie."

"I didn't force him to show up!" Ben shouted.

"No, of course you didn't. But you didn't exactly kick him off the boat, either."

"Oh, what? Was I supposed to just toss him over the edge?"

"No," Julie replied, "you were supposed to tell him 'no.' That we were on vacation. That we were just *relaxing*, just like you said we were doing here."

"And why *can't* we relax here? Why does it have to be on a cruise ship?"

"Why *can't* we? *Why?* Because, Ben, this is now a work trip. You and I both know there's something going on here, and Mr. E and Reggie specifically wanted us here so that we could figure out *what* exactly that was. We're here because *you* told Reggie we'd do it. I followed you, like I always do, and —"

"Like you *always do?*" Ben yelled. "What are you talking about?"

"Ever since we met, back at Yellowstone."

"Excuse me?" Ben asked. "*You* forced *me* to come with you."

"And you would have *died* if you didn't, Ben. Don't deny it."

"But that doesn't mean I *wanted* to."

Julie crossed her arms, ignoring the food and focusing her full attention on the man she'd agreed to spend the rest of her life with. "Yeah. I was aware of that then, and I'm aware of that now. Thanks for reminding me, Ben."

Ben scowled, taking another slice of salmon off the platter.

"You're a piece of work, you know that?"

"What's that even mean?" Ben asked, his mouth full of food.

"It means you're a jerk. And I'm not sure I *care* what the plan is for today, honestly. I'm going to find Sarah."

"Fine," Ben said. "Have a little 'girl time,' for all I care. Reggie and I came here to *work*, to figure out what's going on here. But enjoy yourselves."

There were tears in Julie's eyes now, and Ben tried as hard as he could to not see them. But he knew they were there, and he knew that he'd lost. His stubbornness aside, he knew he would have to be the one to apologize later, whether that was later today or sometime tonight. She could hide, but not forever. He could ignore her feelings, but not forever.

Damn.

Women were tricky. He had never had a relationship before Julie, much less a long-term, serious one. Julie was the love of his life, but he was constantly being reminded that love took effort, and a good bit of pride-swallowing.

He slammed the final rectangle of salmon, ignoring the rest of the mounds of food in front of them, and opened the door.

He walked out into the hallway and turned right, heading toward Reggie's room.

He let the door slam on his way out.

CHAPTER 24

"TROUBLE IN PARADISE?" Reggie asked, as soon as he'd opened the door. Ben's melancholy face stared back at him, and Reggie motioned him in.

"Yeah," Ben said. "To say the least."

"Sorry to hear that, bud," Reggie said. "Want some food?"

Reggie had a spread that was almost as impressive as Ben's and Julie's had been — mounds of scrambled eggs, fresh fruit, strips of bacon and sausage links. Reggie was a self-described 'protein fanatic,' eating just about anything but preferring to start his day off with a healthy dose of animal fats and meat. He'd developed the habit in the military, discovering that his body responded better to a low-carb diet that was high in protein and fat, and he'd never been able to kick it.

And as a man who stretched north of six feet tall and weighed nearly 240 pounds in mostly muscle, he had a ravenous appetite. For as fit as Reggie was, his ability to consume more food than a normal human male should be able to consume was a contradiction.

Ben shook his head and stepped into the room. "I just — I just don't get it."

"Get *it* or get *her*?" Reggie asked.

"Yeah."

Reggie threw his head back and laughed. "Don't worry, my friend. Women were not created to be understood. It's the reason I know that whatever greater entity exists up there has a *strong* sense of humor."

"Or a twisted one."

"Chin up, pal," Reggie said. "You're in paradise, remember?"

"Feels like purgatory."

Reggie laughed again. "Nonsense. We're here to do a job, but it's a simple job. We'll find The Hawk, we'll bring him in, and we'll enjoy ourselves while we do it."

Ben made a noise. "Really? You buy that? We've *never* been sent on a mission that ended with us all relaxed and at ease. You think it'll be different now?"

Reggie sighed. "No, I guess not. If Vicente Garza is here, he's not going to come in quietly. And he'll probably have more than a few of his goonies around him, protecting him. So we're on high-alert until we're done."

"Great. Julie's gonna flip when I tell her that."

"Pal, she already *knows* that. She's not stupid, and you didn't actually think she followed you out here because she thought it would be an extension of her vacation, did you?"

Ben shook his head, swiping at the top layer of eggs on the plate. He didn't use a fork or a plate, just shoveled some into his mouth and chewed them slowly. Reggie watched for a moment, then grabbed a slice of bacon and followed suit.

"I guess not," Ben said. "But — but she was so *weird* about it. Like I'm the reason we're here. *You* were the one who came onto our cruise ship and told us about the —"

Reggie held up a hand. "Yeah, but I didn't *make* you guys come. Ben, she's just *worried*. She loves you. Hell, she's going to *marry* you for some stupid reason. That means she *cares* about you, and she wants to make sure you're doing what's right for *both* of you."

"Reggie, why the hell did you tell us to come here if you don't even think it was a good idea?"

Reggie took a step back, farther into his room. "Whoa, buddy. I'm not saying it was a bad idea to come. It's our *job* to come, remember? We signed up for this."

"Then what are you saying?"

"I'm just saying that she's right about you — you know? She's got you figured out, man, and that's not that hard a thing to do. You're the kind of guy that just won't let it go until you've figured it out. Whatever 'it' is. You won't drop it, even if it means running headlong into danger. It's the greatest asset you have, but it's your biggest weakness."

Ben looked at him like he was about to rush him. Reggie braced, not sure if Ben was going to try to tackle him or burst into tears.

"Thanks. Appreciate the vote of confidence."

Reggie smiled. "Look, dude, I'm not trying to make you mad. I'm just telling you the truth. She's pissed because she knows you, and she knew what you were going to do even before you did it. I don't blame her, and neither should you."

"Well, whatever. Is it too early to drink?"

Reggie laughed. "Never. But we've got something else planned. I figured you and me could head up to Crawford's office and ask him some questions about the park, his background, etcetera. Sarah and Julie are going to check out the staff and employee areas, see about this Dr. Lin fellow."

Ben frowned. "You had that all set up already? Julie didn't mention anything."

Reggie grinned, a sly smile growing on his face. "Julie hasn't heard about the plans yet, but Sarah and I made them this morning, after —"

"Stop," Ben said. "Just stop. I got it. You guys *did* seem like you'd made friends quickly."

"What? Nothing happened. Just two nerdy colleagues, chatting about the mission. We thought it would be best to get a jump on the day, maybe give us some time to hang out and relax this afternoon."

"Right," Ben said. "Fine. Well let's get to it, then. Where's Crawford's office?"

Reggie's grin grew, the enormous smile that had come to define him spreading across his face. "That's the best part."

CHAPTER 25

"I'M WORRIED ABOUT BEN," Sarah said as they walked down the hallway toward the elevators. "He seems so focused on the mission, so intent on finding this guy, Vicente Garza."

Julie waited a moment, thinking. "Well Garza killed his friend."

"*Your* friend too, right? And Reggie's?"

"Yes."

"So why is Ben the one who seems so —"

"Look, *Dr. Lindgren*," Julie said, her words flying out of her mouth. "I don't know you, and I know you don't know my fiancé. He's *fine*. That's just the way he is, okay?"

Sarah seemed to be physically hurt. She slowed. "I — I'm sorry. I didn't mean anything by it."

Julie sighed. "I know. He's just... it's complicated. He's an interesting guy."

"No," Sarah said. "It's my fault. I shouldn't have pried. I know how it is."

"You do?" Julie asked.

Sarah nodded as she pushed the button on the elevator. They were heading down to the sub-levels beneath the hotel, where the map in the room had said they would find the laboratory and scientific research arm of the *OceanTech* facility. Their plan was simple: Reggie and Ben were going to head to Crawford's office and do a little investigating of their own, while Sarah and Julie would check out the staff areas and see if they could find anyone who knew Dr. Lin.

Julie was shaken from last night's revelation on Dr. Lin's phone, but it was too early to tell exactly what was happening, or what it meant. They had little information to make any educated guesses about what exactly they had stumbled onto here, but Julie felt an uncanny sense of dread surrounding all of it. Dr. Lin's face was plastered in her mind. His fear, his frantic muttering, his flicking eyes, seeing everything and nothing all at once.

It was terrifying, and Julie couldn't shake the feeling that something about this place was... wrong.

No one else seemed to share her opinion, at least not yet — but how could they? They weren't there; they didn't see. They didn't know. They *couldn't.* She'd tried to explain it to Ben, but he'd assumed the man was simply reeling from something *he'd* seen.

The truth, what Julie knew without a doubt, was that the man — Dr. Joseph Lin — wasn't just a *spectator.* He was *part* of it. He had a role in it.

She wanted to know what that role was, and more importantly, she wanted to know why. *What is this place?* The question lingered in her mind long after she'd gone to sleep last night, sticking in her subconscious and causing all sorts of odd dreams. Not quite nightmares, but the types of dreams that ended in a cold sweat and waking up with the odd sensation of being someone else for a brief moment.

She thought back to her time in the Amazon rainforest, running from the same man who Vicente Garza had killed. They were studying dreams then, trying to understand an anomalous link between an ancient tribe of people and their descendants using dream-recording technology.

If I only had that technology here, she thought. *Maybe I could make some sense of all this.*

But she also knew that her dreams weren't the cause of the problem. They were simply a reflection of her thoughts, the reactionary machine her biological computer had built to handle strange and unknown circumstances.

"Juliette," Sarah said. "You okay?"

Julie snapped out of her own thoughts and looked over at Sarah. They were on the elevator now, descending, and Julie could feel the gentle vibration of the elevator car as it slid down its cabling. "I'm sorry," she said. "I zoned out. What were you saying?"

Sarah smiled. "Don't worry about it. I just said, 'yeah, I do know how it is.' I had a boyfriend, too. We were close, about to get married if he'd ever gotten around to proposing."

"What happened?" Julie asked.

"He... didn't. Just left."

"Really?"

"Really. It was heartbreaking. I mean, I'm a relatively confident woman, but I've got my share of self-image issues."

"*You?*" Julie asked. "I mean — sorry. Didn't intend for that to sound so rude. It's just... you're... Sarah, you're a knockout."

Sarah looked down at the floor of the elevator. "Thanks. I... yeah, I guess I've never had trouble attracting the boys. It's *convincing* them I'm worth it in the long run that seems to be the trouble."

"You're brilliant. You're beautiful. You probably know kung-fu or something. That's the triumvirate, Sarah. Every man you've ever met has been intimidated by you."

Sarah laughed. "I wish! No, I definitely don't know kung-fu."

"Still," Julie said. "That's how it works. Guys want us all to be weak little princesses who need saving. You don't strike me as the 'cutesy Barbie' type."

"Well thanks. I'm not. Anyway, this guy was similar to Ben in some ways." She froze, her eyes widening. "Not that Ben would do something like that. Just his personality is similar. So focused, so intense. You know?"

Julie smiled. "I know. What happened with your knight in shining armor?"

Sarah struggled with the words, looking around the elevator car as it slid slowly down past 'Sub-1' and then neared 'Sub-2.' "He ran off with another girl."

"I'm so sorry. Did you know her?"

Sarah nodded. "My classmate and then colleague. We were best friends."

Julie put her hand over her mouth. "God, that's terrible."

"Felt like the end of the world."

"What'd you do?"

Sarah shrugged. "What any pissed-off academic would do, I guess. I threw myself into my work, published more papers and research articles than any sane woman should, and started building a reputation for myself."

"That doesn't sound so bad."

"I lost fifteen pounds and almost was hospitalized because I refused to eat."

"Oh."

"No big deal — I got over it, kept working, and eventually became more recognized than her in our field."

"That had to feel nice," Julie said.

"Not really, actually," Sarah said. "That was the biggest surprise. I thought I could 'beat her' by being better than her at our profession. But it was short-lived, the feeling of victory. I still felt robbed, like my life had been stolen from me. I didn't even love him anymore, but it was still... crappy."

"I bet."

The elevator dinged. They'd reached the lowest level, 'Sub-3,' and the doors began to open.

Julie looked over at Sarah. "Hey," she said. "I just want you to know — I'm sorry. I had a bad attitude, and you're new to the group. I think I felt intimidated too. I like you, and I'm really looking forward to getting to know you better."

Sarah smiled, a genuine grin that Julie couldn't help but return. "Me too, Juliette. I'm excited for this trip, and I can't wait to find out what this place is all about."

Julie sighed as she followed Sarah over the threshold and onto Sublevel 3. *I wish I could be excited about that too,* she thought. *But I have a feeling it's not going to be anything good.*

CHAPTER 26

THE MAN SAT FORWARD in his tall, leather chair. Nearly on the edge, he swiveled slowly, rocking back and forth just slightly, enough to notice he was moving but not enough to appear disinterested. There was a calm smile on his face. The dimple was suppressed, still present but not glaringly obvious.

Ben walked farther into Adrian Crawford's private office, Reggie following just behind him. "Good morning," Ben offered.

Crawford's smile grew. "Welcome, both of you! Thank you for taking the time to visit me here."

Is he being serious? Ben thought. *We're the ones on vacation.*

"We know you're busy, Mr. Craw—"

"Call me Adrian." There was no 'please,' no beckoning of politeness, just an assumption between old friends. "I hate when people try to be formal. We're all peers here, wouldn't you say?"

Not at all, Ben thought.

Reggie smiled back. "Of course, thank you Adrian." He walked forward and took a seat in one of the chairs in front of Crawford's desk. Another brown leatherback, but this one didn't swivel and had a lower back. Ben followed suit and sat down in the chair adjacent to Reggie.

"I'm glad you set this up," Adrian said. "I apologize for not thinking of it myself. It will be a *perfect* opportunity to talk man-to-man."

Reggie nodded.

"I do wish your fiancee and Dr. Lindgren could join us, however," Crawford said.

Ben opened his mouth to explain where they had gone, but Reggie beat him to it. "They're taking a little tour of the outer ring," he said quickly. "Sunbathing, swimming, and probably enjoying the morning drink menu."

Crawford laughed. "Of course they are. And quite a menu it is. As I mentioned last night, we're understaffed at the moment, but we're *certainly* not undersupplied. You and the group of investors staying here will have just about free reign of any of our fabulous bars, though — between you and me — I wasn't terribly impressed with the drinking choices of the investors. It's all about one-upping each other on expensive bottles of wine." He made a face. "I'm more of a whiskey man, myself."

Reggie's grin widened, and he sat back in the chair, getting more comfortable. "Well, I can get behind that, Adrian."

Ben nodded.

"Great, well let's get started. Reggie, you mentioned you had a few questions for me?"

Reggie sat back up. "Yes, I — we do. As you know, we're here on behalf of the CSO."

"The Civilian Special Operations. A wonderful group — you're treasure hunters, no?"

Reggie's head tilted slightly. Ben nearly frowned, but caught himself. They weren't 'treasure hunters,' but they certainly had come across what might have been considered 'treasure' in the past. Biological and genetic discoveries, new drugs, and not a small amount of actual cash, in the form of gold and silver. But the main directive of the CSO was to seek out and find the perpetrators of crimes against the American people, domestic or abroad, that fell outside the jurisdiction — or the realm of plausible deniability — of the government.

They were like a private security force, with less emphasis on solving crime cases and more on cases of historical significance. They were led by a philanthropic billionaire, and each of them were board members, along with one member from each of the armed services.

"Sort of," Reggie said. "But the treasure we're usually after isn't really what people would consider 'treasure.' More like 'history hunters.'"

"I see," Adrian said. "And I'm intrigued. That's part of why I was so eager to host you all: I'm a bit of a history buff myself, though my background in is in the applied sciences. I've been following your careers ever since Antarctica, and I must say — your work results and reputation precede you."

Man, this guy's good, Ben thought. He now understood how Crawford had gotten this gig. He may have had a background in the sciences, but he was a killer salesman. The man could probably sell ice to an Eskimo.

"Thank you," Reggie said. "And we are excited to be here. This place is — well... it's amazing. You already know that, but seriously. Well done."

"Thank *you*," Crawford said. "I am quite proud of our work here at *OceanTech,* and I'm hoping *Paradisum* is but one of many such parks we open in the near future."

"Me too." Reggie shifted in his chair, a clear sign that he was about to deepen the conversation. "You mentioned last night that this whole place is right on top of a shipwreck."

Adrian Crawford watched Reggie's face as he spoke, offering nothing.

"...What wreck is it?"

Finally, he spoke. "We don't know, actually. Spanish, of that much we are sure. Probably from one of the treasure fleets that came up from South America, but we have yet to have a definitive match. There's really not much left of it but a shell and some framing."

"Why build it right there? Is it an exhibit?"

"Yes and no," Adrian said. "It's an exhibit, but it's *also* a real, live scientific expedition. We want to know everything about this ship, and we have teams in place beginning to salvage and clear the wreckage, all the while maintaining the integrity of the site. We hope it can serve as a backdrop to the public-facing research we do here at *Ocean-Tech*. The general public has no idea what these sort of expeditions look like, and our dream here at the park is to change that. If the public had a better perception of what 'exploratory diving' or 'anthropological undersea research' meant, there would be many more young men and women taking up careers in those fields. And there would be more publicity, and more funding."

Ben nodded. He fully agreed with Crawford. At Yellowstone he and the other park staff had often complained about the lack of young people interested in the outdoor programs they ran and the decreasing numbers of people interested in careers in national and state parks. They mostly agreed that education was the main issue: if children learned about the outdoors in a tactile, hands-on way from a young age, they would carry that interest and knowledge with them through their adult years.

"So you're planning on *showing* the wreck?"

Crawford's eyes glistened, and Ben sensed his excitement rising. "Why, yes. That's exactly what we're planning." He smiled at each of them, then continued. "Unfortunately the viewing chamber is not ready yet — we'd like to clear the wreckage and pump the room first."

"That's fine," Reggie said. "I'm sure it will be impressive. Crawford — Adrian, sorry — we're actually here for a different reason, as you're probably aware."

Crawford nodded. "I'm aware you're here for a different reason, though your benefactor wasn't willing to confide in me what that reason was."

"He tends to be a bit... reserved."

"Indeed. Well, if I had to guess, based on your prior engagements I've been following, I'd say you're here to investigate our security protocols."

Ben looked around the wall behind Crawford. He saw the obligatory credentials, the framed diplomas from at least three institutions hanging around the huge window. He saw newspaper clippings and magazine articles, apparently declaring something praiseworthy that Crawford had done or been a part of. There were no pictures on the wall, but Ben's eyes fell to the desk.

There was one picture on the man's desk, facing inward toward Adrian's seat but at an angle, diagonal enough so that Ben could see part of it. A man, a younger version of Adrian Crawford, standing next to a boy in a wheelchair. The boy was smiling, but Crawford's face was an emotionless mask.

"Not an investigation," Reggie answered. "Your business is your business. We're merely trying to track down a man we believe the government will be interested in speaking with."

"And what man is this?" Crawford asked.

"He's the head of your security team here," Ben answered. "Vicente Garza."

Crawford closed his eyes and leaned his head back. "Yes, Mr. Garza. Ex-military, somewhat of a strong-arm."

"Somewhat."

"And what interest does the CSO have in Mr. Garza?"

"The government. Not the CSO. But — and I'm sure you can appreciate this — the 'government,' at least in name, wouldn't be willing to make the trip down here. Wouldn't serve their interests, or yours."

"I suppose it wouldn't," Crawford said. "But tell me, Mr. Red, what am I supposed to do in this situation? Turn over Mr. Garza to you two? Let you take him away from his post here at the island?"

Reggie shook his head. "We just want a meeting."

"Of course."

"Of course?"

"Yes, of course you do. And what shall I tell him is the nature of this meeting?"

Ben frowned. "Just... tell him we're here to see him."

Crawford eyed Ben suspiciously. "Here to *see* him. Right."

Reggie leaned forward on his chair more, and Ben felt the tension in the room rising. Ben glanced at Reggie, waiting for some sort of cue, but receiving none, he continued on his own. "Listen, Mr. — Adrian — we're trying to find a man we believe was involved in some less-than-reputable business back in Philadelphia. We're thankful for your willingness to host us here for your soft opening, and — trust me when I tell you this — we've never seen anything quite like this place. But we're here on business. And *our* business is Vicente Garza."

Crawford stared at him.

"Can we meet with him?"

"Of course."

"Really?"

Reggie reached his hand over to Ben and silenced him. "Adrian, thank you. Just tell us when and where and we'll be there."

Crawford smiled at both of them, the tension suddenly lifting and leaving the room entirely. The dimple had returned, and even Ben felt at ease. "Indeed. Gentlemen, thank you. We are already short-staffed here, but there are not very many guests. We're getting ready for our major launch and Mr. Garza will need every bit of time to prepare his team, but I'm sure I can carve out an hour for you."

"I really think we'll only need a half —"

"We run things tightly here," Crawford said, interrupting. "An hour will give him time to take the Subshuttle back here to the central tower. It's a slow beast, but it's efficient. Have you seen it yet?"

Ben and Reggie shook their heads.

"Well, I highly recommend a trip. It's marvelous — a combination of engineering and art, perfectly balanced. Slow, as I said, but it gives you the time to revel in the underwater scenery."

"We'll be sure to do that," Reggie said, standing up from the chair. "When should we expect this meeting?"

Crawford glanced down as if examining some invisible desktop calendar. He looked for a moment then pulled his head back up and addressed both of them. "I'll put a call in now. I believe he breaks for lunch in an hour; will that do?"

Reggie looked over at Ben but was already nodding. "That — that's great, thank you."

Ben stood up to leave, then started walking toward the door. He heard Reggie over his shoulder.

"Where should we meet him?"

"You'll be taking the Subshuttle out to the second ring. Simply walk down to the elevators, take it to the first sublevel, and you'll find the entrance to the Subshuttle right there on your left. There's a map on the wall outside the doors of the elevator on every floor in case you get lost. You won't need any ID or escort to get into the shuttle; I've already disabled the security protocol. When you get to the second ring, you'll find a staff-only dining hall there. Buffet-style. A bit underwhelming compared to the feast we had last night, but I hope that's amenable."

"That'll work great, Adrian. Again, thank you."

Ben had reached the door, but he stopped and waited for Reggie to catch up. He glanced back at Crawford, still seated at his desk. The man was smiling, but his head was down, once more examining the invisible calendar that sat on it.

Reggie made a face at Ben as they walked out of the room. Ben waited for them to leave, waited for the door to close fully. "What?" he finally asked.

"That was easy," Reggie said.

"Too easy?"

"Maybe. We'll see."

"What's the plan?" Ben asked. "I thought we were supposed to grab him in three days, when the chopper comes back."

"We don't have a choice now. We've got a meeting with Garza, Ben. Maybe he shows, maybe he doesn't. If he does..."

Ben looked at him. "Reggie, you haven't been honest with me."

Reggie glanced left and right, up and down the curved hallway. They were standing in front of the elevators now, waiting for it to rise to their floor. "I know..." he started. "I haven't been."

Ben clenched his jaw.

"Look, Ben. Mr. E wanted us to grab Garza, to bring him in. He wanted to turn him over to the authorities; said he and Mrs. E are working on building a case against him that will include evidence from Philly."

"That's... good, right?" Ben asked. He was confused, and Reggie wasn't helping.

"No, Ben. It's not. Not good *enough*, anyway. I want to turn him in about as much as you do."

Ben waited.

"Meaning I don't *want* to turn him in. I don't want *any* chance that he gets off the hook for what he did."

Ben felt the anger returning, the same things he'd felt when he'd watched Vicente Garza — The Hawk — stare him down as he shot and killed their friend, Joshua Jefferson. He clenched his fists, his jaw and his hands in a competition of strength. "What's your *point*, Reggie?" he asked. He couldn't hide the emotion from his voice, and he didn't try to. Reggie knew he wasn't mad at him.

"That *is* my point, Ben," Reggie said, his voice now merely a whisper. "I've got *zero interest* in turning that bastard over to the authorities, just so he can rot in a cell until some high-powered lawyer finds out a way to free him.

Ben's head cocked down and to the side. "You're saying..."

"I'm saying I'm not meeting Garza to try to subdue him. I'm meeting him so I can kill him."

CHAPTER 27

THERE WERE TWO SUBSHUTTLES — one on Sublevel 3 and one on Sublevel 1. Julie and Sarah had ridden the elevator down to the lowest, and were now standing inside the shuttle as it slid through the black, murky water, suspended on its cable. The system was simple in design, both making the Subshuttle an efficient transportation method as well as an inexpensive alternative to something more elaborate. The cable appeared to be nothing more than a stainless stretch of rolled metal fiber, like what Julie had seen propelling ski lifts and gondolas along their course. There was a ballast system as well to keep the Subshuttle from pulling or pushing against the cable. Automated, judging by the label on the floor hatch in the vessel, which apparently led to the innards of the Subshuttle and allowed for maintenance.

The roof of the shuttle was glass, which bubbled around to the sides and halfway down, where the glass terminated into thick, dark plastic. The entire submersible was rectangular-shaped, with rounded edges. They stood on a plastic floor, like the hull of a boat, and everything appeared to be bolted down and waterproofed.

In spite of the earthquake-proof space, the engineering and design of the vehicle was impressive. The glass ceiling and walls gave

Julie the feeling she was traveling through space, the only light coming from the submersible itself and whatever rays of sunlight reached them from the surface of the water, forty feet above them. The front and back of the craft were identical, the sloping plastic beneath the glass windows curving gently into the long, flat floor. Seats had been placed across an aisle from one another, two on each side, with three total rows.

"Impressive," Sarah said.

Julie nodded. It was a little unnerving, being this far underwater inside a submarine. She'd never been in one, and the closest thing to it she could imagine was walking through a glass tube that sat underwater at an aquarium she'd visited as a kid.

"Nervous?" Sarah asked.

"Huh? Oh, sorry. No, just... yeah, a little, I guess."

Sarah smiled. "It is a bit weird. Even though we're only thirty or forty feet under, it seems like much more."

"Yeah," Julie said. "Only forty feet." She peered out the glass on the starboard side of the vessel, watching the water change from dark blue to black to blue again. Suddenly a shape passed near the window.

She jumped back, gasping. "Wh — what was that?" she asked.

Sarah looked puzzled. "I didn't see anything. Where were you —"

She froze. Julie watched her. She was looking out the opposite window.

"I saw something, too," Sarah said.

Julie walked to the front of the vessel. "Is there a throttle or control panel anywhere. I'd like to end this trip as soon as possible."

"I'm with you," Sarah said, walking toward the back. "Nothing back here."

"Nothing up here, either. Not even an emergency stop."

"Guess we'll just have to hope that whatever's out there *stays* out there."

Julie nodded, swallowing. She was watching the shuttle's

progress from her perch at the front of the boat. The wide glass windows swelled outward here, and the water pressed back in toward her, causing the floating particles and streams of light from the surface to be skewed and magnified.

It also caused everything *else* floating around out there to be magnified.

She jumped again when she saw another shape. A shadow, flicking left to right across her vision. It was *huge*, and she caught a glimpse of a tail streaking past the glass.

Sarah had seen it, too. "Okay, what the *hell* is that thing?"

Julie shook her head. "I have no idea, but I want out. Now." She started backing away toward the center of the shuttle, holding onto each of the chair backs as she passed. She met Sarah there, and both women looked straight ahead, at one another.

"Shouldn't be too much longer, right?" Sarah asked. "And there's... no way they could get in —"

"No," Julie said. "I'm sure this thing is made of something stronger than whatever's out there."

The shuttle creaked and shook a bit, then Julie felt it rise in the water. They were traveling upward now on a shallow rise.

They stood, silent and still, until Julie felt the shuttle lurch again, then a mechanical catch banged through the hull of the vessel and they came to a stop. Julie looked back to the front of the boat, out the glass wall. The water was falling, draining around the sides of the shuttle and being replaced by a bright white light.

"I guess we're here," Sarah said.

"I guess we are. Wonder how long it takes to pump the water out of the room."

Her question was answered soon — less than a minute, thanks to a pair of massive pumps that sucked the water out from the floor and back into the sea. The Subshuttle itself formed the seal for the fourth wall, and within another thirty seconds the door on the side of it slid open, revealing a long, brightly lit hallway.

"We're here," Julie said, stepping out. "I guess this is the lab."

The ring was much larger than the central ring that housed the hotel, so the hallways seemed to be straighter, even though Julie could see the edges curving around on both sides of her. Sarah stepped out and stood next to her.

"So," she asked, "where do we start?"

"We're looking for anyone who knows Dr. Lin," Julie said. "And preferably anyone who knows what he was working on."

"Right," Sarah said. "But I'd be happy to bump into anyone who knows something about what's floating around out there, too."

"Can't argue with that. Let's start by finding *someone* in general. There can't be too many people here, right? They'll surely know something about this place, and probably Dr. Lin as well."

Julie walked to the left, with Sarah Lindgren at her side. Julie shuddered once more, thinking again about the mysterious creature that had buzzed their shuttle on the way in. The long, slender tail, dark body, blacker even than the water it was traveling through.

I hope we figure this out soon, she thought. She was starting to think this *Paradisum* was less of a paradise than the name implied.

CHAPTER 28

BEN WAS REELING, his head spinning. He felt the same way he felt after he and Reggie had one too many glasses of bourbon at night. He was a rum and Coke sort of guy, and he and Julie enjoyed a glass of red wine together most nights, but when Reggie was staying with them he brought out the bourbon.

And right now he felt drunk. He wasn't stumbling, nor was his perception compromised, but he felt the same floating lightheadedness of too much alcohol in his system.

He's going to kill him? he thought. Ben wanted Garza out of the picture just as much as Reggie, and he knew Julie felt the same way. Joshua had been a close friend to all of them, and they all wanted justice to be served.

But they weren't mercenaries. They weren't cold-blooded killers. Ben knew how he'd felt in that moment; he remembered it like it was yesterday. He remembered where he was, lying on the floor in the gymnasium, injured from his own gunshot wounds. He remembered not being able to see Julie, not knowing whether she was okay. He remembered The Hawk standing over him, smiling.

And he remembered Joshua falling to the floor, fading away. He'd died young, older than Ben but younger than Reggie by a few years. A stand-up guy, tricked into serving for an organization he thought was worthy of his loyalty, up until their expedition to the Amazon months ago convinced him otherwise and he joined the CSO as the de facto leader.

He closed his eyes as they rode the elevator down to Sub-1, identified by the large, lit circular button on the panel. That's where they would catch the Subshuttle to the second ring, where the staff quarters, research labs, and their rendezvous with Garza would take place.

Ben squeezed the area around the sides of his nose with two fingers, trying to push away the growing anxiety. *We can't do this,* he thought. *We can't kill a man for no reason.*

He knew there *was,* in fact, a reason. But how would it look to the park staff? To the investors visiting the park, if word got out? How would it look to Adrian Crawford?

And most importantly, what would happen when Mr. E found out? The man was a docile, reserved gentleman, not without his quirks but certainly above cold-blooded murder from a team he was in charge of.

He turned to face Reggie. They were eye-to-eye, Ben just a fraction taller. He was bigger, though. Stocky and intimidating when he wanted to be. And right now he wanted to be.

"I can't let you do that Reggie."

Reggie grinned, then frowned. Unsure of what game he was playing, Ben figured.

"I can't let you murder Garza."

"Ben..." Reggie sighed. "Ben, this is *Garza* we're talking about. The H —"

"I *know* who it is, Gareth," Ben said. "I was there too, remember?"

Reggie stepped up closer to Ben. His grin faded. "What are you saying?"

"I said it twice already. I'm not going to let you kill —"

"You're not going to *let* me?"

"That's what I said."

The elevator dinged, but neither man moved. Ben caught a glimpse of the shoreline, now above them, smacking against the very top reaches of the glass elevator. The deep blue of the ocean outside the window hovered, pressing in around Ben. He felt constricted, claustrophobic even.

"You're going to *prevent* me from killing Garza. That what you're saying?"

"Reggie, I told you already. You can't just walk in there and kill him. He's — I mean, he's not innocent — but you represent the CSO now. You're not just some guy hellbent on exacting revenge, damn all the fallout. I know that was your background, and —"

Reggie laughed, a snickering grunt. "You know *nothing* of my past, Ben. I told you pieces of it, and the report you probably read has the basic details. Army, sniper, worked as a hired gun for awhile. That it?"

Ben nodded.

"Well you don't know the *half* of it. Here's the deal, pal: when I'm faced with doing the right thing or backing down because I can't figure out how to make it sound palatable, I *do the right thing*. I thought you were the same type of guy."

The doors opened, then closed again. The elevator didn't move.

Ben clenched and unclenched his fists. He felt like punching him.

"Ben, I'm going to walk into that room, and I'm going to avenge the death of my friend. You can try to stop me, but I can *guarantee* you that it's a very bad idea. You're tough, but you're a capable fighter because I *made you that way*. Got it? So if you think —"

Ben lashed out with a right hook, aiming straight for his friend's jaw. *Do it the hard way, then,* he thought.

Reggie sidestepped the blow easily, brought his elbow up and smashed it down on Ben's outstretched right hand, crushing his forearm. Ben immediately fell to his knees, unable to control the pain searing up his arm and shoulder.

Reggie held Ben's fist, still pressing down with his own elbow. "Try it again, Ben."

Ben glared up at him.

"Go ahead. Try it. See what happens. You've seen me upset. I'm getting there, quickly. You sure you want to be on the other side of that?"

Ben struggled against Reggie's grip, but he had him in an unbreakable hold. Without twisting his own arm out of its socket, Ben was completely unable to move.

"I'm going to let you go now, Ben," Reggie said. "I don't want to hurt you, and I'd like a bit of backup in there. But I'm telling you, right now: if you try anything, or get in my way..."

He stopped. Ben waited, still glaring. "What?" he asked. "You going to kill me too?"

Something flashed in Reggie's face. Red, dark, brooding, it was there and then it was gone. Just a slight notion that the man was thinking — feeling — something besides what he was outwardly trying to portray. Reggie's grip loosened a bit. Not enough for Ben to break free, but enough so that he could twist around and stand back up. Reggie allowed it.

"I — I'm going in, Ben," Reggie said. "Please don't stop me."

Ben stood there a moment as Reggie mashed the button to open the elevator car's door. He stepped out, turned left, and disappeared.

Ben waited until Reggie was out of sight before letting out a breath. He sucked in two more, quickly, trying to recover. Trying to figure out what he wanted to do. He wanted to scream. He wanted to chase after his friend and apologize, or tackle him. He wasn't sure which.

Instead, he took a third breath, this one deeper, and held it as he crossed the threshold and exited the elevator. He turned left to follow

Reggie and found the man waiting for a door that led into an antechamber, the door and the wall around it made of glass.

The sign above the door read 'Subshuttle 1,' and just as Ben stopped next to Reggie, the door slid open.

Reggie looked at Ben, then at the waiting capsule on the other side. He strode forward.

"Your call, friend. You coming?"

CHAPTER 29

THE SUBSHUTTLE RIDE was impressive but uneventful. Like a married couple overcoming a quick spat, neither man spoke during the ten-minute ride. Reggie felt something he wasn't used to feeling. He was angry, but in a disappointed sort of way. Anger was an emotion he could deal with. Anger was a known entity, a *comfortable* entity in some ways. He was used to it. But this anger wasn't one-dimensional. It wasn't based on a single fact, or focused on a single idea.

This anger was based on betrayal. Ben was his friend, by his account even the best friend he had. He trusted him, and he knew Ben respected him as well. When they were together they were inseparable, and they had been since they'd walked out of the Amazon rainforest after a successful mission.

So Ben's refusal meant a lot more to Reggie than just a simple disagreement. They were leaderless on this mission, and Reggie had assumed a lot of control already. He had always looked up to Ben for the man's resilience, sense of justice, and his loyalty to those he was closest to. He had always looked to Ben for the right thing to do, since he knew Ben would do whatever needed to be done, no matter what, as long as it was 'right' in the man's mind.

So now, to be so sure of himself only to be disregarded by his best friend, was a strange emotion for Reggie. He wanted to please Ben, wanted him in his good graces, and yet an opposing force inside his mind told him to forget about it, to ignore Ben altogether and push forward with what he knew was right.

And killing The Hawk was, without a doubt, right. Reggie knew the moment he'd taken Julie hostage that Vicente Garza would die. And the moment The Hawk had pulled the trigger and ended his friend's life, Reggie knew he would be the man to kill him.

He sped up, unsure of Ben's location behind him and not caring enough to turn around and check. For a man as large as Ben, he moved stealthily. Reggie curved around the hallway and toward the glass doors at the end, labeled 'STAFF DINING' in plain-white block vinyl lettering. There were a few other people in the room, sitting at tables around the interior, and Reggie pushed the doors open and walked in.

The room smelled like a cafeteria: many interesting and delicious smells wafting together and creating a not-so-delicious overall effect. The warm heat of the room added to the high-school cafeteria feel, the effect of ovens that had been cranking out dishes since early that morning. The humidity in the air even felt higher here, surprising considering they were in the middle of the ocean to begin with, but Reggie hardly noticed or cared about any of that.

He scanned the room. A group of three scientists, all men, each wearing the obligatory white lab coat, sat at a round table in the corner off to his right. Another group, this one made up of two women and a man sat at the table directly in front of him, the group he'd seen through the glass.

I'll have to make sure we're subtle here, he thought, already calculating positioning and tactics. He didn't want anyone to panic, and he certainly would not be happy with any collateral damage. *Find The Hawk, isolate, take him out.* That was the working plan, at least. In his experience, however, he knew that plans were destined to change on the fly. And in his experience, his greatest skill was in adapting those plans on the fly.

He didn't see any semblance of security in the room. There were support columns, three in total that he could see, holding up the ceiling in the large expanse of a room. The dining hall had probably two-hundred tables inside, each with four or five chairs, but only the two in front of him and to his right were occupied.

He walked farther into the room. Ben appeared at his side, silent as usual. Reggie strode forward and saw another group of five, all wearing casual clothes, to his left, about halfway down the room. They had been hidden from view by the column in front of him, and he realized then he would need to do a full reconnaissance scan of the area. He couldn't afford to not see who all was in here.

"Over there," Ben said, his voice low.

Reggie looked to where Ben was facing, and then he saw it. Sitting with his back against a window, facing them. Looking at them, but not truly seeing them. Or if he was, not revealing his thoughts about them.

Reggie increased his pace.

The Hawk watched him approach.

Ben kept up, walking alongside his friend. Reggie had a moment of doubt as he wondered what in the world Ben was thinking. *Would he try to sabotage this?* Reggie disregarded the thought. Ben could be rash sometimes, but he would never purposefully endanger his friends. And even though their little spat was unfortunate, it wouldn't have been nearly enough impetus for Ben to abandon their friendship entirely.

No, Ben would play a different game. Reggie thought it out. Planned against the contingencies and possibilities, trying to understand Ben's perspective. Ben would try to prevent Reggie from taking action against The Hawk, but he wouldn't go so far as to put their lives in danger. He might argue, might even plead, but he wouldn't allow The Hawk to attack Reggie.

So go fast, make it count, and do it before Ben has a chance to open his mouth.

Good a plan as any, Reggie reckoned. He was unarmed, but that had never been much of an issue. His background in the Army, his later missions working as a gun-for-hire, and his years spent running a survival training camp and shooting range in Brazil had molded him into a killing machine, no matter the situation.

The table was sparsely set. No food, but a cup of coffee sat in front of Garza, mostly full. Silverware at all four seats, rolled inside thick cloth napkins. A paper napkin dispenser, which seemed somewhat redundant, sat on the edge of the table against the wall, flanked by a salt and pepper shaker on either side.

He'd killed someone before using the watch he was currently wearing, so any of the items on the table were possible tools.

He approached the table, seeing out of the corner of his eye the larger group of five people, casually dressed, standing up and walking their dishes toward the bucket of dirty tableware near the buffet line. They were laughing about something, completely unaware of Reggie's and Ben's presence in the room. Two buffet line workers stood still, poking at something with tongs, wearing hairnets and ignoring everything else happening in the room. They joked and laughed, set their dishes down one at a time, and exited the room the same way Reggie and Ben had entered.

Across the room behind Garza, he saw a janitor, mopping up a spill still farther into the curved, wide room. The glass windows The Hawk sat in front of stretched all the way around the room, probably a quarter of the way around the entire structure itself. It was a massive hall, and the relative emptiness of it was somewhat off-putting.

"Hello, Gareth," Garza said. He was alone, his thick, black hair pressed back on his head, a new hairstyle Reggie wouldn't have been a fan of even if the man wearing it wasn't was a murderer.

"Garza," Reggie said.

"And you brought Harvey with you as well. Welcome, Mr. Bennett."

Ben glared at The Hawk. "I think we're on a first-name basis by now, *Vicente*. Wouldn't you say?"

The Hawk nodded. "Sure. Of course, Ben. Please, sit." He beckoned with his hand at the chairs opposite him at the table. Reggie examined the gesture. They would be sitting facing the gorgeous ocean view, the deep blues of the underwater scene broken up by brilliant rays of sunlight that tore through the water, lighting the near surroundings. Fish danced and swam outside the windows, oblivious to the tension mere feet from them.

Rather than oblige, Reggie pulled his chair around and sat with his back to the glass, opposite the table from Garza but facing the same direction. If the table hadn't been between them, the two men would have been shoulder to shoulder. Ben sat in the chair next to Reggie, pulling it out diagonally so he was facing Garza.

"Thank you for meeting with me," Garza said.

Reggie smiled. "Thank you for meeting with *us*. Glad you found time in your busy schedule to sit down with us."

"Of course," Garza said, returning the smile. "It's been in my calendar since you all got here."

Ben shifted in his seat. "It — it was?"

Garza threw his head back and laughed. "You think I don't know *everything* that's happening here at *Paradisum?* This is my security team. My protocols, my contracted installations of every camera and security measure. All of it, mine. I know *everything* that happens on any of the rings."

"So... you already planned on meeting with us?"

"I made the appointment with Crawford the minute you landed. I told him you'd be along sooner or later to ask for a meeting, so I had this time and place carved out."

Reggie looked over at Ben. *Something doesn't feel right about this.*

"Listen, Garza. We're here to talk to *you*, and you alone. That's it. We have no interest in this place, or Crawford, or —"

"I know what you're here for, boys."

Reggie glared at him. *We may have walked into a trap,* he thought.

"I know you want revenge. You want to kill me, is that it?"

Reggie felt his fists clenching into tight balls. "That — that's a start. And your men, eventually."

"Right. You want to get back at me for offing your friend back in Philadelphia. Jefferson, right? Joshua? Seemed like a good kid. Good soldier, even. He'd have done just fine in —"

Reggie slammed his fist down on the table, the silverware from a previous place setting clinking and rattling. The napkin dispenser slid a good five inches toward Ben. "Don't you *dare* talk about him like you knew him, you bastard. You *murdered* him, and I'm here —"

"I know, I know," Garza said. "You're here to kill me." He sniffed, sat up a bit in his chair, and took a sip of the coffee sitting in front of him. "I got that. Here's the thing, though. I'm one step — at least — ahead of you. Always have been, always will be. No changing that, so you might as well stop trying to get the jump on me."

"I could kill you right now, asshole," Reggie said. "Pick your weapon. Fork? Knife? How about this for a blunt object?" he grabbed the black metal napkin dispenser and rotated it in his hand.

As he did, he noticed something else in his peripheral vision. The scientists who had been sitting in the corner of the room had stood up and started walking toward their table. They were grinning, but it wasn't the sort of grin one used when appreciating a friend's joke.

And, worst of all, Reggie realized he recognized one of the men.

We definitely *walked into a trap.*

"Ben," he said.

Ben looked at him. The Hawk's smile grew.

"Ben," Reggie said again. "We need —"

He never got the rest of the sentence out. The man closest to them opened his lab coat, a convenient disguise for what he was hiding beneath it, and pulled out a small subcompact machine gun. The other two men sped up, their long white coattails floating along behind them as they took up positions on either side of the table.

The janitor suddenly seemed to be interested in the goings-on at The Hawk's table. The short, mustached man placed the mop he had been using down and leaned it against the cart. He stared at the scene for a moment and then began walking over to the table.

You've got to be kidding me, Reggie thought. *Him, too?*

The janitor unbuttoned the top two buttons of his one-piece blue uniform and reached into the area in front of his chest. He withdrew his hand a moment later, revealing a matching submachine gun.

"So," Garza said, capturing Reggie's attention once more, "are we ready to talk?"

"We have nothing to talk about," Ben said.

"In that case, this meeting is adjourned. I *am* still quite busy with the soft launch happening next week."

The men surrounding the table stepped closer at The Hawk's words, lifting their weapons and aiming them directly at Reggie and Ben.

Ben's head dropped. "Looks like our little plan failed before we even got here, buddy."

"*Our* plan?" Reggie asked.

"Take them to the security main," The Hawk said. "We can leave them in the brig until Crawford has a better idea of what to do with them."

Two of the men stepped forward and grabbed Reggie's shoulders, riveting him in place. The janitor and the third scientist held Ben down as well.

"I'm assuming you boys aren't actually scientists?"

"Or janitors," the janitor said.

"Reggie, Ben," The Hawk said. "You remember my boys from

Ravenshadow? They were really looking forward to meeting you once again. The rest of my team is also looking forward to meeting the rest of *your* team as well. You wouldn't happen to know where they are?"

Ben flashed Reggie a glance that said, *when this is all over I'm going to kill you, too*. But there was also a hint of fear in the man's eyes. He was thinking about Julie.

Reggie was, too. And he was thinking about Dr. Sarah Lindgren, as well. The women were somewhere in this ring, looking around the laboratories and trying to discover whatever they could about Dr. Joseph Lin and his creepy pictures. Whether they had made any progress on that front or not was unknown to Reggie, but of one thing he was certain.

If the women in their group were seen by any of the Raven-shadow crew, this mission was as good as over.

CHAPTER 30

THE LABORATORY AREA beneath the surface of the second ring was mysteriously empty. Julie had expected a bustling community of scientists and researchers, running around the curved level as they worked on whatever experiments and projects they'd been assigned. But there was no one in the hall. No doors opened, and no sign of life whatsoever greeted them as they walked along.

In spite of the brightly lit corridor, Julie was a bit creeped out. "This is weird," she said aloud.

Sarah nodded. "You got that right. There's no one here."

"Maybe they're all inside? Working?"

"Maybe," she said. "But it seems like we'd hear talking, or see something, right? At least —"

She stopped. She turned to her left, looking at the wall. In this section of the ring, the wall was made of glass, and the view allowed Julie to see into the dark blue waters of the ocean waiting just outside the hallway.

"What is it?" Julie asked. She shuddered, thinking once again of their encounter with the strange beasts they'd seen from inside the Subshuttle.

"I — I think I saw... *there*!" she cried out and pointed up at the top edge of the glass wall.

"What was it?" Julie asked. All she saw was something whitish in color, floating gently upward until it was gone.

"A jellyfish," Sarah said. "I think. I couldn't get a good look —" she interrupted herself again, studying the glass. Julie waited, her face plastered to the glass. "There's another one!"

Julie saw where Sarah was pointing. Sure enough there was a small, semi-opaque jellyfish swimming in their direction. Two more floated behind it, each following the natural forces of the water that guided them, oblivious and incapable of controlling their direction. One of the specimens floated close to the glass, providing both women with an up-close examination.

Still, it was hard to see the jellyfish. The entire bell was only a few millimeters wide, and they were only visible when the tiny creatures were just about pressed up against the glass. They may have been small, but Julie had to admit they were strikingly beautiful. Bluish in color, with a hundred or so strands of tentacles piling out from beneath them, and a heart-like reddish object pulsing from within the center of the bell.

"Those are the stomachs," Sarah said. Her voice was filled with reverence, her eyes wide and glistening as she pressed up against the glass to get a better look. "*Turritopsis dohrnii*, I believe. Found in the Mediterranean Sea and off the coast of Japan. It's no surprise they're able to survive in these warmer waters."

As if the jellyfish were putting on a show for the two women, the area on the opposite side of the glass suddenly lit up in a brilliant display of blues and reds. The three they'd been watching suddenly turned into hundreds, all of the specimens floating toward the glass and spreading out to fill the entire window. The stomachs, the reddish heart-shaped portions of the minuscule creatures, flitted around the glass, their long, blue tentacles following behind wherever they went. The lighting from inside the hall seemed to have been designed to reflect the glorious colors and opacity of the creatures.

"It's beautiful. And interesting," Julie said. "But why are they on display? They're almost microscopic. If you're going to have jellyfish at an ocean park, why not get ones you can see?"

Sarah smiled. "No idea. These are fascinating creatures, though. Lots of marine biologists are studying them right now, due to their ability to live forever."

"Wait, what?" Julie stopped looking at the jellyfish dancing around on the other side of the glass and turned to face Dr. Lindgren.

"Yeah, they're called the 'Immortal Jellyfish.' Somewhat of a misnomer, too, really. They have the ability to regress back into their polyp state if they want."

"If they want?"

"Well, under special circumstances — temperature changes, environmental threats, predation. Yeah, they basically can flip a switch and 'start over' from scratch. Technically the cells are what start over, not the organism itself, so saying that they're 'immortal' is, like I said, a bit of a stretch."

"How do you know about these guys?" Julie asked. "You have a PhD in marine biology too?"

Sarah laughed. "I wish. No, I've been interested in them from an anthropological standpoint. They're called the 'Immortal Jellyfish' because of their unique properties, and those properties aren't terribly removed from what some scientists think stem cells are capable of."

"Wait," Julie said. "You're saying that *people* might be able to do that, too? Revert back to a previous state? Like turn into a fetus once again?"

"Well, no. But it's intriguing science nonetheless, and the fact that we don't know *how* these jellyfish cells are able to operate is grounds for plenty of research funding. I'd bet *OceanTech* is doing just that sort of research — maybe hoping to study these creatures and be first to market with a new form of medication or healing procedure for damaged skin cells, for example."

Julie nodded, looking once again out at the tiny little red and blue orbs dancing across her vision. "They're cute, I guess. Still, it seems like sort of a waste. All this water, and they fill it with super-tiny jellyfish?"

Sarah shrugged. "This isn't technically the park, remember? This area is for research and study. I doubt the public will even be able to come over here." She paused, a slow grin growing on one side of her mouth. "And besides, these jellyfish aren't the *only* things *Ocean-Tech's* got on display."

Julie knew immediately what she was talking about. "You know what those things were?"

"I think, yeah," she said. Her face turned upward and to the side, deep in thought. "It's just a hunch, but I think they were crocodiles."

"*Crocodiles?*" Julie was incredulous, but she realized that every-thing she'd seen from within the Subshuttle fit that description. The long, slender tails, the whip-fast way they slid through the water.

And the size.

"They were *huge*," Julie said.

Sarah nodded. "Yeah, I noticed that, too. And it's saltwater out there, so I'm guessing they were saltwater crocs. The kind found off the coast of Australia, usually in swamps and low-lying areas."

"But again, why here?" Julie asked. "Wait, don't tell me. Salt-water crocodiles have a special ability as well? They can regenerate?"

Sarah laughed once more. "No, thank God. They're just animals. But they're still interesting, the little that I know about them. All crocodiles, and especially the saltwater ones, seem to have been stuck in an evolutionary standoff. They haven't really changed in millions of years, which is odd. They've gotten a bit smaller I believe, but that's about it."

Julie thought about the ones she'd seen in the shuttle. *They're still humongous.*

"So *OceanTech* has them here, because why not? They've got microscopic jellyfish and saltwater crocs. Every kid in America is going to be *dying* to come visit, in that case. Who cares about Disneyworld when there's a hard-to-reach floating theme park featuring obscure animals and lots of learning nearby?"

Sarah laughed, harder this time. "I was thinking the same thing, actually. Seems odd they'd build it here, on top of a shipwreck, then spend all this money building individual enclosures for these animals."

"Odd, to say the least. It doesn't make any sense." Julie paused, taking one last look at the beautiful jellyfish floating around mere inches from her. "Want to keep moving? We need to figure out if Dr. Lin is still around, or if anyone's seen him. And I'd bet the boys are making good progress. I'd guess they'll be ready for a drink soon."

CHAPTER 31

THE RAVENSHADOW TEAM surrounded Ben and Reggie and led them back through the main doors of the cafeteria, toward the elevators. Before they reached the entrance to the elevators and the Subshuttle, however, The Hawk turned left and swiped a security card over a panel mounted on the wall next to a door.

The door was unassuming, a slightly off-white color compared to the curved wall of the inner ring, giving it the look of an afterthought. It hadn't been designed and pored over like the hotel and tower's interior.

Security, Ben thought. It looked like the entrance to a janitor's closet, which he knew would be a perfect location for the entrance to a security headquarters.

He was proven correct as he stepped over the threshold and noticed what was on the inside of the room. White walls, fluorescent lights, and a simple desk off to one side with a man sitting behind it, a couple computer monitors in front of him. Nothing else on the walls, nothing else in the room. No fake plants or standing lights suggesting that at least *some* effort had been spent decorating the room.

Ben had seen rooms like these before. He had spent plenty of time in government offices as a park ranger, briefing someone on this or that petty crime or being debriefed on this or that new policy change. Government offices, especially the public-facing ones like the Department of Motor Vehicles, Social Security Administration, or public health facilities, all gave the same, bland, stale-out-of-the-box impression.

This room was hardly better, but it wasn't government. The *other* place he'd seen rooms like this were deep inside organizational headquarters, hidden to most of the world. Casinos had them, just past the wall of smoke, and after the last row of penny slots ended in a linoleum-marked pathway to the restrooms.

It was a security room. Specifically, it was the room *before* the actual security vault began. An entrance to a larger facility hidden behind, this room was simply a staging area for whatever security the organization required. A desk jockey — in this case the Ravenshadow recruit sitting behind the desk, warily examining the two new faces — and a computer were all that was typically required.

When Ben and Reggie were finally in the room, the man stood and saluted Vicente Garza.

Garza ignored the show of respect. "Any update?" he asked the man.

The man shook his head. "No sir. The rest of the group was last seen leaving their rooms this morning. We believe the women may have headed out to the outer ring for some sight-seeing."

Garza glanced at Ben and Reggie. "I highly doubt they're here to *sightsee*, Jacobs. Don't we have a feed from the tower and hotel floors?"

The man gulped. "Those — those feeds aren't quite ready yet."

"Not *ready* yet? Why the hell not?"

"We're waiting for the tech. He's scheduled to be here tomorrow afternoon, when they fly in supplies for the soft launch, and —"

"Get over there and *fix it*, Jacobs. Yourself. Get my cameras online or you're going to be on that same flight *off* this station."

"Yes, sir," Jacobs said.

Garza turned to Ben. "I apologize, Harvey. It appears your friend Juliette is currently missing. We have a pretty good idea of who's doing what inside the walls of this facility, whether in the hotel tower or the rings, but apparently our systems aren't *quite* ready for use just yet.

"Rest assured, my men *will* find them. And then we'll all be together again."

He paused, ran a hand through his thick, black hair, and smirked at Reggie. "Together again, just like in Philadelphia."

Ben lunged forward but felt the vice-grip clamps of the two Ravenshadow mens' hands holding him back. Reggie was similarly detained, but it didn't stop him from struggling against the bonds.

"I'm going to kill you," Reggie said.

Garza turned and stared at Reggie. "I'm not sure your reputation lends much credibility to that statement, Gareth. Wasn't only a few years ago you were begging me for a slot on my team?"

Ben knew it had been longer than that — Reggie had tried to become a Ravenshadow member following his military service, before he knew what sort of a company it was, but he hadn't made it through the gauntlet of tests the organization required.

Reggie spat. "Day I fight for you is the day hell freezes over."

Garza laughed. "You didn't have the mettle, son. It's fine — not many of our recruits do. You know that firsthand, don't you? You took out quite a few of them back in Philly."

"What's this all about, Garza?" Ben asked. "Where are you taking us?"

Garza motioned toward the door at the back of the room, and the guards holding Ben and Reggie pushed their captives toward the door. Garza reached it first and opened it, then stepped aside and waited for them to walk through.

The real *security chambers,* Ben thought. Casinos loved to do this, as well as hospitals and other places where public impression was of high importance. Having *Mission: Impossible*-level security chambers tended to put people on edge rather than at ease, so having the bulk of the tech and systems behind a second set of doors was common practice. *OceanTech*, apparently, was no different.

On the other side of the door the room opened up into a larger space, probably three times the size of the reception room they'd just left. It too was brightly lit, but this room was filled with computer workstations, blinking monitors on each desk and a wall-sized display to their right showing at least thirty feeds from cameras around the facility.

Ben saw movement on one of the miniature screens and watched as a group of civilians — likely the group of investors Crawford had mentioned — traipsed around the outer ring, making their way from the artificial beach toward one of the cabana-style bars.

In another image, Ben saw the cafeteria they had just left. It was nearly empty, no one but the cooks and servers standing around, moving a bit to grab a dish or prep some meal. All of the images were black-and-white, but of the thirty or or so screens, none were low-quality. Every screen appeared to have a perfect high-definition feed with no jumping or signal loss.

The far wall, opposite the door they'd entered, was solid glass, broken in places only for the structural support beams holding the panes together. They were on the first sublevel, so the ocean filled all but the last foot of space at the top of the other side of the glass. A few fish darted back and forth in the water, uninterested in what was happening inside. The light-blue hue of the sunlit water was more than enough color for the otherwise white room, but the bright fluorescents above their heads seemed to be constantly fighting with the streaking lines of light pouring through the glass.

"Crawford didn't spring for a designer for these parts, I guess," Reggie said.

"No need," Garza answered. "No one's supposed to see the inside of this room unless they're invited guests or security."

"I figured. I guess that makes us invited guests?"

Garza grunted, then walked farther into the room. The glass wall curved inward, the gently sloping concave shape of the inside of the ring revealing just how large the central ring really was.

The two men holding Ben pushed him forward, and the two holding Reggie followed suit.

"You planning to hold us against our will?" Reggie asked. "That's against the law, I'm sure."

"It is," Ben added.

"I'm sure you're right," one of the Ravenshadow men responded. "But where? America? I'm not sure we're technically *in* America."

Ben considered that. Technically the man was correct, but he wasn't sure how a company like *Ocean Tech* could operate outside the laws of *any* country. Surely they had to be in compliance with *some* governing agency?

Garza spoke over his shoulder as he led them through the long room, the desks on both sides forming a narrow hallway between security personnel at their stations, monitoring different areas of the park. "Adrian Crawford and I are not fans of 'loose ends,' as you no doubt have come to know. He and I agreed at the beginning of this project that the security components of the operation would be left to me and my team."

"Plausible deniability for him," Reggie said.

"So you can do whatever the hell you want with us, and he can say he had no idea," Ben added.

"Let's not get out of hand, boys," The Hawk said. "I'm not going to *do* anything to you. There's no reason to suspect you've harmed me or this park in any way. But we will have to *detain* you for some time."

"For how long?"

"Until we can find your partners, Juliette and Dr. Lindgren, and get you all safely out of the park."

Ben glared at The Hawk. "What makes me think you've got *no interest* in our safety?"

Reggie was less subtle. "I'm going to kill you, Garza. I told you that before, and I mean —"

"Stop being rash, Gareth. It doesn't suit you. Get in the cells, keep your mouth shut, and you just might make it out of here without your arms being broken."

Reggie's expression shifted. "Yeah, what's up with you guys and arms? Everything we've seen around here is just... creepy. Is Crawford into that sort of thi —"

He never got the rest of the sentence out. The submachine guns the men were carrying weren't long enough to be a terribly effective bat, but they were sturdy enough to prove an effective blunt object against Reggie's side. He went down in a heap with a groan.

Ben watched on in silence, feeling the tightening grips of the men holding him and knowing he couldn't do anything for his friend.

The guards picked up Reggie from the floor and tossed him like a rag doll into the open door behind him. Ben's guards shoved him along behind Reggie, and he had to stumble to the side to not lose his balance.

The guards left, leaving Ben and Reggie alone in the sterile, white-walled room, and The Hawk appeared at the door. The expressionless facade the man had been wearing, the nonchalant attitude he'd been selling, disappeared. "You two are lucky we're not back in Philadelphia," he said. "You killed my men. I killed yours. But that debt hasn't been paid on my side, and it's clear you feel the same. If it weren't for Crawford calling the shots around here, I'd have you both thrown into one of the exhibits and be done with it."

Ben knew his expression did little to hide his rage, but he didn't care. "I'm warning you, Garza. You even *touch* her again, and —"

"And what?" Garza asked. "You're going to kill me, just like you did back in Philadelphia. Harvey, there are *many* men who want me dead, and every single one of them have so far failed. Most of them aren't around to talk about it. I want *nothing more* than to add you two wash-ups to that list, so *please* don't test me.

"If you so much as *attempt* an escape, my men will hurt you. We won't kill you, but we will start killing the rest of your team. That pretty doctor you brought along? She goes first. Juliette? I've had my eye on her since she landed here. But I'm not going to just let her off the hook as easily as Dr. Lindgren. I've got quite a few men here who have *also* had their eye on her, if you know what I mean."

Ben rushed the door. He wasn't as fast as Reggie, but he was larger, and when he got moving he knew he was about as easy to stop as a freight train.

The problem was that The Hawk was standing outside the door, while Ben was inside. He only made it halfway to it before Garza slammed it shut, the lock mechanism immediately engaging. Ben tried to slow himself, but he crashed against the heavy door and his face smacked against the reinforced rectangular glass window. The Hawk was staring at him from the other side, a sly grin on his face.

"As I said, Ben," Garza said, "behave. If you don't, you're going to start looking a lot like those bodies down on Sub-3."

Before Ben could respond, The Hawk turned and walked away, leaving Reggie and Ben inside the silent, empty room.

CHAPTER 32

THEY SAW the first employees on the second ring at the end of the hallway. The hall ended at a set of glass doors which opened when they drew near. On the other side of the doors was a large, open room, set up with tables and chairs lining three sides of the room. A large, open conference room. A stage — nothing more than a simple panel of risers and a podium, sat in front of the tables. A man and a woman looked at Julie and Sarah as they entered.

"Hello," Julie said. "We're looking for —"

"You shouldn't be down here," the man said. "This is restricted area. The entire facility is closed off to guests."

"Right," Julie said. "I know, I'm sorry. But the Subshuttle took us here, and we're Crawford's guests. We're just looking around."

The man exchanged a glance with the woman he was standing with, but his expression soured. "Mr. Crawford is looking for you, in that case."

"Is he?" Sarah asked.

"Just called it in. He wants all of the guests back in their rooms within the hour. Something about a security breach."

Julie felt a moment of panic, but she forced herself to play it cool.

"That — that's why we're here. We're looking for an employee. A scientist who works for *Ocean Tech*, I think. Dr. Joseph Lin."

The man swallowed, his eyes widening ever so slightly then narrowing once again. The woman took a faltering step back. "You — you know where he is?"

"No," Julie said. "That's why we're here. We're trying to find him."

"Where did you meet him?"

Julie looked over at Sarah, unsure of how much she should reveal.

Thankfully Sarah spoke up. "We ran into him in the hotel, actually. Said he was working on something down here we should see. I'm Dr. Lindgren, maybe Mr. Crawford mentioned I'd be here?"

Julie almost smiled. Sarah was smooth and confident, that was clear. She held herself well, and maybe her ruse would help them out. Whether or not the two employees would buy it remained to be seen.

"I'm sorry. He didn't," the woman said. "And as Dr. Jones just said, this area is restricted. Now, if you don't mind heading back the way you came, you can find the Subshuttle entrance —"

"We're going to take a quick look around," Sarah said. "If it's okay with you."

The woman frowned. "No, it's *not* okay, actually. There is very delicate research here in the lab, and Mr. Crawford won't be happy to know that you just walked in and starting poking around." She took a step forward.

Going on the offensive.

Julie knew they were in the right place. These people, while not necessarily criminals, knew something about Dr. Lin, and why he had been acting so frantic. She wasn't about to accuse them of anything, but they were certainly withholding information. It was more than a simple misunderstanding — they were actively trying to cover something up.

"Is this where they keep the bodies?" Julie asked.

The man looked shocked. The woman stood ramrod straight, as if she hadn't heard Julie correctly.

"The bodies," Julie said again. "The ones with missing limbs? Who are they, anyway?"

The man's mouth opened, then closed again. "I — you... what are you talking about?"

"Too late," Sarah said. "We're going to 'poke around' a bit. Call Crawford if you must. We'll be out of your hair before he can send his security down here." She stopped, looked both of them up and down, sizing them up and not trying to hide it. "And if you think you two are going to stop us, well —" she looked over at Julie, possibly for some reassurance — "I'd be impressed with the commitment. But it would be a mistake."

Julie allowed the smile to slip out at that comment. She stepped forward, around the side of the first row of tables. The man and woman had been sitting at the end of the row of tables and chairs to her left, up against the window that looked out into the ocean. There were curtains drawn, covering the view and basking the entire room in a dim yellow light. She assessed the situation. The pair might come toward them, but they would have to contend with a set of tables before they could get to Julie and Sarah.

And by that time, they'd be in the next room.

Julie started toward the door on the opposite side of the room, next to the portable stage. Since the rings were circular, her best guess was that this door led further into the laboratory facility, bending around the left until they eventually would end up right back where they'd started at the elevators and the entrance to the Subshuttle.

Sarah was right beside her, and Julie could see a hint of a smile as they sped up and headed toward the doors.

She's going to be a great teammate, Julie found herself thinking.

The man was yelling at them, calling them back, and the woman was working with a cell phone she'd retrieved from her pocket. Julie couldn't hear her exact words, but she got the gist: *security, Sub-1, two women.*

Now we're being chased, she realized. *That adds a level of drama I don't want.*

"They're calling security," Sarah said.

"Yeah," Julie answered. "I heard. That means we're even more in a hurry than we were before."

"Any grand plan?" Sarah asked. "You've been in a situation like this before, right?"

Julie continued to run, but she looked over at Dr. Lindgren. "You mean running from a security team through a research station? Yeah, I've been there."

"What'd you do in that case?"

"We had lots of guns, and we had more people."

Sarah didn't respond to that.

"But they did, too. Far as I can tell this is a smaller operation. So run faster, and let's see if we can figure out where Dr. Lin's office or lab is."

They found it behind the next door. The single glass door led into an anteroom with another door on the opposite wall, and a sign next to the door that said *LABORATORY: MAIN.* There was an ID reader affixed to the wall near the door, but the LED light on the panel was green.

Unlocked.

Julie pushed it open and barreled into the room, followed closely by Dr. Lindgren. There were two people, a man and a woman, in the room, both hunched over a metal table with a body laying upon it.

"Where's Dr. Lin?" Julie asked. The woman jumped, both of them looking up at the intruders. The man cocked his head to the side, trying to understand what was happening, why two strange women had stumbled into their lab.

"Dr... Lin?" the woman asked.

"Yes," Julie answered, breathless. "Dr. Joseph Lin. Where is he?"

"I — I'm sorry, ma'am," the woman said, "but he's... not here. Is there something we can help you —"

"You two are not supposed to be in here," the man said, interrupting his coworker as he started to walk toward them. "I'm going to have to ask you to leave."

Julie stepped toward him, her shoulders broadening and her chest expanding as she held in a deep breath. She raised her chin, preparing to stand toe-to-toe with the scientist.

"We'll leave when we find out what happened to Dr. Lin. And I'd *love* to see what you two are working on in here as well."

Sarah modeled Julie's confidence, and the man seemed to realize he wasn't going to win without reinforcements. "I'm calling security, and —"

"They've already been called," Sarah said. "Your friends out in the large conference room weren't too happy with our barging in, either. I'd expect them to be here any minute."

"What are you working on?" Julie asked again. She directed her question toward the woman still standing near the table, as she seemed to be more concerned with her own safety.

"We —" she glanced at her male coworker — "we're just working on our... assignment. We're under a tight deadline here. Dr. Crawford has us all working around the clock, and —"

"*Dr.* Crawford?" Julie asked. "like, *Adrian* Crawford?"

The woman nodded. "Yes, of course. He's the lead researcher for this department of *OceanTech*. It was all his brainchild. Everything here. Including —"

"Susan," the man said, his voice raised a bit in warning. "Don't."

"No, *Susan*," Julie said, stepping up to the woman. She was short, her black hair tied back in a tight ponytail. If it wasn't for her loose-fitting lab coat and black slacks, she might have been an attractive woman. "*Please* do. Tell us: what is th —"

Julie stopped, stumbling backwards a step. She had looked down at the person on the table as she spoke to the woman, and what she saw had caused her to stop short.

It was a woman, young and dark-skinned like the rest of the people they had seen on Dr. Lin's phone. Her eyes were closed, but Julie could clearly see her naked chest rising and falling. *She was alive.*

And her arm had been halfway removed. A line of blood marked where the pair had been sawing, and the saw itself, metallic and shining with the sheen of crimson, sat nearby.

"Wh — what are you doing?" Sarah asked.

The man's face darkened. "As I said, you two are *not* supposed to be here. I need you to leave, *right now.*" The man rushed forward and around the table toward Julie, his arms extended. Julie anticipated the attack and was prepared. She crouched, then plowed upward with her head, aiming directly for the man's chest. She made contact and the two of them fell, the man landing on his back with Julie on top. He groaned and she felt and heard the air leaving his lungs.

"I'm not going anywhere," she said. "Tell me *right now* what this is all about. Dr. Lin came to our room last night and gave us pictures — pictures of people whose limbs had been removed. Much like this one almost is."

The woman was shaking, but Sarah had stepped up next to her and placed her hand on her shoulder. "We're not going to hurt you, but we're serious. We need to know what this 'laboratory' is all about. We're afraid there might be lives in danger."

The woman began to sob. "It's — it's too late," she whimpered. "Crawford... he won't let us..."

"Let you what?" Julie asked. She kept one eye on the woman and one on the man groaning and trying to catch his breath on the floor.

"He won't let us... leave. We're here under his orders. We're paid well enough, but we're contracted into service, and there's no breaking it."

"You're slaves?"

"No, not really. But he's a bit paranoid. He wants to know everything we're doing, and when. We have reports to send every day, detailing every hour. And we're not allowed to leave the island until the project is over."

Julie took a deep breath. "And the project; what is it? Cutting people's arms off?"

The woman seemed saddened. "It's not — it's not what you think. There are amazing things being done here. But we... we weren't aware when we were recruited what exactly we'd be doing."

Dr. Lindgren walked closer to Susan, gently squeezing her upper arm. "Susan, we're here to help. You *and* the people you're... working on." She swallowed. "But we need to know *exactly* what it is Crawford is making you do."

The woman nodded. She opened her mouth to speak, but there was a loud crash from behind them.

Julie turned and stared. Two guards were standing inside the anteroom, and one of them was banging the butt of a mean-looking submachine gun on the thick glass wall that led into the laboratory space. The other guard was working his ID card into the slot.

They must have locked everything down, Julie realized. After their Subshuttle ride and the security call from the other employees in the conference room, someone higher up must have locked down the entire facility.

"We're out of time," Sarah said. "Let's go, Julie."

Julie took one last look at the unconscious, breathing body of the woman on the metal table, her arm halfway removed from her torso, then at the woman standing scared nearby and the man trying to recover from Julie's blow to his chest.

This is getting more interesting than I thought.

She turned and began running around the long, curved laboratory room. Sarah was right behind her the entire time, and surprisingly, the woman named Susan was as well.

CHAPTER 33

"AT LEAST THEY could get us something to sit on," Reggie said, crouching with his back against the wall.

"Shut up, Reggie," Ben responded. He was standing, leaning against the wall in the back corner of their makeshift jail cell. "This is your fault."

They'd been sitting, standing, and pacing in the room for nearly an hour now, and neither of them had any idea what Garza's plan was. They could hear nothing, see nothing, and nothing in the room gave them any clues.

"*My* fault?" Reggie said. He stood up. "I didn't drag you here. I didn't *make* you do anything you didn't want to —"

"Yeah, well you may as well have. You didn't have *half* a decent plan, and even then you didn't think to share it with us? What, you thought you could walk in here and just *kill* him? Come on, you're better than that."

Reggie seethed, but he didn't approach Ben. Ben waited for Reggie to move, to do something, but the man just stood there, empty and silent.

"You brought me and Julie into this, and now Dr. Lindgren is involved as well. Best of all, they're somewhere out there, somewhere in the park, and the Ravenshadow guys are looking for them."

"Maybe they'll be able to get off, find a ride out or something."

"Are you insane?" Ben said. "We're on an *island*, Reggie. A man-made floating hotel. What are they going to do, wave down a fishing boat?"

"Stop," Reggie said. "None of this is helping. The least we can do is put our heads together and figure out what we're dealing with. Julie's smart, she'll be able to stay ahead of them."

"Yeah," Ben said, "*if* she knows they're after her." He started breathing heavier, trying not to think of his fiancée running blind, somewhere in a hostile environment in the middle of the ocean.

"She'll figure it out. Dr. Lindgren's got chops, as well. They're not naive, and there's no sense worrying about them. We figure out whatever we can here, and then we figure out how to get out."

"What is there to figure out?" Ben asked.

"Like this place — *Paradisum* — it's a theme park, but it's also *not*. It's clearly something else entirely, either as a cover up for the park, or the other way around."

"You mean a place where they cut people's arms off?"

"Well, yeah. But *why*? Why would Crawford put it all here, right on top of some ancient shipwreck and then build a luxurious hotel and fake beaches all over it? If he wanted to hide it, why *attract* attention?"

Ben shrugged. "Maybe he's telling the truth — maybe it's a research facility because he's *actually* trying to build an 'education-based theme park,' or whatever he called it."

Reggie shook his head. "It still doesn't explain the creepy arm-farm downstairs. And we know Crawford's a bad apple, anyway."

"We do?"

"Remember when we met with him? He *knew* we'd be coming, asking for a meeting with The Hawk. He was prepared, because Garza told him about it. He even had it pre-scheduled."

Ben thought about it for a moment and realized Reggie was absolutely right. "We walked into a trap. I knew it when we were in the cafeteria, but I didn't really realize Crawford was *part* of it."

"Right, but we know he is. He *has* to be. All of it — this place, the dinners, schmoozing us and the investors — it's all a game. He's playing us, but I don't know why. The Hawk probably wants our heads on a platter, but Crawford shouldn't care about us one way or another. He should be neutral, but he's not. He's doing exactly what The Hawk is telling him to do..."

"Which means *Garza* is the one calling the shots," Ben said. He let out a breath of air and rubbed his forehead with a hand. *This just got way worse.*

"Which means we're *way* out of our element here," Reggie added. "And it didn't just start with the meeting with Garza. It started the moment we set foot on *Paradisum*. From the moment we got here we've been playing in Garza's game."

Ben nodded. "I agree. But what game is it? Why the hell would he have us come all the way out here? Lure us out here in the middle of the ocean... for what?"

Reggie looked around the room, the makeshift cell they were in. "I don't know. Seems a bit over the top, you know? If he wanted us dead, why not just kill us somewhere else? Why work with Crawford, agree to have us come all the way out here, and spend all this money and attention on us? If it were me, I'd just have killed us on the cruise ship. Or back at the cabin. Much easier to hide the bodies there."

Besides the macabre analogy, Ben knew Reggie was right about that, too. Crawford and The Hawk were working together on something, but it was impossible to know what it was. It was impossible to understand the men's motive without having more information, but it was absolutely clear to Ben that Garza and Crawford were playing them. They'd lured the CSO team here, and now they just needed to figure out why.

And how to get out of this room.

"The girls are going to need help," Ben said.

Reggie nodded. "They will, wherever they are. They're probably walking into a trap right now as well."

"So we need to get out of here."

"You see any way of doing that?" Reggie asked. "No windows, one door — I'm guessing locked — and not even any ceiling tiles. Can't do any Hollywood-style escapes with this."

"Maybe we can get a guard to come over here, open the door. You know, trick him or something."

"Trick him?" Reggie scoffed. "You realize we're dealing with the best underground security force in the country, and probably one of the best in the world. Garza's men run the gauntlet, literally, in order to get in. They're not just going to waltz over here and open the door because we start yelling."

"No, but maybe we —"

"No, Ben," Reggie said, cutting him off. "We're screwed. We're at Garza's mercy, and Crawford's too. The only way we're getting out of here is if —"

The door clicked, and started to swing open. Two armed guards appeared in the hallway, each holding one of the ubiquitous submachine guns Ben had come to recognize. The first man stood to the side, aiming his rifle in the space halfway between Ben and Reggie. *One quick jerk to the left or right and we're toast,* Ben thought. *This guy is trained well.*

The second man looked at each of them in turn, focusing on neither. It was as if they were simply robots, not men. Prisoners, not humans. The man had no telling expression on his face, and Ben wondered if that was just how he looked or if he was playing a game. Continuing the ruse Garza had started back in the cafeteria.

"Move out," the man said. His voice was gruff, hard. This man had seen some action, and Ben recognized the military all over his face and the way he held himself. And not just regular grunt-level work, either. This guy was special forces, hardened and molded over years of service and plenty of battles into the deceptively plain-looking soldier that stood before them.

"Where?" Reggie asked.

"Doesn't matter, does it?" the man responded.

"Depends."

"I can *make* you move, or you can do it yourself. I'd welcome either option."

Reggie looked over at Ben, then shrugged. Ben got the point. *This might be our chance.*

"Fine," Reggie said, taking the lead. "I'll play."

He walked out of the room and into the hallway, and Ben followed behind. Ben stopped when he realized the hallway wasn't empty.

"Change of plan, boys," The Hawk said, standing in the hallway, his wide stance nearly covering the space from left to right. "Crawford decided he'd like one more word with you."

"What's Crawford got to do with this?" Reggie asked. "You're the one who wanted us here, right?"

Garza didn't respond.

"You lured us here. You *wanted* us to come out, to see what this place was all about. You probably leaked the fact that it was Raven-shadow's new contract, made sure it was seen by our benefactor so he'd send us down here to check it out."

Again, Garza just stared, silent. He crossed his arms in front of his chest, waiting. After another moment of silence on both sides, he grinned. "Crawford has more to do with this than you might think, boys. But let's not get ahead of ourselves. I am *certainly* excited you're here, as I feel there was some unfinished business back in Philly. I plan to make good on my promise to you, but I also have a boss. Crawford's in charge for now, so I'd suggest we all just play nice."

Reggie set his gaze straight ahead, and Ben simply watched on, trying to piece things together.

It didn't work. He was just as confused as he had been inside in the room.

Garza turns and began walking away, and Ben felt the nose of the small weapon in the guard's hand on his back. He started forward, following behind The Hawk as he walked on into the main security chambers, a few men looking up from desks as they passed. He exited the room into the antechamber, and Ben saw the first person they'd seen at the desk on his right, his head buried in his computer as they passed.

The Hawk led them out into the hall, almost exactly the reverse of the path they'd taken to get here. They headed toward the elevators, moving quickly. Apparently Crawford was impatient, or The Hawk was just trying to make up for lost time.

Ben was still confused, but he was confident about one thing:

If they were going to try anything, this was their chance.

CHAPTER 34

THE WOMAN, Susan, proved to be a valuable asset even after only a few minutes. They were running through the large, curving laboratory that followed the structure of the ring they were in, but they were running blind. Susan took the lead after a minute of jogging through rooms separated by glass doors and identification checkpoints, and Julie was immediately happy that she had decided to come along.

She had questions, but they could wait. Susan was quick with her ID card, clearing them into each section the deeper into the laboratory they got. Dr. Lindgren and Susan ran ahead of Julie, who decided to keep an eye out over her shoulder for any of the guards she knew were heading their way.

They didn't have much time, and — worst of all — they had no plan. Without getting Susan safely into a locked room, Julie didn't want to risk stopping to talk. Her questions and the woman's answers would have to wait. They needed to stay ahead of the guards, and they *really* needed to find Dr. Lin.

If anyone knew what was going on, it was the man she'd met in the hotel last night. Dr. Lin may have been frantic and difficult to communicate with, but she doubted that was his nature. Something had seriously spooked him, and it had been a big enough deal that he'd wanted to share it with the outside world, not the fellow scientists and researchers he had been working with.

Susan turned left into the next room, an odd choice of direction considering that the ring and sub level they were in was curving around to the right.

"You know where you're going?" Sarah asked.

Susan nodded, swiping her ID card on the front of the door without slowing down. She waited the two seconds for the green light to appear, then she pushed the handle down and threw the door open.

Dr. Lin was inside, sitting in the corner. The room was a closet, nothing but three walls of shelves with laboratory equipment, cleaning materials, and old computer monitors gathering dust. The shelves extended out more than a foot into the room on all three sides, leaving little room in front of them for anything other than a single chair.

But there *was* a single chair in the room, and on that chair sat Dr. Joseph Lin. His black hair, previously parted on the side and combed perfectly, with a bit of mousse to hold everything together, hovering over the rest of his head, was now disheveled. It looked as though he had run his hands through it over and over again until the hair was so badly messed up the man was nearly unrecognizable.

"Dr. Lin?" Julie asked. Susan had opened the door and held it, standing like a sentinel outside in the main room as Julie and Dr. Lindgren fell upon the man in the chair.

The man nodded. He sniffed, looking up at each of them. He didn't speak.

"Are — are you okay?" Julie asked.

He stared. His eyes were empty, devoid of emotion, but Julie thought she could see a slight shake to the man's hand. He was resting the hand on one of the shelves next to him, while his other sat in his lap.

"Dr. Lin," Sarah said, "we came here to find you. I'm Dr. Sarah Lindgren, and this is Juliette Richardson. We're with the CSO, and we — we saw the pictures on your phone, and we —"

"So you know," he whispered. "You know now." It was a question, just a hint of raised inflection. He wasn't sure *what* they knew.

"No," Julie said. "That's why we came. We *don't* know. What is this all about? Dr. Lin, if you could just —"

"*She* knows," he said. He pointed a long, scraggly finger at Susan. Julie hadn't noticed how gaunt the man seemed before. Or he had somehow lost a good portion of his body weight in a day.

Julie and Sarah turned and looked at Susan. Julie waited, raising an eyebrow.

"I — I'm not sure what he's talking about," Susan said. "I'm here with them, Dr. Lin. I came to help them, to try and figure this —"

"You know they took your sister," Dr. Lin said. "Elizabeth. She's gone. Removed."

Susan shook her head. "You don't know that. She told me she was going to be reassigned, that they'd be taking her —"

"Susan," Dr. Lin said. His eyes were bloodshot, pleading. The mask of emotionless nothingness had lifted and Julie saw in the man's face the look of someone who knew something was going to happen to them, and that something wasn't going to be good. He was resigned to his fate. "Susan, you know the truth. You *have* to know. The signs have all been here from the beginning. From your recruitment — do you remember that?"

Julie watched Susan's face. The woman was middle-aged, probably nearing her mid-fifties judging by the creases surrounding her eyes and the way she carried herself. To her credit, however, she looked far younger than that, and Julie knew she could pass for mid-thirties with a good stylist on her team. Her blond hair was pulled back tightly into a bun, and she wore wire-rimmed glasses on the tip of her nose. She was short, shorter than Julie, and a bit stocky. The way she looked down at Dr. Lin, though, told Julie everything.

She has no idea what he's talking about. She's innocent.

"They took Elizabeth. Told me she was going to be removed."

Susan swallowed. "Wh — why?"

Dr. Lin shook his head. "There was a... lapse. The same reason they came for me." At this, he flicked his eyes left and right at the shelves on the walls, as if trying to see beyond them. "It's why they're *still* after me. You — all of you — need to leave."

"Not until you tell us what's going on here," Sarah said. "The people in the pictures — who are they?"

Lin shook his head once again. "I don't know that. They were here when I got here. All related, or at least from the same demographic, I believe."

"South American, by the looks of it," Dr. Lindgren said.

Lin's face registered surprise.

"I'm an anthropologist," she said, answering the unspoken question. "I'd guess Peruvian, or somewhere around there."

"I believe you're right," Dr. Lin said. "It would match up with what we believe was found in the wreckage beneath the hotel. The ship; has Adrian showed you that?"

They shook their heads. "No," Julie said. "But we heard. From the Spanish Treasure Fleet?"

Dr. Lin nodded. "We think so. The skeletons we found there have been a core component of our research. The DNA samples we were able to extract were... odd, to say the least."

"How so?" Sarah asked.

"They differ slightly from that of what we would call 'normal' humans. As if there was a step missed in their evolution. Something that should have been switched off never was, and Dr. Crawford believed it allowed them to have some unique characteristics. He thought the Spanish, way back then, thought so as well, and that was why they were taken."

"And why were the *live* people taken?" Julie asked. "There's no excuse for that."

"No," Dr. Lin said. "Of course not. But as I said, they were here before I got here. All of them."

"Why?" Julie asked. "For what purpose?"

Dr. Lin turned his head to the side and looked at Julie. "For more research, of course."

"Research. Right. What *sort* of research is going on here, Dr. Lin? What kind of research would require the skeletons of centuries-old Peruvians, and modern-day ones? And you —" Julie looked at Susan — "how are you involved in all of this?"

Susan's eyes widened. "I — I'm not. I mean, I am, but not at the level of Dr. Lin. He's in charge of the entire laboratory. It's his research we're working off of."

If Dr. Lin was upset with the woman for her betrayal, he didn't show it. Instead, he lowered his head. *She's telling the truth,* Julie realized. *She has nothing to do with whatever Dr. Lin got himself into.*

"This station — the entire park," Dr. Lin began, "is just what Dr. Crawford says it is. It's a park meant to tie together education with entertainment, in a way that's never been done before."

"We heard the marketing pitch," Sarah said. "Impressive stuff. But it's not true, is it?"

"It's very much true," Dr. Lin answered. "Very much. But it's not *all* this park is. The funding — the investors that are here, the people behind it all, the board — they're all in it for a different reason."

"Research?" Julie asked.

"Yes."

"Research about how to remove peoples' limbs?" she asked. It was a crude follow-up question, but there were people searching for them. They were running out of time.

And they needed answers.

"No," Dr. Lin said. "That is but one component of the research that *OceanTech* is involved in. It is a brutal, albeit necessary component."

"If it's brutal, why is it necessary?" Sarah asked. Susan and Julie nodded. Julie was somewhat surprised that the new addition to the group was as in the dark about all of this as they were, but she wasn't going to question it. Chances were good that Crawford had plenty of safeguards in place to prevent employees from sharing their trade secrets with one another. Keep everything compartmentalized and it was easier to control the flow of information.

Keep people in the dark, and it was *way* easier to control everything.

"A component of what, Dr. Lin?"

Dr. Lin sighed, looked around again, then looked up at Julie. "We are not *removing* limbs here, Ms. Richardson."

Julie frowned. *Those pictures on your phone are telling a very different story,* she thought.

"We are growing them back."

CHAPTER 35

"YOU'RE... *WHAT?*" Julie and Susan said in unison.

Julie heard a crash from behind her. The closet faced the entrance to this section of the lab, and before Julie turned around to see what the commotion was, she knew. *Too late, we're out of time.*

"Let's go," she said. "Dr. Lin, you too. We need to get moving." She crept out of the closet and saw that there were two soldiers waiting for a command from somewhere else in the park to unlock the door. Apparently even the guards did not have access to these internal laboratories. Julie made a mental note of that, further adding to her suspicion that there was something seriously wrong going on down here. *Even the Ravenshadow men are banned from accessing Crawford's secret lab.*

Dr. Lin started to stand, then collapsed back onto the small chair. It swiveled around and his knees bumped into the shelf, and he looked up at Julie. "No, it's too late, as I said. There is no hope for me to continue my research."

Susan stared down at her coworker. "You can't just abandon us now," she said. "This is all your research. This is what you've been working on, and we can help you if you will only tell us what it is you are trying to do."

Dr. Lin shook his head. "No, it's too late. This was and always will be Crawford's research, and he won't let someone like me — or any of you — get in the way of completing it."

The guards had the door open and Julie pushed both women out into the main laboratory to the left. "Go, now," she said. "Keep moving, deeper into the labs. I don't think they can get through the doors without help from someone else remotely opening them.

Sarah Lindgren looked shocked. "But what about you?" she asked. "They're almost inside."

"Don't worry about me," Julie said. "I'll be right behind —"

The sound of gunfire cut her off. Susan screamed, but Dr. Lindgren grabbed her arm and the two shuffled away farther into the lab. Julie turned back to Dr. Lin. "I know these men," she said. "They're going to kill you. Come with me, now."

To her surprise, the man stood up shakily and began walking to the closet door. The guards were moving along the right side of the room, closing in on a direct shot of the closet, but focusing their attention on the two women making their way across the room farther away. Julie stepped out softly and snuck around to a rolling whiteboard set up a few feet away from the wall next to the closet. Its legs were a couple of feet off the floor, so her feet would be hidden, but with any luck the men were scanning top to bottom and she would be well-hidden. She waited an extra second for Dr. Lin to see her, then she ducked behind the whiteboard. He followed her, and she appeared out the other side of the board and waited for the men to pass. Susan and Dr. Lindgren were already through the glass doors separating this segment of the lab from the next. Julie had the odd realization that this laboratory was set up like nothing she had seen before, as if it's designer had intended each section to be accessible yet mutually exclusive from each other part. *Yet another mystery.*

But she didn't have time to dwell on the characteristics of the space and its architectural anomalies. The guards were nearing the door, the man on the right with his hand on the handle and the man on the left speaking into a microphone he wore on his wrist. Within seconds, they would be through those doors as well, and Julie realized something else:

We're going to get locked inside this room.

She turned to Dr. Lin. "Please tell me you have an ID badge that opens the doors down here."

He nodded. "Of course. But if I use it, they'll see it on the control screen. There are no cameras in this section of the labs, for obvious reasons."

Those reasons weren't yet obvious, but Julie didn't have time to press him.

"We need to get into the next space, where Sarah and Susan are," Julie said.

"That's where the guards are going," Lin replied. "Like you said, they'll shoot me —"

"They'll shoot *them*, too. And I'm not going to let that happen."

"What do you suggest?" Dr. Lin asked. "They're armed. We have nothing to fight them with."

Julie thought for a moment, watching the guards in the next room through the glass. They were about a hundred feet away, but they were standing still, looking the other direction. *Looking for the two women.*

"Let me distract them. I can get them to at least come back into this room," Julie said. "You take your badge and sneak along the side of this room." She pointed. "Crouch in the corner over there, behind that desk, and as soon as they both get back into this room, *run*. Get through the door and then keep going until you catch up."

Dr. Lin looked troubled for a moment. "I — I can't. I'm not sure..."

"*Go,*" Julie said.

He shook his head, then dropped it, looking down at the floor.

The brightness of the room didn't reach them, and his dark face fell into shadow. "I need to stay. Take my card, and let me distract them."

"No," Julie said. "It's too dangerous. You can't —"

"They're going to kill me anyway. Crawford had me removed, and the board approved the motion."

"Removed?"

"Removed from my post as lead researcher."

Julie was confused. "So? That's a good thing, right? Will they let you leave?"

He shook his head. "No, 'removed' means they're removing everything about me. All records of my working here will be erased, if they haven't already been, and any publications that include my name as a mention related to this research will be changed to 'et al,' and again, my name erased."

"But that's... who cares?" Julie asked. "Is it really about the vanity? You'll lose a few years of your life, but then you can start over, right?"

His face told her that she was missing something.

"No," he said. "I'll continue to be a part of the research here, just not as a *researcher.*"

Julie frowned, then her jaw dropped. *Oh.* "You mean..."

"Yes," he said. She thought she caught a glimpse of a tear in his eye. "I will be removed from my role, but I will thereafter become a subject for study. Just another nameless person in a cage."

Julie was about to ask a follow-up question, but Dr. Lin shoved his ID card into her hand. "I'm not leaving this place, Ms. Richardson. That's why I came to find you in the hotel. I knew you and your team would be able to help, somehow. What's happening here is not okay, and the world needs to know about it."

Julie swallowed, then nodded. "We — we'll do our best."

"No," he said. "You *have* to do better than that. You have to stop Crawford. No matter what. He doesn't understand what he's doing here."

He placed his hands over her clasped fist, still gripping the ID badge. She had the keys to the kingdom now, and the trust from the lead researcher that she would bring Crawford down.

All she needed now was to make good on that promise.

CHAPTER 36

REGGIE LEANED over and whispered to Ben. "Not yet. Let's see what Crawford has to say first."

Ben nodded. He was still mad at his friend, but at least they weren't going to have to wait around in the jail cell. The Hawk led the way, with the two armed guards following behind Reggie and Ben. They hadn't been bound or handcuffed, and Reggie assumed that meant the Ravenshadow men were confident in their abilities with their compact assault weapons.

Reggie was certainly confident in their abilities. While he didn't recognize any of the Ravenshadow crew they'd seen so far save for The Hawk himself, Reggie knew all about their recruitment tactics. Vicente Garza had started the company years ago, luring young soldiers into the security company's fold by offering a much better benefits package than their government's military. It was a huge draw for the grunt-type young men, the ones who wanted an excuse to use their weapons. They often had no family or nothing to tie them down, and many of them even had had more than a few brushes with the law in their time.

The Hawk would offer to pay the men a bonus for leaving the military after their commitment term had been completed, and even pay for training programs while they were enlisted. Then he would send them to his grueling form of bootcamp, a program he'd designed with physiological and physical torture in mind.

Reggie knew about it because he'd *done* it.

The Hawk had tried recruiting him years ago, just after he'd finished his term and just before he was going to try out for the Special Forces Qualification Course. Reggie had jumped at the opportunity to 'fast-track' his training and experience by joining up with a group that promised better options than the Army. He left his unit and traveled to the backcountry of Canada to start the first phase of the training.

It was after this first phase that Reggie discovered more about who The Hawk was, how he had received his reputation, and just what exactly the Ravenshadow crew was involved in.

Only a few recruits each year passed through 'The Gauntlet' successfully and came out the other side as a full-on Ravenshadow soldier. The Hawk had designed the intense program to try each man as much as the famed Navy SEALs' BUD/S training program, but with a bit more physical abuse and torment thrown in, and yet just about every young man that went through the program and failed wanted more. They were addicted to the fight, to the pain of it all, and The Hawk's company thrived on that adrenaline.

Garza kept a running list of recruits that had tried and failed to run 'The Gauntlet,' and he often called on them to help on missions when he needed to bolster his crew. Reggie had no doubt that there were quite a few of those exact types here with him now, possibly including the men that were escorting them to Crawford's office.

But like Reggie himself, these men were far from 'unqualified.' They could shoot, fight, and think like any of the best soldiers Reggie had met, and they were in peak physical condition. They had been given a taste of what freedom was like, dangled over their heads by Vicente Garza, and they were hooked. They'd fight any war he ordered them to, no matter where or against whom.

And *that* was the reason Reggie had thrown in the towel. He'd seen firsthand the sort of battles The Hawk wanted them to fight, and he wanted nothing to do with it. Companies paid good money for a bit of 'forceful security,' and many of them could not care less what measures were taken to protect their interests. He'd been to Africa with The Hawk and come out the other side shaken, morally confused, and angry.

And he *hated* being angry.

So he quit. It wasn't as simple as just putting in a letter of resignation — The Hawk was smarter than that, and Reggie knew the man would be able to find him anywhere in the world he thought he could hide, and there would be consequences to pay. Instead, Reggie had purposefully failed a crucial mission parameter just before he was up for completion of the bootcamp course.

The Hawk was furious, firing Reggie on the spot, and Reggie took the tongue-lashing and went on his way, eventually settling in Brazil and starting his own survival training camp for corporate executives. He'd pushed The Hawk and Ravenshadow out of his mind, focused once again on his personal life for the first time in years, and had nearly forgotten all about his experiences with the private security sector.

Until Philadelphia. The Hawk and his men had walked back into his life at the request of their newest benefactor, a woman who wanted protection for her company during the creation of a serum and drug that needed to be kept under control. Reggie had nearly lost his life then, and many people had, including his close friend, Joshua Jefferson.

He'd never forgive The Hawk, and he'd sworn at that moment to kill the man who'd caused so much suffering in so many lives.

But now was not the time. Another threat, this one by the name of Adrian Crawford, had walked into their lives. Crawford may not have been the soldier type, but he was every bit as cunning as Garza. He'd successfully lured them into his realm, buttering them up with fancy food and accommodations. On top of that, he'd perfected his 'nice guy' appeal and charisma, and Reggie had fallen for it.

They were about to come face-to-face with that man, and Reggie wanted a chance to tell him *exactly* how he felt about his new park.

He knew Ben wanted to as well, and he didn't want to take that opportunity from him. Crawford would get an earful from them, and *then* they would try to escape. Julie and Dr. Sarah Lindgren were still out there somewhere, exploring the park and hopefully enjoying themselves, but they were in danger now. Reggie would do whatever it took to protect them, knowing that he could never forgive himself if something happened to another member of his team.

And he didn't even want to *think* about what Ben would do if something happened to Julie.

He looked over at Ben as they approached the elevator that would take them to the top level and Subshuttle entrance, and examined his friend's face.

Ben appeared stoic, but Reggie knew there was a lot going on under the surface. He wanted revenge as much as Reggie, and he would get it. He would protect Julie, but until he knew for a fact she was in danger, his focus would be on Crawford, then The Hawk.

For a moment, even in spite of the guns and the grunts behind them, and the all-too-capable leader of those men walking in front of them, Reggie felt pity for them all. Harvey Bennett hadn't started as a fighter, but he'd become one.

And he hadn't lost an ounce of the resilience and strength that had gotten him this far.

They're dead, Reggie thought. He didn't know how, or when, but he knew it was a fact. *They're all dead.*

CHAPTER 37

JULIE RAN. There was no choice now, and there was no turning back. She would be shot on sight, knowing The Hawk. Garza had probably ordered the shoot-to-kill before they'd even descended down into the laboratory space beneath the second ring.

Dr. Lin had made his choice, as well. He stood in the center of the room, nothing but empty space and a thick sheet of glass between him and the men in the other room. One of the men turned, saw him, and shouted to his teammate.

The two Ravenshadow guards hustled to the door and one of them called it in again, waiting for it to open. He stepped through, his gun raised.

Julie waited, crouched behind the desk, watching. They hadn't seen her earlier, and she was sure they hadn't seen her now. Still, she'd need to time things perfectly for her plan to work, and even then it was a long shot. These men were trained killers, soldiers-for-hire that had been further tested by The Hawk himself. She'd met the group in Philadelphia, and had withstood a grueling night alone in a gym, tied to a chair, awaiting torture from The Hawk or one of his men.

She wanted to kill them — all of them — even though she didn't directly recognize these two. She knew what they stood for, and whom they worked for, and that was more than enough.

But not now, she thought. She wanted to, but there was no way to take them down without a weapon. And Susan and Dr. Lindgren were still in the laboratory somewhere, and she owed it to at least Dr. Lindgren to help.

The second guard entered the room, and both men pointed their submachine guns at Dr. Lin. Dr. Lin looked pitiful, his disheveled hair still mussed, his hands raised in defeat. "I — I want to talk to Crawford," he said.

The man closest to Julie laughed. "Too late for that, Doc." He fired, two quick shots. The first spun Lin around, while the second lodged into the left side of his upper back. The two guards stepped forward, walking toward Lin.

Lin wavered a moment, then fell.

Now, Julie thought. The moment had arrived, and she bolted up from her crouched position on the floor and ran to the door. She held out the dead man's card and watched impatiently for the light to blink green and the door to unlock. It took a grueling two seconds, and she forced herself to not look over her head, to not look at the two armed men standing barely twenty feet from her.

Nothing I'll be able to do if they see me, she thought.

The door clicked — loudly — and slid open. It was a soft click, but to Julie's adrenaline-amped ears it sounded like the entire park could hear it. She knew for a fact at least one of the Ravenshadow guards would have heard it.

She waited just long enough for the door to open wide enough for her to slide through, then she twisted and rolled alongside the glass on the opposite side of the wall.

And it was just in time, too.

A spattering of gunfire hit the glass where she had been standing only a split-second before. The glass held, but Julie felt the rippling impacts of the absorbed shock throughout her body. She forced herself to breathe. *I'm still alive. I'm still fighting.*

She wasn't going to back down, but she also wasn't going to rush headlong into a battle without arming herself. This was the wrong time and place for a standoff, so she did the only thing that made sense.

She ran.

She ran as fast as her legs would carry her, deeper into the curving laboratory, and she ran for her life, and for the lives of the two women she'd only just met. The walls banked around to the right just like they had in the earlier sections of the lab, and she assumed she was about a quarter of the way around the ring. They were on Sub-1, beneath the surface of the water, and she suddenly felt the weight of the water surrounding her, separated by only a wall on each side. There was a palpable tension in the room, even though she hadn't checked to see if the two guards had joined her or were still in the previous lab segment.

She didn't care — it didn't matter where they were. She needed to find Sarah and Susan and get them to safety. Dr. Lindgren seemed tough, but Julie wasn't going to assume she had ever been in a situation like this. Not many people had, and she was positive Susan would fare even worse.

She didn't worry much about Reggie or Ben, knowing that they were capable of taking care of themselves, but she did hope they'd figured out that Crawford was just as terrible as The Hawk.

She hoped they hadn't walked into a trap.

It was after running into the next segment that she realized *she* had walked into a trap. Not one in a physical sense, but certainly one in a psychological sense.

The laboratory segments had so far been typical of what Julie might expect: rooms with shelves and cupboards lining the curved walls, tall metal tables and stools spread out throughout the rooms, microscopes, beakers, graduated cylinders, and computers. Very typical of what she remembered from her own experience in chemistry class in college.

But this segment was different. First, it was darker. It was lit poorly, either by design or from ignorance, but she guessed the latter. Second, the room felt completely unlike the rest of the laboratory rooms. It was humid, the climate control system working on overdrive to catch up with the added moisture in the space. Finally, it had a completely different layout. The tables and stools had been replaced by a long, slightly curving space, and the computers were absent, replaced by a massive monitoring station made up of a bank of display screens that was angled downward, mounted above her on the ceiling and wall.

Lastly, there were no shelves or cupboards. Instead, there were cages.

Inside the cages, people.

She stopped, unable to help herself. The cages — all of them, to her left and right, stacked one on top of another in individual glass-faced compartments — were filled with people. One person per cage, each of them sitting or crouching in a very uncomfortable position, looking out at the room.

Not at her, but at... nothing.

They were as empty as shells that had washed up on the beach. Signs of prior inhabitation, but devoid entirely of life. She stood still, stunned. She looked at each cage on her left, as far as she could see, then she turned and looked at the cages on her right. All of them full, all of them empty at the same time. The people inside stared back out, none of them showing any sign that they had even noticed her entrance to their miniature prison.

She wanted to run back the way she'd come, but the guards were still back there, still chasing after her. They would likely have called it in by now that they were after three women, one scientist employed by *OceanTech* and two civilian visitors. The doors wouldn't be a problem for them after that, she guessed, assuming that they wouldn't need to stop outside each segment of the laboratory and wait for the control room to let them in.

She had to continue forward, had to continue moving. These people — whoever they were — needed her help. The two women waiting for her up ahead needed her help.

Reggie and Ben, wherever they were, needed her help.

She looked once again at the first cage on her left, preparing to start running once again. She saw the man's old, wrinkled skin, his blank, empty eyes, his hands, weathered and cold, sitting lifelessly at his sides. She watched him for a moment, unsure if he was actually breathing. Maybe they were all wax sculptures, some form of cruel joke put on by *OceanTech* and Adrian Crawford.

But then she saw his chest move, quickly and sharply, once, then again. He sucked in a breath, not diverting his stare from the point he'd chosen directly in front of him. *Maybe he couldn't see through the glass,* she thought.

She started to move, slowly at first.

But then his eyes moved.

Tracking her.

Watching her.

She nearly fell down, and had to catch herself by reaching out for the next glass cage in the line. She caught her balance and straightened, looking back at the man in the first cage. *It's an illusion,* she thought, *like how a person on television seems to always be staring directly at you.*

But she knew it wasn't true — this wasn't a two-dimensional version. The man's eyes held steady, examining her, coming to life and watching her stare back at him. They looked at each other for mere seconds, but to Julie it felt like an eternity. Captive and observer, man and woman.

And then he reached up and placed his hand on the glass. His eyes softened, and Julie's heart skipped a beat.

He pleaded with her, no words exchanged, but she knew exactly what he was trying to say.

Help.

CHAPTER 38

"HARVEY, GARETH, COME IN!" Crawford's voice had not lost any of its characteristic charm, but to Ben it now felt contrived. Well-rehearsed, certainly, but contrived. The charismatic man standing in front of them, behind his desk, was a brilliant strategist.

And Ben and Reggie had played right into his trap.

"Shut it, Crawford," Reggie said. "Enough with the games — what's this all about?"

Crawford feigned concern for a second. "Has my security team not treated you well?"

"I'm not going to tell you again, *Adrian*. Cut the bull—"

"Enough," Crawford said, holding up a hand and silencing Reggie. "Fine. All honesty from here on out."

"Like I'm going to believe that," Reggie said. "There's no way I'm going to trust —"

"You're here because Vicente Garza told me it would be in my best interest to rid the world of the Civilian Special Operations," he said.

Damn, Ben thought. *That* was *honest.*

"Really?" Reggie stammered.

"I told you, all honesty from here on out."

"Fine," Reggie said, turning to face The Hawk, who was standing next to him. "Why'd you hire these guys in the first place? They're criminals. The government finds out who's running your security, you're shut down within an hour, guaranteed."

Crawford smiled, and Garza grinned. The two Ravenshadow guards had entered with Ben and Reggie, but were standing behind them. Ben got the feeling they weren't laughing or smiling.

"You assume this place is under your government's control," Crawford said. "We have very minimal operational requirements from the United States and Bahamian governments, and *OceanTech* itself is registered as a corporation in Ireland."

"So you're running a tax-free and regulation-free business," Ben said.

"Not out of the ordinary for a corporation," Crawford said. "But that's not the point. The point is that there is a lot of research here that will not be understood — or accepted — by typical government regulating bodies."

"Because you're killing people?" Reggie said.

"*Because* it's cutting-edge," he responded. "And it's state-of-the-art, and therefore it's *valuable*. Ravenshadow has a proven track-record of protecting many assets that require care, discretion, and anonymity."

"What research?" Ben asked.

Crawford flashed him a dimple-laden smile. "Glad you asked. As I said, all honesty here. *OceanTech* has always been a company working on the forefront of genetic research. *Paradisum* will still be a park, intended first and foremost for entertainment through education, but *OceanTech* has built its flagship product on *this* location because of the raw materials available for continuing our research."

"Saltwater?" Ben asked.

Reggie shook his head. "The shipwreck."

"Indeed."

"But why *that* shipwreck? Surely it's not just about finding *any* shipwreck and building a hotel on top of it."

"Of course it's not. This *particular* shipwreck was part of a Spanish Treasure Fleet in the 1700's. One that started its voyage with a very special cargo."

"You're mining Spanish gold and silver from the wreck?" Ben asked.

Crawford shook his head. "No. Though we *have* found a few hundred thousand dollars' worth of gold and silver artifacts, the 'precious cargo' this vessel was carrying was *people*."

Ben's mind immediately flashed back to Sarah's mention of the *human cargo* she believed was on the ship. The article she'd read — the one that had nearly immediately after been removed from the publication — had mentioned that the ship was found with the skeletons of people inside not belonging to the actual Spanish crew.

"Incan?" Ben asked.

Crawford squinted. "Yes, precisely. Good guess?"

Ben shrugged. "Dr. Lindgren is a capable anthropologist, I guess."

Crawford seemed impressed, then his face darkened. He looked up at Garza. "Do we have a location yet, Garza?"

Garza gave a quick shake of his head.

"Fine. Keep looking. But I *need* them found."

"Of course. It would be easier to find them, however, if you had allowed me to install surveillance equipment in the —"

"Not in the lab, Garza. We talked about this."

Garza nodded, but Ben could tell he was unhappy to be told what to do. It was probably an uncommon feeling for the man.

Crawford recovered, taking a step sideways and turning slightly to once again address Ben and Reggie. "Indeed she is. Quite fascinating individuals, both her *and* Ms. Richardson."

Ben waited for the man's tell.

"I hope we'll all be together again soon," Crawford said.

"What's this about, Crawford?" Ben asked. "What do you want with us?"

"I told you. I want to ensure that the CSO will not interfere with our research here in any way. You have the unique ability to operate somewhat outside of any sort of direct oversight, which worries me."

"Fine," Reggie said. "We'll stay out of it. Let us off the island."

Crawford shook his head. "I'm very sorry. I can't allow that."

"What's with these skeletons? Why build a park on top of them?" Ben asked. He was intrigued by the entire idea, but Crawford's words were only causing him more worry.

"They are a very special find," Crawford said. "The Spanish discovered the members of this tribe and immediately wanted to explore the possibilities garnered by their unique capabilities. They were, of course, a bit too *primitive* to make any successful medical leaps."

Medical leaps? Capabilities?

"What capabilities?"

"The people of this tribe, one of the many that made up the Incan civilization, were thought to be descended from the Incan gods themselves, or so the story goes. They were capable of regeneration."

"Regeneration..." Reggie said. "Like zombies?"

"No, no. Not at all. I meant *limb* regeneration. They were believed to be able to regrow arms, legs, fingers, and toes. Sometimes both, but most records state that the tribe was reclusive and kept to themselves. They were mostly unknown, and the Incan civilization usurped their lands without their even knowing about it. They were technically an uncontacted tribe within the larger geographic area of the Incan population, and they remained a mystery to the Peruvian inhabitants. Simply a myth, a legend.

"But the Spanish apparently found them — they were the *real* gold the Spanish crown was after. Can you imagine? To be able to recreate the process of limb regeneration in humans?"

Ben was somewhat fascinated, but *very* disturbed. "So... what? You were able to extract DNA from the skeletons and try it?"

Crawford shook his head. "No, unfortunately. Though we tried for a couple years. But the DNA was too old, the samples too worn. There was nothing useful available to us within the ship's decayed hull, so we decided to pivot and build on the knowledge we *already* had. The information that linked this tribe to the legends."

"And where was *that* information?" Reggie asked.

Ben knew Reggie was a history buff, and from his time living in Brazil, this all would be piquing his interest. Still, it sounded quite far-fetched, and Ben knew Reggie was skeptical.

"Most of it went down with the Spanish ship," Crawford said. He looked down at his desk, in a sort of feigned reverence. Solemn, chewing the inside of his lip and and shaking his head. *What an actor*, Ben thought. "But there was a set of documents my company found in Peru. In an old Jesuit church, written on parchment that was crumbled and faded."

Man, this guy has a way with words, Ben thought. *He's still playing us, even though he has no reason to.*

"The parchments were examined by my science team, and I myself compiled them into workable documentation of the period just before the Fleet left port. The priest who wrote them was acting as a sort of quartermaster for the ship's captain, apparently, as he kept a ledger and a manifest, and one particular paragraph seemed to imply that the Spanish ship was bound for the Florida coast, then on to Spain, as quickly as the weather would allow.

"They were loaded down with 'items of the crown's interest, including possessions of silver and gold and —' I quote — '*inhabitants of the Tribe of Legend, for purposes unknown to me.*'"

"So this priest got a little pen-happy. How do you know that he was telling the truth?"

"It was an educated guess," Crawford said. "But it was a correct one. The skeletons were useful to us, if only to point us in the direction of finding *more* of them."

Ben frowned. "*More?*"

"Yes. More. This time with the skin attached. We needed *fresh* subjects, if you get my drift."

Ben's eyes widened, and he looked at Reggie, but his friend was glaring at Crawford. Ben imagined Reggie lunging for the man's throat, knowing it would only take a few seconds for Reggie to end him. But that would be a mistake, as Garza and his men were standing by. Julie and Dr. Lindgren would only be in more danger if they did something rash now.

"Why are you telling us this?" Ben asked. "Why reveal your hand?"

Crawford laughed. "*Reveal my hand?*" he asked. "I'm not revealing *anything*, Mr. Bennett. This is going to be common knowledge in a month, possibly less, when we publish our initial findings. But it won't matter — no one can touch *OceanTech* anyway, as I explained earlier, and there will be *thousands* of organizations and pharmaceutical companies interested in our research. It won't matter how we *obtained* the research."

Ben was growing more and more upset, but he knew Crawford was right. Once it was out that *OceanTech* had figured out the secret to human limb regeneration, no one would care about the means to get there — the end result would justify nearly anything.

But *he* knew. And that was Crawford's first mistake.

The second was telling Reggie.

CHAPTER 39

SHE FOUND them around the next bend, behind the next set of glass doors. She was breathless, her heart pounding, still thinking about the laboratory worker named Susan who was huddling behind a table next to Dr. Sarah Lindgren, waiting and watching the doors. Julie used Dr. Lin's card and waited for the door to unlock, once again thanking whoever it was in the facility that hadn't yet seen Lin's access and shut it down.

"Dr. Lin?" Susan asked.

Julie shook her head. *No more explanation needed,* she thought.

The two women stared at her, but neither asked a follow-up question.

"Why did you stop?" Julie asked.

"We were talking," Susan said. "This is halfway around the ring, so it's the farthest we can get from the elevators on the other side."

Julie saw that she was right; there were no elevators on this side of the ring. However, there was a set of doors, unmarked, behind Sarah's and Susan's location. She wasn't sure where the doors led, but they were solid, thick doors, and an ID reader mounted next to it. *Wherever those doors go, they don't lead into a broom closet.*

The rest of the room was relatively bare, a few metal tables and stools, but the tables were empty and the stools had been tucked beneath each table. It looked as though no one had been in here since it was set up.

The two walls on the outside and inside of the curved room were metal as well, and upon closer inspection Julie noticed that the walls weren't a solid, singular sheet of metal, but box-like sections of metal, hammered into place at the corners. The sum effect was a mural of silver, the metallic sheen of the faces of the squares bouncing the dim light back into the room.

It was an odd design for a room, Julie thought, and it was even more odd that someone had decided the room *needed* to be designed. She examined the wall more closely, feeling around the edges of one of the squares of metal.

"We didn't know where the guards were," Sarah added. "We figured it was safest here, away from where they'd likely be coming from."

"They're behind me," Julie said. "They don't have a card, though, so they're going a bit slower. We need to keep moving."

"We shouldn't go around all the way, though," Susan said. "There are cameras outside the elevators. They'll know exactly where we are as soon as we get close to the front of the ring."

Julie figured the scientists were used to calling the side of the ring that featured the elevators and Subshuttle entrance the 'front,' which meant they must have been standing somewhere in the back side of the submerged ring. "Okay," she said. "But they don't have cameras down here?" she subconsciously began examining the walls and ceilings, looking for the small, black surveillance cameras she'd seen in the hallways of the hotel in the central ring.

Susan shook her head. "No, not down here in these back labs. Crawford wouldn't allow it, and Dr. Lin probably agreed, knowing what they were working on."

"Yeah," Julie said, "I saw a bit of what they were working on. I'd want to hide it, too." She said the words and meant them, but she was a bit surprised at how much they seemed to sting. "Sorry," she added. "I'm not sure how much of it you knew about."

Susan swallowed, then looked around the room. "Not much, honestly. Dr. Lin had just made me his replacement assistant, which is why I have access to these back rooms. But I didn't even get to speak with him about anything before... earlier."

Julie knew what the woman was talking about. She hadn't needed to explain anything, knowing that Susan was intelligent enough to put two and two together. *Dr. Lin is dead. Her boss is dead. She knows that.*

"So you had no idea about the... cages?"

Susan paused a beat, then nodded. "I knew they were testing on people, of course. I thought they were sick, or had volunteered, or something."

"Easy excuse," Dr. Lindgren said. Julie flashed her a glance. *Not now,* she thought. *We need this woman to cooperate.*

"Susan," Julie said, keeping her voice flat. "We need your help. Whatever you know about this... lab. Anything you can tell us. No one's accusing you of anything."

Susan nodded, then looked at Julie and Sarah. "I was originally brought on to create a synthetic component of a drug they're administering to the test subjects. Or that's what I was led to believe. That's my background, my area of expertise — genetic medicine."

"Genetic medicine?" Sarah asked. "I haven't heard of that."

"Stem cell research," Susan said. "But the medicine form of it. I build chemical compounds that can be administered to patients to help with all sorts of genetics-related diseases."

"Are the people in that other lab diseased?" Julie asked.

"No. Well, I don't know. But I don't think so. I never interacted directly with them."

"What did you do?" Sarah asked.

Julie looked around the room, listening carefully for any sign of the guards that were tailing them. If Susan was right, this was the best place for them to wait, to regroup, but it also meant that they were sitting ducks.

"Where do those doors go?" Julie asked, interrupting Susan's answer.

"That's the Subshuttle exit for this level," Susan said. "The shuttles run on a straight line, remember. They start at the elevators and run to here. There's one that runs perpendicular to this one on the next level down. Slow, but it works for shift changes, since we all typically head down together."

Julie thought for a moment. "Any way to get on it? Can we call it from this side?"

Susan nodded. "Yeah, I can swipe my card, but I don't think it's a good —"

"Do it," Julie said. "Now."

She listened again, hearing the telltale sound of the guards. Crashes as the men ran through the laboratory segment to her left, knocking over tables and chairs as they ran along. They were obviously more interested in finding their escaped prisoners than in leaving the lab in proper shape.

Susan walked over to the ID reader and swiped her card. "It might take a bit," she said. "I don't know where the shuttle is."

"Doesn't matter, Julie said. "We're just using it as a decoy."

"How's that?" she asked.

"Watch, and follow me."

Judging by the sound, the men were outside the glass doors leading into this 'back' segment of the circular laboratory ring. Julie poked her head up and could see them working the controls to the door. The first guard stood by, gun raised, as the second communicated with his control center by speaking into his wrist-mounted mic. She figured they had fewer than thirty seconds to act, possibly less if the control room had anticipated the guards' movement through the labs.

For the first time since they'd started moving through the labs, she thanked Crawford for the tight security protocols that were in place. He didn't trust his own security team enough to allow them uninhibited access to these sub-level labs; Susan, on the other hand, had no trouble moving around freely thanks to her access card.

Julie ducked back down and moved back to the wall. *Please, work.* She pushed on the surface of one of the squares that had been hammered to the wall and felt it give a bit. There was a clicking noise and then the square pushed away from the wall, revealing an open, empty space inside.

"What the —"

"We're not in the lab anymore," Julie said. "We're in the morgue."

CHAPTER 40

"SO AGAIN, CRAWFORD," Reggie said. "What do you want with us? You've played your hand, and it's impressive. Not quite a Royal Flush though, you know? What, you expect you'll just kill us and hope our benefactors don't come sniffing around?"

Crawford looked confused. "Really, Gareth, I expected more from you." He turned to Ben, then back to Reggie, sizing them up. "No, I'm not going to *kill* you. That would, as you said, be far too easy."

"Then... what?" Ben asked. "Our leadership team already knows we're here. They'll start —"

"What?" Crawford asked. "Their hands are tied, Bennett. You know that — you're on the board of the CSO, both of you. You signed the contracts. Hell, you helped *write* the contracts. The entire structure of your new organization was designed to be transparent. So transparent it's invisible. Plausible deniability isn't just an idea, gentlemen, it's a value. And your organization *defines* that value.

"You won't be missed, because you won't be *allowed* to be acknowledged. You know that. A simple helicopter crash off the coast, a breached and flooded compartment, a fire — there are plenty of ways to explain your deaths with your board. And while they may be suspicious — military types are that way by design — they know they can't ask questions. They created your organization in that way, on purpose."

Ben listened, trying to find fault with Crawford's argument. He couldn't. Adrian Crawford was correct on every count: the CSO's structure was created around the idea of a bridge between the military and the civilian sector, with the ability to deny any interactions in any operating theater the team found itself in. It was a risky business, running into fights the military couldn't be involved in and the private sector wouldn't want to be.

"So that's means you're here as my *guests*," Crawford said. "And nothing more, nothing less. And suffice to say I've suddenly felt a lot less hospitable."

Ben watched Reggie's face. *What's our move, buddy?* He thought. Reggie, unfortunately, gave him nothing.

"Mr. Garza and his men are going to escort you down to our labs," Crawford said, continuing to address them both. "You will stay out the rest of your time down there."

"In the laboratory?" Reggie asked. "What the hell? What are you getting at, Crawford?"

Crawford looked down at his desk, feigning the same examination of an invisible calendar Ben had seen before, then looked up at Garza. "I have another engagement," he said. "I'm sorry, but I must leave you now. Garza?"

Garza nodded to his men and Ben and Reggie were grabbed and spun around and pushed to the door. Ben caught one last glimpse of the immaculate office. The clean, organized desk, the framed degrees on the wall behind Crawford, and the picture of Crawford and the boy on the edge of his desk.

"You won't find the accommodations down there quite so...

accommodating, but I do hope you'll take some solace knowing that you are contributing greatly to the advancement of science."

Reggie didn't struggle, and Ben took the hint. *Not now,* he thought. *Let's get them when they're least expecting it.*

Ben wasn't sure *when*, exactly, that would be, but he knew one thing for certain: Reggie was not in a million years going to let anyone lock him up to be used for any sort of experimentation.

Ben had no doubt that when and if he wanted, Reggie could fight off all three of these goons, including Garza. It would be a hell of a fight, but he'd seen his friend come out against longer odds.

This time, too, Ben would be involved. And while Ben wasn't the trained killer Reggie was, he was a capable hand in a brawl and a decent contender in hand-to-hand combat.

And to top it off, he knew he was just as pissed off as Reggie was.

"Take a right, head to the elevators," Garza ordered. "We'll head down to the Subshuttle and take that across. I just got word that your fellow companions are heading here on the shuttle as we speak."

This was news to Ben, and judging by the look on Reggie's face it was news to him as well. *This changes things,* he thought. *Doesn't it?*

He was still thinking, planning, and trying to piece everything together when the elevators dinged. The guard behind him pushed him, hard. He felt himself thrown against the back wall of the elevator, the side that faced the open oceans and the concentric rings down below. He wasn't focused on the beautiful view, though. The glass was cold against his face, and his forehead hurt from the sudden impact with the hard surface.

Reggie had fared no better, and Ben caught a glimpse of his friend's head striking the glass and bouncing backward, then the man falling to the floor.

Ben watched, stunned. The two guards entered the elevator and one turned to mash a button on the panel. The second held his weapon ready, aiming at Ben's gut. An impact from this range may not smash through the glass, but it would certainly smash clear through Ben's body.

Garza did not enter the car with them. He looked down at Reggie, who was laying on the floor of the elevator, his eyes closed. There was blood on his forehead and Ben wasn't sure if the man was passed out or worse.

"You got it from here?" Garza asked.

The soldier holding the gun to Ben's stomach nodded once. He was a young guy, blondish-brown hair, and his face said he couldn't be much older than eighteen, but his build was that of a thirty-year old bodybuilder who'd been working out three times a day for twenty-nine of those years. He could barely nod, the muscles in his neck and shoulders permanently flexed. His bear hands looked as though they could tear the gun into ribbons of aluminum foil, and Ben wasn't certain he couldn't.

He watched Ben as the elevator doors closed. Garza watched until the doors were shut completely, and Ben felt the car shift as it began to descend.

He looked down at Reggie. *Wake up, man. Come on.*

Just then Reggie's eyes shot open and he stared up at Ben. Both the soldiers were focusing elsewhere — the blond linebacker at Ben's face, the other man out the window, taking in the view. Reggie blinked once, caught Ben's eye, then winked.

Then his eyes closed once more.

Got it, Ben thought. *This'll be fun.*

He was no longer mad at his friend. Reggie had duped him, withheld information, but he couldn't fault him for it. He understood why, and he may have done the same thing had he been in Reggie's situation.

They were a team once again, and that was bad news for these guys sharing their elevator ride with them.

"Think you can take me?" Ben asked.

"Huh?" the blond man asked. His clueless grunt didn't do much to change his all brawn, no brains impression.

"I said, do you think you can take me?"

The guy smiled. "Yeah."

"You're Ravenshadow," Ben said. "I've taken a few of you guys before. Turns out you're not all that hard underneath that rock-solid shell."

"Wanna try me?"

Ben made a face as though he was contemplating it. The elevator descended, slowly, the ocean growing as they drew near the surface.

Reggie's legs flipped, twisting sideways. They caught his guard behind the knees and the man went down, hard. Reggie followed through with the motion and crammed his elbow onto the back of the man's neck.

"What the —"

Ben's guard turned and pointed with his gun. Ben lunged forward, leaning back with his upper body and letting it lag behind his legs just a bit. *Winding up.*

He threw his head forward and aimed. His forehead hit, right onto the man's nose. It was a disgusting sound, but the feeling inside Ben's head was worse. It was like he could feel each and every bone in the man's face smashing beneath the impact, the structure of it all crumpling and caving in.

Blood went everywhere, or at least that's what it looked like to Ben, who had it all over his field of vision.

The man groaned as he went down, suddenly far weaker than his body implied. His muscles were useless to him now, and the gun fell out of his hand and bounced around on the floor.

Reggie was already kneeling, holding the other guard's submachine gun and aiming at the man's head.

"Don't," the man said. He rolled onto his back and looked up at Reggie, his hands above his head, palms out. "The Hawk will just kill us. "Don't try to get any information out of us. There's no —"

Reggie fired, two shots in quick succession. The man bounced once, then lay still. "I wasn't going to," he said.

Ben opened and closed his mouth, trying to bring back his hearing. The shots, even from a relatively small round such as that from the subcompact, was deafening in close quarters.

Reggie walked over to the second guard, writhing on the floor and holding his busted face. He fired two shots into him as well, this time aiming at the man's chest. "Thanks for the offer," Reggie said. "But I already know everything I need to know."

CHAPTER 41

THE GUARDS ENTERED the room only a second after Julie pulled herself inside the rolling, human-length cabinet. It was difficult at first to move, but the rollers had been well-maintained and likely had been greased with graphite recently, so once she got a finger hold on one of the structural supports on the ceiling, the cabinet rolled back into place and closed.

The silence and blackness was immediate, and total. It was unnerving, really, going from an open, ambient space with a normal amount of reverberation allowed to work through the room into a closed, tight, space.

She wasn't claustrophobic, but a space like the one she was now in — not to mention what it was typically used for — was constricting enough to make *anyone* feel anxious. She hoped Susan and Dr. Lindgren were faring well next to her.

She slowed her breathing, trying to get a feel for where the guards were in the room. After a few seconds she thought she heard one of them shuffling by, stopping in front of the wall of cabinets, moving on, then stopping again to Julie's right in front of the doors to the Subshuttle.

Julie had quickly opened three of the cabinets along the bottom row and — luckily for Julie — they were empty. She wasn't sure what she would have done if all of the sliding containers had been filled. Not only would they once again be in the line of fire from the Raven-shadow guards, she would have to face the cold, dead bodies inside the cabinets.

Her mind had flashed to a similar moment in Antarctica, when her team had discovered row after row, floor to ceiling, of humans in cabinets. That room hadn't been a morgue, however, and those humans were *not* being stored in anticipation of a mortician's scalpel.

Susan was wary about lying down in the cabinet, but Julie and Sarah had persuaded her that it was the only choice. The Subshuttle had been docked at that entrance, the doors had slid open, and Julie had dashed in and back out of the anteroom after pressing the 'depar-ture' button. She had just enough time to insert herself into her own empty cabinet when the guards made it into the room. Julie had anticipated not being able to get back out, so she'd made sure to leave a small crack open when she'd shut herself in, hoping that the guards wouldn't notice.

She could hear their voices cutting through the silence.

"They're on the shuttle," one of them said.

"Call it in," the other responded.

"We've got confirmation," the first voice said. "They're on the Subshuttle at Sub-1, backside. Should be fifteen minutes before approach to the front. Can we assemble a team there?"

A pause.

"Confirmed, yes. We will make our way around. Out."

Julie let out a breath, waited more, and then heard the sound of their boots clanking along the metal floor of the morgue segment to the opposite entrance. The guard called in his location and asked for the door to be opened, and Julie listened to the sounds of the men leaving the room and the door sliding shut once again.

She let out a larger breath. *Thank God.*

She waited a few more seconds to be sure, then pushed her

cabinet back out on its rollers. It took some maneuvering but she slid up and out of the drawer and back onto the cold, hard floor. She immediately pressed open the next drawer and helped Susan out of her cabinet.

"Did they buy it?" Susan asked.

Julie shrugged as she moved to help Dr. Lindgren. "So far, I guess. They'll figure it out soon, though, so we should probably think up a better plan than 'wait around here.'"

"Agreed," Sarah said as her cabinet slid open. "Any ideas?"

Julie looked at Susan. "You know of any way up or down a level, without using the elevators?"

Susan looked at her like she was crazy. "Yeah, of course."

Sarah and Julie stared at her.

"The stairs, obviously."

CHAPTER 42

REGGIE KNEW The Hawk would know about his mens' deaths soon enough, if he didn't already. He'd seen cameras just about everywhere in this central ring, in every hallway and public room, save for the restrooms and Crawford's office.

While he hadn't seen any in the elevator, he hadn't been able to get a close look, and many times the cameras inside elevators were far more subtle than the typical closed-circuit monstrosities mounted above doors and windows. Somewhere on the control panel, perhaps, or even hidden between the cracks in the decoupage-style ceiling.

It didn't matter. They were outlaws now, on the move. If The Hawk's men weren't already on a shoot-to-kill mandate, they would be now. There would be no scheming, no stopping to plan, no thoughtful posturing.

They were at war.

Crawford and The Hawk were at the top of his list, followed by the rest of the guards and soldiers-for-hire Garza had brought along. Finally, if there was time and it proved necessary, all the scientists who had participated in the research.

Before any of that could happen, however, they had a simpler mission: find Julie and Dr. Lindgren, and get them to safety. Julie at least would force them to let her fight with them, and Reggie knew she would be an asset. But that didn't preclude the fact that they were his teammates, and they could be in danger right now. He needed to find them, then figure out what to do next.

Besides, there would be no arguing with Ben, and he would be focused only on finding Julie.

"They're at the Subshuttle entrance," Ben said, proving him right. "We're going to go down there and find them."

Reggie nodded. "Not arguing with you, pal. But which shuttle? There are more than one, remember?"

"We'll start with Sublevel 1, then," Ben said. "That makes most sense anyway. Post up outside the doors and wait for it to open, then shoot anything that moves unless it's Julie or Sarah."

Reggie smiled. "A *bit* rash, perhaps, but I like it."

They had removed the weapons and extra ammunition from the guards, and Reggie had been slightly disappointed to learn that the Ravenshadow guards around here were packing light. No sidearm, no combat knives, and no vest.

He'd learned about the latter characteristic when he'd shot the second guard, aiming at his chest. The rounds would have knocked him out from that range if he'd been wearing body armor, but instead they punched right through his rib cage, lungs, and probably lodged somewhere near the back of his torso. The coroner around here would have a heyday with the jumbled remains of the guy's guts.

Reggie's only regret was that he'd put the big man down so quickly. These Ravenshadow guys deserved long, slow deaths, no matter how new to The Hawk's crew they were. By the time they'd successfully completed The Gauntlet, interviewed with The Hawk, and participated in a few missions, they knew all about the less-than-reputable type of operations The Hawk threw them into.

There was no excuse for any of them, and that was all the justification Reggie needed.

"Let's at least take a second to make sure there aren't any civilians inside," he said. "Those investors, or whoever they are, are in the hotel somewhere too."

"Fine," Ben said. "But if I see another Ravenshadow ass—"

"I know," Reggie. "Trust me, brother, I know. They're dead. All of them."

The elevator reached its destination, and Reggie and Ben stepped over the dead bodies inside the car and out into the hallway, each man taking a position facing opposite directions.

"Clear," Reggie said.

"Clear," Ben responded.

Reggie walked to the left, aimed down the curving hallway, then stopped in front of a set of doors. "This is the antechamber," he said. "Should be opening when the shuttle's here."

"Perfect," Ben said. "Let's wait down the way a bit. Should we split up?"

Reggie shook his head. "No, we're stronger together. And I don't want us to get separated. You watch my back, though, and I'll keep a bead on the shuttle doors."

"Sounds good," Ben said. He knew Ben wouldn't argue with that command, either. Reggie was a sharpshooter, and even though these lightweight subcompacts were far from the heavy-duty snipers he was used to lugging around, he could probably still shoot the head off a cockroach from across the hallway with it.

Ben kneeled with his back to Reggie's. Reggie took the down-time to get a bearing on their surroundings. This hallway looked exactly like the one directly above, with two elevators emptying out in a wide, curving stretch of hotel lobby. The difference here was the Subshuttle entrance, and Reggie noticed now two sets of stairs, farther apart than the two elevators, but across the hall from them.

There were two unmarked doors, but they were single, hollow-core doors that appeared to be simple closets.

Finally, there were two sets of restrooms — men's and women's — just outside the sets of stairs.

It was unlikely there would be any soldiers bursting out from the restrooms and storage closets, but that still left the curve of the hallway on both sides of their location, the stairs, and the elevator. At least with the elevator they would be alerted to its motion by the dinging arrow as it lit up, announcing its arrival.

Still, a lot to be cognizant of.

"We'd be better off in the stairs," Reggie said.

"Agreed. There's a lot to aim at up here," Ben said.

Reggie gave him a nod, and Ben bolted across the hall and swung the heavy, wide door that led to the stairwell open. He stepped in, aimed down the stairs and over the ledge, then turned and nodded to Reggie.

Reggie ran into the stairs, making sure the door stayed open. It would mark their position if any guards strolled down the hallway, but it would also give them the upper hand if anyone did step out of the Subshuttle.

"You got the stairs?" Reggie asked.

"Affirmative. You got the shuttle?"

"Couldn't miss it if I tried, friend."

"Well do your best to not shoot my fiancée," Ben said.

There was not more time to chat, for as soon as the words left Ben's mouth Reggie saw a light above the Subshuttle antechamber illuminate.

"They're here," he said.

Ben didn't say anything.

"If I start shooting, forget the stairs and help me clear the antechamber."

"You got it."

The doors opened. Slowly. Unlike the elevator doors, which crept open slowly at first then sped up until they'd reached the end of their tracks, the Subshuttle seemed to have been built more like an industrial freight elevator. It was efficient, and slow. Powerful, but not much care had been taken in designing things like ensuring the doors opened quickly enough for guests to not have to wait around.

Reggie felt like one of those guests, waiting around. The doors slid apart in slow motion, the ever-increasing crack of light from inside growing wider with each passing second. But those seconds felt like minutes.

"See them yet?" Ben whispered.

Reggie shook his head. He didn't care if Ben couldn't see it.

The doors widened. He tightened his grip on his weapon. It suddenly felt good in his hands, like it had grown to be a part of him. He was ready.

Julie and Dr. Lindgren weren't on the Subshuttle. If anyone was, they were hiding behind the thin sections of siding behind the open doors that were out of his line-of-sight.

Smart, he thought.

He crouched lower, ready and anxious for the battle. There were guards in there, he could feel it. They were waiting.

He waited.

He could wait all day.

"Cover the stairs," he whispered to Ben. "But get ready."

"You got it."

Reggie squeezed the trigger, instinctively knowing just how far to pull it in so that his shots could be unanticipated by his conscious mind. He was steady, breathing with his weapon, fully aware of everything in his field of vision and peripherals, and subconsciously feeling the area directly behind him as well. The hair on the back of his neck would warn him of any approaching danger, as it had so many times in the past.

He was in his element, and the Ravenshadow men weren't going to stand a chance.

He continued to wait, but no one came out of the Subshuttle's anteroom. He could see the machine inside, the gondola that slid on its cable beneath the water, but it was empty.

Were they lying down? Reggie thought. It would have been an effective hiding spot, but it would make them vulnerable as well.

He double- and triple-checked the spots across the hallway in the anteroom he would consider hiding, trusting his instincts that they were, in fact, empty.

That left the floor of the craft, and possibly the very rear end of the shuttle behind a chair on its starboard side. Those were the only two blind spots, therefore those were the only two places anyone could hide.

Time to move out, he thought. "Ben, cover the hallway, I'm going across to check it out."

"Yep."

Ben followed him out, and they executed a clean sweep in both directions before Reggie sprinted across the hall and slid to a stop, feet-first, directly in front of the shuttle.

And he discovered that it was very much empty.

"Clear," he said. His voice was calm, but hesitant. *How could that be?* The women must have faked it, not even getting on the shuttle at all.

"No one?" he heard Ben's voice ask.

"Nope. All clear."

Reggie walked through the open antechamber doors and onto the Subshuttle. He didn't need to check under every chair — the thing was small enough that he knew it was empty.

Ben stepped in beside him, watching the hallway but glancing over his shoulder. "You sure? Nowhere else to hide in here?"

"Nothing, man. I'm positive."

"But The Hawk said his men called it in. They saw Julie and Sarah get on, right?"

"He said they *believed* they got on. Or it could have been a ruse, to —"

Shit.

"Ben, gun's up. Get ready."

"For what" Ben asked.

He didn't need an answer. A trio of bullets pinged into the sidewall of the antechamber.

"Down! Now!" Reggie yelled.

CHAPTER 43

BEN HIT THE FLOOR, and Reggie stepped over him, straddling the man's prone body. Ben was a solid shot, and he'd be even more effective lying on the floor with some ability to support his arm. Reggie was ruthless in any position, so together they — hopefully — would form a deadly pair.

The first two guards came into view on Reggie's left. He forced himself to turn to the right, and he was glad he did.

Ben shot at the men on the left, and Reggie shot at two more guards advancing from the opposite direction. He knew Ben would take the bait, so he had made sure to detect any threats coming from the other side.

Their weapons fired at the same time. Two men went down, one on each side. Their partners stepped backwards, possibly not having anticipated anyone firing back. Reggie took the opportunity to down his second man, then he turned to see how Ben was faring.

Ben missed, and Reggie tried to follow up with a kill shot to the man's head, but it missed. The man ducked out of the way behind the curve in the wall, and Reggie checked to see if he needed to reload.

"Reggie, we got company." Ben said. His voice was low, tense.

"Let's take them out. We're better protected in here, anyway."

"No, not what I meant. Look."

Reggie looked up, watching the area where Ben was staring. "You've got to be kidding," he said.

Julie and Sarah were in the stairwell, the same one they'd previously been posted at, watching the hallway. Julie waved, but Reggie held up a hand.

"Not the best time to come up here, ladies," he shouted.

"Figured that," Julie said. "But I'd feel much better being in the same room as you two once again."

Reggie nodded, then looked down at Ben. "And probably not just because we've got the guns, huh."

"Bad time for jokes, bud," Ben said. He was still aiming at the bend in the hallway where the guard was waiting.

"We'll cover you, but you need to run. *Fast.*"

"Got it," Julie said. "Try not to get shot?"

"Exactly. Ben, lay covering fire that direction on the count of three. Nothing crazy, we don't have all the ammo we'd like to have. Just make sure no one gets off a pop at our girls."

"Understood."

He aimed the other direction, then counted it down. He spoke the words clearly and loud enough that they could hear him across the hall, but he didn't yell. No sense broadcasting their next move to the bad guys, he figured.

"One... two... *three!*"

Ben opened fire. Julie and Sarah shot out of the stairwell — followed by a third woman. Reggie watched the hallway to his right, but didn't shoot. He didn't want to waste ammo.

Julie made it across and jumped over Ben, landing in the center of the Subshuttle. Reggie leaned out of the way for her to pass, just as Sarah leaped from the hallway.

She's going to land right on top of —

She made it to the space right behind Ben and took a deep breath.

"That was one hell of a long jump, Doc," he said.

"Track star. All through college." She smiled and winked at him.

The last woman was slower, and Reggie watched the hallway in both directions. She didn't try to jump for it, but she hustled toward the end, feeling the pressure and seeing the guns. She made it to the shuttle just as Reggie hit the button to shut the doors.

And just as three more guards, jogging in front of Vicente Garza, came into view. They started firing, and Reggie pulled the third woman out of the way.

"Get back, Ben. We're hot, to the right."

Ben nodded and slid backwards, but he didn't move from his spot lying prone on the floor of the shuttle.

The rounds pinged off the metal doors to the anteroom, and a few lodged between the shuttle itself and the anteroom's walls.

Now would be a great time for these doors to start moving faster, he thought.

Unfortunately the doors were every bit as slow closing as they been opening.

"They're not going to close in time," Ben said.

"Slide back a little more, Ben," Reggie said. "Let's hope this shuttle's bulletproof."

He hit the next button on the panel — there were only three — and the door to the Subshuttle started closing. It was only marginally faster than the antechamber's doors, but the space it had to travel was far smaller.

The doors closed, and a few rounds ricocheted off the glass and door panel. None were direct hits, but none even made a dent. *Let's hope they don't start shooting at the same spot from up close,* Reggie thought.

The antechamber doors closed, but not before The Hawk

stepped into view. Reggie watched him from inside the Subshuttle, his gaze on the man's eyes.

The Hawk smiled, the same cold, ruthless grin he'd seen so many times before. It said both 'that was a mistake,' and 'I'll see you again.'

He wasn't sure about the first sentiment, but he was *absolutely* positive about the second.

Reggie turned and faced the three women, huddled together in the center of their new home for the foreseeable future.

"We're going to be sitting ducks in here," Julie said.

"Better than being sitting ducks out there," Reggie answered.

Ben shrugged, joining them. "Maybe. I'd have rather fought for it."

Reggie walked over to the wall panel and pressed the third button. It did exactly what he expected. The first button was to manually close the antechamber doors. The second was to close the Subshuttle's.

The third was simple: GO.

Water began rushing in around the shuttle's glass walls, and he felt the vehicle listing slightly as it raised up with the water level before its ballasts kicked in. It didn't take longer than a minute to fill the tank, and then the opposite doors on the other side of the antechamber opened and dumped the Subshuttle out into open waters.

Then, with a quick lurch, the shuttle started inching along its cable.

They were moving, but Reggie felt little relief.

This thing only goes one direction, he thought. *And they'll be waiting for us there.*

CHAPTER 44

BEN LEANED down and kissed Julie, hugging her. *Too bad we can't just stay here forever,* he thought.

"I take it you two know each other," Sarah joked.

"A bit," Julie said. "But *you* two don't." She pulled on the third woman's shoulder. "Ben, Reggie, this is Susan. Dr. Susan Richards. She's a researcher at the lab."

Reggie strode forward, ignoring the woman's outstretched hand. "Then I guess you have some explaining to do. You're a criminal, you know that?"

The woman retreated, head down.

"No, Reggie," Julie said. "It's okay. She's with us. She was working on some stuff she's not proud of, but she wants out."

Reggie glared at her, but he didn't try anything. Ben waited, knowing the exchange wasn't over.

"What kind of stuff were you working on?" Reggie asked. "Did you know they were growing limbs? *After* they chopped them off live people?"

She shook her head, still sheepish. "No — yes. No, I mean I didnt' know they were trying to grow them back, but I had heard stories of what they were doing in the deeper labs."

"So you were okay with it?"

"Of course not," Susan said. "But I couldn't do anything. They wouldn't let us out; they still won't."

"Crawford?"

"Crawford, the board, all the higher-ups here. They're keeping a lid on all of it, and those of us who ask too many questions get removed."

"Removed?"

"Shown the door, I guess," she said. "But not in a *nice* way, probably."

"Probably not," Julie said. "Ben, Reggie. They *captured* people against their will. They're still down in the sublevel labs."

"We know," Ben said. "And Crawford's been pulling the strings."

"We know."

"So anything we *don't* know?" Reggie asked, looking around the small room. The Subshuttle had started working its way along the cable, and they were well away from any structure by now. The water was thick and dark around them, and very little light made it to them from the surface.

"A lot," Julie said. "Like the giant tank of saltwater crocodiles?"

"Saltwater *crocodiles*?" Ben said. "You've got to be — that's a thing?"

Reggie and the three women nodded.

"I have a theory about that," Dr. Lindgren said. "I think it has something to do with the genetic material in the crocs. Something dormant in their genetics that's been there since they first evolved. For whatever reason, they essentially *stopped* evolving some-odd millions of years ago."

Susan nodded. "She's right. I'm not sure exactly what they're using them for here, but my own research is in genetics. I'm focusing on trying to isolate the genes and chemical structures in the jellyfish."

"The *Turritopsis dohrnii*?" Sarah asked.

Susan seemed shocked. "Yes — how'd you know?"

"We saw a tank full of your little pets back in the lab area," Julie said. "The '*Immortal Jellyfish*,' right?"

"Yes," Susan said. "But it's not an accurate name. The specimens themselves don't live forever. But they do have a weird characteristic that lets them 'hop' from one life stage to another. Like an egg becoming a tadpole, then becoming a frog."

"Only the frog could choose to become a tadpole once again?"

Susan shook her head. "No, it would essentially be *forced* to for predatory or environmental reasons, and it wouldn't become a tadpole — it would just break up into a bunch of little eggs, and the process would start all over. But there would be more tadpoles the next time, you see..." she let her voice drift off.

"Right, so this little jellyfish can become — an egg?"

"A polyp," Susan said. "Or rather, a bunch of polyps. The life-cycle would start all over again, and technically speaking it would be made up of the same stuff the jellyfish was made up of, so..."

"Immortality," Reggie said. "Creepy."

"Definitely weird," Julie said. "And you're trying to figure out how to make that work in humans?"

"What, like we'd just turn into fetuses again?" Reggie asked. "That's gross."

"No, nothing like that," Susan said. "It's far more... complicated. With humans, we're not as simple as a jellyfish, and even with the *dormi* it's a complicated task. Isolating genes is tricky business, because life works in mysterious ways. One thing affects another, so you can't just remove one of the things and expect it to function properly."

"Right," Dr. Lindgren said. "So you're trying to figure out how to recharge human cells into their previous state — making new stem cells?"

Susan looked at Sarah, smiling. "Close, but no. Stem cells are a completely different field of research, and aside from the political and social fallout of admitting to studying it, we're pretty close already to cracking the code.

"But what we're trying to do here isn't *changing* the human genome at all."

"It's not?" Julie asked. "If you're playing with stem cells, and other stuff in the human body, then —"

"We're not. We're trying to activate what's already there."

BEN WAS LISTENING to the conversation, but his focus was out the window. He didn't like being in the water — swimming wasn't really his thing. He could do it, of course, but he felt it was like running. The only time it should be truly necessary to run was when being chased, and the only reason it should be necessary to swim was when one found themselves in the water without knowing how they got there.

In short, he didn't like this Subshuttle thing. He hadn't paid it much thought before, but he felt the ominous pressing of the sea, mere feet from him, trying to get in and —

He shook his head. There was no point in thinking about it. He could compartmentalize his fear of 'death by drowning' into its special place in his mind for a while, until they figured out what to do to get out of this mess.

And that was a *far* better topic to be thinking about, mostly because he had *no idea* how to solve that problem.

The women and Reggie were still discussing the research, trying to piece everything together, but Ben couldn't help but stare out the window. And *everything* was a window. They were standing in a window, a bubble of glass that trudged along underwater like a slow, stupid tugboat.

He wondered why it had to be *under*water. *Why not just have a ferry?* he thought.

But he knew the answer: this was an *experience*. Besides an easy way for people across the park's three rings, it would be something that added perceived value to Crawford's offerings here. Like the monorail at Disneyland, this little 'ride' would attract all sorts of people who had always wanted to be in a submarine.

This would be the closest they would ever get, but it would be enough. Crawford was sitting on a gold mine *without* the research that lived and breathed in the laboratories beneath the second ring.

"...the jellyfish is like a salamander?" he heard Julie ask. He turned around and saw the four of them sitting, each of them appearing comfortable, as if there *wasn't* an entire ocean sitting right outside the bubble, trying to get them.

"Sort of, but instead of recreating itself into a completely different life stage, the salamander has a unique ability to regrow arms and legs."

"Like some lizards' tails," Reggie said. "We used to pick them up by their tails when we were kids, shake them around, see which ones fell off first. It was a game. I was pretty —"

He looked around. Ben smiled. *Wrong crowd for that story,* he thought.

"In a way, yes," Susan said. "But the salamander does it in a different way. It's really quite fascinating."

"It is," Julie said. "So you're building a medication that will give humans that ability?"

Susan shook her head. "We don't need to. As I said before, we're activating what already exists in our DNA. The salamander has mastered this through its evolution — it's called a *blastema*, and it's sort of like a ripe stump — a mass of cells — that can regrow complex multi-tissue components. Crawford believes humans already have this ability, it's just been repressed into our evolutionary history."

"Wait, humans *already* have the ability to regrow limbs?"

"They do, but for whatever reason that ability was stifled and shut off by our own evolution at some point along the way. It's there, coded right in our strands, but it doesn't *work*."

"So you're working on how to activate that," Sarah said. "Absolutely fascinating."

"Yeah, if you don't mind the methodology for testing around here," Reggie said.

Susan hung her head. "I told you, I've been involved only for a short time, and most of that was working on just the chemical compounds. I never knew until recently what it was all for, and that we were actually *using* it on people."

Julie swiveled around in her seat to face Susan. "Is that what you were doing when we found you? With that other doctor?"

She shook her head. "That woman was already dead, if you remember. We were trying to see what effect the serum would have on her, if any. It's supposed to do two things: allow for the creation of a blastema, allowing the stem cells to do their work to regrow the limb, and it acts as sort of an anesthetic, preventing the subject from feeling."

"*Feeling?* You're taking away their ability to *feel*?"

Susan shook her head. "It's not a bad thing — it's the only way we've found for the medication to do its *other* job. The brain must not be allowed to think something is wrong, that some foreign chemical compound has been introduced, or it will shut down the processes."

"So the people in the cages," Julie said. "You were regrowing their limbs, but you were *also* taking away what made them human."

"No, I wasn't involved in that. Not directly, at least. I didn't know they were *using* it on live test subjects, like I said. It was all — it still is — theoretical."

"Well *something's* going on in that lab," Reggie said. "And those people don't deserve that."

Dr. Lindgren put her hand on Susan's shoulder. "Does it work? The medication?"

Susan nodded. "From what I have seen, yes. Sometimes we can restart some basic growth in dead species of frogs, fish, some mammals, even long after they've passed."

"You're building zombies," Ben said. "Great."

Susan smiled. "Not at all. No one is coming back from the dead, not by a long shot. But we might be able to get a finger to twitch for a minute, unrelated to any brain and nervous system activity. Or we've seen hair start to grow again, at least until the cells die from lack of supplementation."

Reggie shook his head. "The end doesn't justify the means."

"No," Susan said. "Of course not. That's why I'm here with you. I want out. I started working for Dr. Lin, and that gave me access to the deeper labs. The ones in the back."

"The ones where they're keeping the bodies," Julie said.

"Yeah," Susan replied. "Those. The first time I saw those tanks, I was absolutely horrified. I didn't — I still don't — believe what they're doing here."

"What *you're* doing here," Reggie said.

"Enough, Reggie," Ben said. "She's out, she said so. You want to kill her? Do it."

Reggie fumed, but he didn't get up.

"That's what I thought. Give the lady a break. She's obviously been through — and lived in — hell. Best we can do is get her off this island and back into the real world."

"Yeah," Julie said. "About that. We're not going to get off this shuttle by just walking off on the other side. The Hawk's going to have his entire team waiting for us, and I'm sure they're not going to let us explain ourselves."

"We already tried the 'explaining ourselves' bit," Reggie said. "It went about as well as you might think."

"Is there any way to manually drive this thing?" Julie asked. "Maybe we can start going back to the other side, where we came from. Might be able to get there faster, before The Hawk can assemble his crew on that side."

"No," Susan said. "It's manually controlled from somewhere in the central ring, or by the control panel outside each entrance, like an elevator. Keeps things running smoothly."

"Yeah," Reggie said," except in an elevator there's at least an emergency shut off button."

"No," Julie said, shaking her head. "A lot of times those are just there to put peoples' minds at ease. They don't do anything except alert the control desk that there's a potential problem, and *they* can control the elevator's movement."

"Great," Reggie said. "So we're screwed. We're floating right toward Crawford and Garza, nice and slow, giving them enough time to get ready to pepper us with holes."

Ben felt the Subshuttle lurch, and he involuntarily grabbed the chair in front of him. He caught his balance again, but noticed something after.

We're no longer moving.

"Well, speaking of having no control," Reggie said. "Seems like we've been shut down."

"Wonderful," Julie said. "Just great. *Now* what the hell are we going to do?"

Ben thought for a moment. He knew there was only a small amount of oxygen left inside this machine, but it should last a decent amount of time since there were only five of them inside. The problem was that he had no idea how much time a 'decent amount' was, and if it would be enough oxygen to keep them alive until The Hawk decided to start their shuttle moving again.

Or if they'll start moving it at all, he thought. It wouldn't have been a bad strategy to just let them sit there, slowly asphyxiating, choking on their own expelled breath. It would save resources, and his crew could essentially go back to what it was doing without even giving the people inside the Subshuttle a second thought.

We suffocate or we get shot, he realized. Those were the two options that made most sense to him, were he in The Hawk's position.

Neither sounded very fun.

Ben looked around, sighing. He had an idea, and he knew none of them would like it.

Worst of all, he liked it the least.

CHAPTER 46

JULIE HAD KNOWN Ben for nearing two years by now, and she knew him well. He was a capable man, able to do things that 'normal' people couldn't, just due to the man's sheer willpower and resiliency. In every other way, however, Julie would have defined the word 'normal' by holding up a picture of Ben. He was no superhero.

And he wasn't a leader.

Not that he wasn't *capable* of being one, but Julie had only seen Ben step up and take charge a few times. He was more than happy to play shotgun to someone else's leadership role. It had been Joshua Jefferson at first, when the CSO had been officially formed, but throughout their relationship he had allowed Julie herself to take charge numerous times. When Reggie had walked into their lives, guns blazing, Ben quickly stepped aside to allow Reggie to take point when it counted.

But this was a different situation, and Julie was somewhat surprised to see Ben taking charge. Something came over him there, standing in the Subshuttle in front of the rest of the team. He had a certain decidedness to him, a drive. It was in the way he was standing, his nostrils flared, his jaw set, and his hands confidently resting on the seat back he stood in front of. He looked like he knew exactly what he was about to do, that he had mapped it all out, planned for every contingency, and was about to act on it.

She had no idea what that plan was, but she was interested to find out. She'd never seen him like this before. It was impressive.

She hoped it would pay off.

Ben looked around the Subshuttle, his eyes searching. He took a few steps down the center of the shuttle's fuselage, toward the back, everyone stepping out of his way.

"What do you have on your mind, big guy?" Reggie asked.

Ben ignored the question, deep in thought.

"Anything we can help with?" Julie asked.

Still, nothing.

Ben reached up and pressed hard against a curved panel of plastic near the floor. It separated from the wall, revealing an open space behind it. A drawer, similar to the cabinets Julie had found in the morgue. A simple door that slid back and clicked into place, no handles or knobs necessary.

Ben must have spotted the hairline cracks around the cupboard.

"There's an oxygen circulation system in here," he said. "On the floor, but it pushes the air out and up, see?" He pointed at one of the tiny vents between one the chairs and the wall of the shuttle. "There would have to be, assuming these things were ever full of people. No way to keep all that breath from turning into carbon dioxide without scrubbing it or at least expelling it out into the water, then replacing it with the good stuff."

"What are you getting at?" Reggie asked. "You want to try to use the oxygen tanks as a weapon?"

Ben shook his head, walking across the back of the shuttle to the opposite side, feeling around for another hidden cupboard. "No, I just wanted to make sure. There's also a small LED panel on it — the tanks are about eighty percent full. I'd guess the antechambers refill them whenever the shuttles are docked. Not sure how long eighty percent will last us, but I'd guess it's not much."

Julie frowned. "What — what are you planning, Ben?"

Still, he didn't respond. Finding what he was looking for, he reached down and pushed against the panel, opening yet another plastic cupboard. The door, like the previous one, conformed to the shape of the wall around it, curving upward and to the right, to match the bubble-like interior of the craft. The top edge of the drawer ended at the glass wall that extended upward until it rounded up and over the ceiling.

Ben reached around inside and finally found something. He pulled it out. "This'll have to do," he said, talking mostly to himself.

Julie, Reggie, Sarah, and Susan all watched, interested in Ben's sudden fixation on the small object. It was a miniature metal broom, short and stubby, with a set of bristles in the shape of a triangle. The type of hand broom used to sweep up small messes, the type Julie might have expected to find in a boat or a car.

Or a shuttle, I guess, she thought.

Ben examined the broom. Whether it was what he was looking for or he was about to MacGyver something was unclear.

Until he twisted off the rubber cap at the end of the broom's handle and held up the open end of the hollow tube to his eye. "This will work," he muttered.

He dropped the broom, then jumped on the handle, landing on the very end of it with his heel. He repeated the procedure, then a third time, and finally picked up the broom and held it up again.

It was now a tube with a squashed end. He appeared to be satisfied, as Ben then carried the broom over the nearest chair and knelt down. "These chairs are bolted to the floor on two legs," he said. "I think we can get the bolts off with this makeshift wrench." Julie wasn't sure why it mattered, but she watched anyway. The chairs indeed only had two legs — the back legs — and they were bolted on heavy-duty steel to the fuselage floor of the Subshuttle.

Julie watched, intrigued but still very confused, as Ben worked at the first of the two bolts holding one of the two legs of the chair to the Subshuttle's fuselage. He tried a few times to fit the smashed head of the broom over the bolt, then began to twist. He grunted with the effort, but Julie watched as the triangular set of bristles rotated ever so slightly. *It's working.*

He continued twisting, and the head of the bolt loosened enough so that he could work it completely loose with his hand. He moved on to the next bolt, finding this one a bit easier. Within another minute he had the leg of the chair completely separated from the floor.

He slid over to the next leg. "Let me help with that," Reggie said. "I don't know what the hell you're planning, but I don't care. If you're this focused on something, it's going to be good."

Ben nodded, handing Reggie the broom-turned-wrench. Reggie worked at the bolt, finding this one to be a bit trickier as the leg of the chair was set up against the side of the Subshuttle and getting the broom to fit over the bolt was difficult.

After five minutes, the second leg was free. The Subshuttle still hadn't started moving, and Julie was beginning to worry. *They're going to let us suffocate down here,* she realized. It wasn't a bad plan at all — simply turn off the Subshuttle and wait until it ran out of oxygen inside. They'd all be killed without The Hawk's team ever having to fire a bullet.

Ben and Reggie stood up, and Reggie walked over to the open panel that contained the oxygen display. "72%," he said. "It's moving down quicker than I thought it would."

"The ballast system might be tapped in as well," Ben said. "It can use oxygen to help with the buoyancy so there's not as much weight on the cable."

"Whatever the case, we need to get this thing moving again. We can take our chances with Ravenshadow once we're —"

"No," Ben said. "We're not going to win that one."

"Then what's the plan, Ben? You have a better idea?" Reggie asked.

Ben shook his head. "Not a better idea, necessarily," he said. "But it might work. And it doesn't involve a shootout with two guns against thirty."

"I'm all ears," Reggie said. Julie nodded.

"No time to explain," Ben said. "We're already depleting too much oxygen. And we're going to need it."

Julie stepped forward and watched as Ben lifted the chair up from the cam bolts that had previously held it into place. The bolts dangled through the holes. Ben hefted the chair, feeling its weight and solidity, then nodded. "I think this will work," he said. He looked over at the glass wall, where two sections of the glass had been glued together. There was a line of clear silicon caulking covering the glue, stretching from the top of the ceiling to the place where the wall of the Subshuttle met the plastic near the floor.

Suddenly Ben tipped the chair sideways. The bolts had been in the square-shaped foot of the chair leg in a section of metal perpendicular to the leg itself. The small lip fit into the small crack between the two panes of glass.

"Ben, what —"

He struggled with the weight of the chair for a moment, then he set it down on the chair in front of it. The chair Ben and Reggie had removed was now sideways, the foot of one of its two legs jammed inside the gap between the two panes of glass, the rest of the chair balanced on top of the chair in front of it.

Julie stared at it for a moment. And then she realized what was about to happen.

CHAPTER 47

"BEN, NO!" she shouted.

Ben ran forward, swinging his heavy leg up and toward the sideways chair. He landed the kick on the side of the chair, on the square metal frame that surrounded the seat cushion. The leg and glass made a cracking sound and the chair slid a bit forward.

"What the hell are you doing, Ben?" Reggie asked.

Ben kicked again. This time there was a much louder crack, and water began spraying into the Subshuttle.

"Stop, Ben! You're going to break the glass."

"Exactly," he said. He kicked one more time, and this time one pane of glass completely cracked and fell away. Water slammed inward, and Ben was hit and thrown sideways.

Susan and Julie screamed, and Reggie jumped forward to pull Ben backwards. The pressure wasn't great enough to hurt him, but the amount of water plowing into the interior of the shuttle was frightening. Julie watched, knowing that it would be less than a minute before the entire shuttle was full.

She heard a groaning sound and felt the shuttle list to the side, then buck down a few feet.

"We're sinking, Ben!" she yelled. The torrent of water was deafening, and already her legs were soaked to her knees. Ben and Reggie were completely wet from head to toe, and Sarah and Susan had jumped up and onto chairs to try in vain to escape the rising water level.

"That's the plan!" Ben shouted back. "I thought the ballast would kick in, pushing us up. By flooding the inside, we might be able to override the control and force it to lift us up to the surface."

"That's the stupidest thing I've ever heard!" Dr. Lindgren shouted. "You've got to be kidding me! We're all going to drown down here now."

Ben looked directly at Julie. His eyes were wide, pleading. He needed her to agree. He needed to know the plan wasn't completely insane.

But she couldn't. She *didn't* agree. He had acted rash, popping a hole in the only thing keeping them alive, and now there was water spilling in, already up to her waist.

Worst of all, the Subshuttle was sinking. As the water poured in, the weight of the craft couldn't compete with the cable. She wasn't sure how deep it was in this part of the ocean, and she *really* didn't want to find out. There was only so much give on the line, and she knew they were going to hit it.

Unless the ballast system kicked in and Ben's plan worked.

And if it didn't...

"Ben, I hope you have a backup plan," Reggie yelled. He was treading water on the other side of the shuttle.

Ben nodded, but there was fear in his eyes. "I do," he said. "But it's worse than this one."

Julie felt the water hit her bellybutton, and the sudden shock of everything hit her at once. The water was warm, as they were in the Caribbean, but to her it felt ice cold. She started shaking. She couldn't get to Ben if she tried, as the gaping hole in the Subshuttle's glass prevented them from moving from one side of the vessel to the other.

She was going to die down here, they all were.

And she was going to die alone.

She looked around the flooded Subshuttle, wondering how she'd ended up here. It was surreal, everything happening in slow motion. Susan was standing on a chair, but the water was higher than her knees anyway. Dr. Lindgren, a taller woman than Susan, was also standing on a chair, her head nearly touching the ceiling. She was watching the water rise, calculating their odds. Julie could see it on her face, the calm assurance that they were out of options.

She wanted to scream. She wanted to reach across the center of the shuttle and punch Ben. She wanted —

She saw a flash of darkness out of the corner of her eye. A whipping motion, a swift kick as it passed through the water right above her head, just outside the glass. Then it was gone.

Oh, God no.

She hadn't even considered where in the park they might be at the moment.

Another wraith appeared, then disappeared. Like an apparition, it was only visible when she wasn't focusing on it. She spun around in a circle, the cold water growing even colder as it lapped against her chest. A few stray drips lanced upward and splashed onto her throat. Her throat constricted, her breathing grew heavier.

Again, she spun. Sarah was looking at her now, her head turned, trying to determine what it was that had Julie so terrified.

Then she knew, and Sarah's face melted into an expression of pure fear.

Julie nodded.

And another slender, black shape flew by.

CHAPTER 48

BEN LOOKED across the pool of water and saw Julie's face. It was masked in a glow from the floor lights that surrounded the interior of the vessel, and the light was eery and dispersed in the five feet of water. He watched her, trying to see if she would look his way.

She didn't.

He turned to Reggie. "Any minute the ballast should kick in," he shouted. The sound of the water rushing in had been lessened now that the hole in the glass was below the waterline. But the ocean couldn't fill the Subshuttle fast enough, and the water was rising an inch every few seconds.

We're out of time, he realized.

The shuttle lurched, pulling downward on its cable.

Shit.

He had calculated poorly. His plan had been based on knowing that the shuttle was automated, that the ballast tanks would fill and empty based on the weight of the vehicle, so as not to disturb the cable line and put too much downward pressure on it as the submersible slid through the water.

He had hoped that since the lights in the craft were still working that the Subshuttle itself was still in working order, that the ballast tanks would do their job. He'd hoped — counted on — the reason they had stopped dead in the water was that The Hawk or Crawford had ordered it.

He had *not* counted on the ballast system completely ignoring their rapidly sinking vessel.

The shuttle groaned, the water reached Ben's chin, and Reggie pulled Ben around, a uselessly slow movement in the thick seawater.

"It's too late, Ben," he said. His voice was calm, but Ben read the fear in the man's eyes. Reggie was a fighter, but he wasn't rash. He wasn't insane, either. Fear was a part of him as it was every other man. If Ben was terrified, he knew Reggie was at least frightened.

Ben nodded. He didn't want to admit defeat. He looked around at the two women standing hopelessly on their chairs, their hands up and pressing against the glass roof. He saw Julie, still not making eye contact with him, as if she were watching something outside the shuttle.

"I'm sorry," he said.

Reggie shook his head. "Enough of that crap, brother," Reggie yelled. "You had a plan. A halfway decent one, too. I'd have done the same thing if I'd thought about it."

Ben nodded again.

"But you said you had a backup, right? Something else we could try?"

A small wave caught Ben's arm as he slid it through the water and a bit of saltwater splashed up and into his mouth. He spat, then caught his balance once again as the shuttle fell backwards, now sinking stern-first into the depths. The cable, somehow, was still attached, so he knew they would only be able to sink as deep as the cable's slack allowed.

"I did, but I don't — we can't. Reggie, it's too late."

"I didn't trust you earlier," Reggie said, talking into his ear so Ben could hear him clearly.

Ben frowned. *What is he talking about?* "You're bringing this up now?"

"Yeah, man. I owe it to you. You need to hear it."

"Hear what?"

A pop sounded from somewhere below the waterline, and Ben felt the pressure change around his legs. Another pane of glass had blown somewhere, and the craft was going to be filling even faster. He worked his way up and onto the back of a chair, crouching down so his head wouldn't hit the ceiling. Reggie followed suit, but Ben knew it was only a matter of seconds before the entire shuttle was filled.

Another pop, another groan. This time the shuttle fell three or four feet straight down, sinking faster than Ben thought possible. A louder creak sounded from somewhere above him, outside the shuttle.

The shuttle strained on its cable, its lifeline.

Their lifeline.

It sank, pulling the cable with it.

Wherever the cable was anchored on opposite sides of the long expanse, Ben hoped it would hold.

"You're in charge now."

Ben looked at his friend. Completely soaked, his head the only thing above the water.

"You're the leader, Ben. You always have been, really. You're the guy holding this thing together. Joshua was a de facto leader, but you're the guy we were always following."

Ben shook his head. "We don't have time for this right now, Reggie. We need to —"

"Save it. One more second," Reggie yelled. "I'd follow you to hell and back, brother, and I just wanted you to know that."

"Thanks. Means a lot to me," Ben said. "I'll keep that in mind as we die on the floor of the ocean."

"Knock it off," Reggie said. "I'm serious."

"So am I, Reggie. We need to get out of here!"

"What was your plan?"

The women were listening in as well now, all eyes on Ben.

"It — it wasn't much," he said. "I just thought we'd wait for the thing to fill up, then swim for it."

Reggie's eyes bulged. "That — that was your plan?"

Ben shook his head, with what little of his head was left out of the water. "No, that was the *backup* plan, remember?"

Susan shouted over the sound of the hissing water and groaning shuttle. "It's our *only* plan now. Who wants to go first?"

Julie finally looked at Ben. He wouldn't be able to hear her from across the craft, but she wasn't trying to talk.

She simply shook her head.

No.

He frowned. "Why?" he shouted.

She apparently read his lips. *No.*

He had nothing to go off of, no information to help him understand what she was trying to say.

Too late.

"We have to try," he yelled, to whoever could still hear him. He moved to the left, toward the center of the Subshuttle, stretching his left foot across the aisle underwater so he was straddling the backs of two of the chairs. There was about eight inches of air left at the top of the shuttle, where the bubbled part of the panes of rounded glass met on the ceiling. The others followed his lead and soon the five of them were all stretched across the aisle, one leg on each side standing on the backs of the chairs.

"Susan," Reggie shouted. "You're first."

She nodded, a terrified look in her eyes but her chin held high. Whether it was because that was the only way she could keep her mouth above water or it if it was her confidence, Ben didn't know. He didn't care. He reached out a hand, waiting for her to grab it.

He pulled her close. "The hole is down to my right," he yelled.

"You're going to have to take a huge breath and swim down first, but Reggie and I will help you out."

She nodded, her eyes nearly popping out of her head.

"Once you're out, the air in your lungs should help you up. Use your legs more than your arms, so you don't burn through your oxygen too quickly. Just use your arms to guide you so you don't run into anything."

Ben looked up and out the glass ceiling. He could see the rays of light piercing the blue water above them. "We're only about ten feet from the surface." It was a guess, and he hoped it was right.

He hoped it was at least close.

He couldn't afford to continue being wrong.

"You ready?" he asked.

She looked at him. There was water on her face, and her eyes were glistening. She was either in tears or the water had splashed her face. "I — I have to be."

"Damn right you do," Reggie yelled.

She took a huge breath.

"Sniff when you're done," Ben said. "You'll get a little more air."

She nodded, sniffed, then immediately fell beneath the surface of the water. Reggie and Ben had her arms and half-guided, half-pushed her down and toward the hole. They couldn't afford to waste time, but Ben didn't want to hurt her, either.

They found the hole just as the shuttle filled up completely. He hoped the others had heard his instructions, but he knew they would at least have taken a huge, deep breath just before the water hit the ceiling.

Hopefully not their last.

CHAPTER 49

SUSAN'S BODY was nearly through the hole. Ben and Reggie gave her a final push, and she popped through the hole and immediately began her ascent to the surface.

Julie was there next. They hadn't discussed a particular order, and Ben didn't care. He would have wished his fiancee go first, but he knew Julie would have forced Susan through the hole first anyway. He took a bit of satisfaction knowing that Julie had a strong chance at survival going second in line.

They were only ten or twelve feet underwater, he was sure of it now. They would all be able to get out of the shuttle and safely to the surface, where they could swim to shore. Assuming The Hawk's men were still waiting outside the doors on the opposite antechamber entrances around the ring, that meant Ben's team and Susan would be able to swim safely to the shore, get out of the water, and have a fighting chance at saving themselves.

They were still unarmed, as Ben and Reggie had discarded their weapons on the floor of the shuttle and focused instead on helping the women out first. He wasn't sure if they would still work after being submerged. Reggie would know, but it may not even be worth the risk trying to find them and get them up out of the water. He certainly wouldn't want to rely on the weapons firing properly, so they would need another option.

They were somewhere between the hotel and the second ring, Ben thought, possibly closer to the second ring. There was no artificial beach there like on the outer ring and he hadn't paid enough attention to what the inside and outside perimeters of the second ring looked like, so he only hoped there was an easy way up and out of the water there.

It didn't matter now. They had no more options. There was nothing to do but swim for it, holding as much of their breaths inside as their lungs would allow. He could only focus on the present, on the task at hand. He had no plan except to get out of the shuttle, after the rest of his team was safely out and swimming upward to the surface.

Julie's face came up to face his. He looked at her underwater. Her hair floated around her head, small bubbles caught between the strands. The light hit her from behind, darkening her face. Her eyes, however, were lit from somewhere deeper, possibly the lights around the floorboards inside the shuttle. They sparkled with a fiery intensity, the light browns exploded into a million smaller greens, blues, and oranges. He knew those eyes better than his own. He could read them even when they weren't open.

And right now he was reading volumes. She was trying to tell him something. She didn't need to shake her head, but she did anyway. *No.*

There it was again. *What the hell is she trying to tell me?* he wondered. *Why doesn't she want us to leave the shuttle?*

This was their only option. He'd taken their options from them, ruined their chances. He alone had made a rash decision, betting on something that had failed miserably. *Is she trying to remind me of that?*

Julie was stubborn — nearly as stubborn as he was — but she

wasn't petty. She wasn't the type of woman who would play the 'I told you so' game. She had no interest in making him feel bad for no reason, and certainly not in a situation like this.

No, she wasn't trying to rub it in. She wasn't trying to make him feel like he'd made a terrible mistake — she knew that he already knew that.

She was trying to communicate with him.

No, she was saying. *Leaving the shuttle is a mistake.*

He couldn't imagine why.

Dying was a far worse option than attempting to escape, in his mind.

He shook his head and shrugged, then helped Reggie push her out and through the hole.

They had just finished with Julie when the Subshuttle jumped and snapped sideways, a gigantic crunching sound following. Ben was holding his breath and the sudden movement startled him. He released a few bubbles of air from his mouth, then cursed himself for allowing it to happen.

The shuttle rocked on the cable, then swung violently sideways. He felt the cable snap before it happened, feeling the tension ratchet through his body even before he reached to the glass wall to steady himself.

No, he thought. *Please, no.*

The cable snapped. It was a strange, otherworldly sound from beneath the water, a bright, zinging high-pitched sound followed by a duller, deeper thud. The shuttle hung for a brief moment, suspended like it was nothing.

And then it dropped.

It began to fall through the water, gravity finally achieving its goal and the ocean claiming its prize. Ben looked at Reggie, but the man was holding tightly to the seat back with one hand, his other hand flailing around underwater.

There wasn't going to be enough air left in Ben's lungs, and they still had to get Sarah out.

Reggie looked at him. He knew it. The truth of it all hit Ben harder than the jolt of the Subshuttle snapping off its cable.

We're out of time.

Down here, trapped inside a glass bubble that was completely full of water and quickly falling to the ocean floor, air was time. And time was life, and they were running out of all of them.

He wanted to cry. It was an unnatural emotion for him, but it was there. Truer than anything, he felt like he had failed not only his best friend and fiancee, but his teammates and an innocent civilian. He wasn't sure which of those stung worse; which failure gripped him more with the fear of knowing he wasn't strong enough to prevail and save them.

If Julie made it to the surface without him, he'd have failed her, leaving her without the man she'd committed the rest of her life to.

If she *didn't* make it to the surface — that was even worse.

But there was still a job to be done, and he wasn't dead yet. The others often talked about his 'resiliency,' a word he'd only recently come to understand. It wasn't about being able to overcome adversity, or stand up to a foe or a demon or a challenge. It wasn't even about being to bounce back and continue fighting.

To Ben, resiliency meant something far simpler: it meant he was totally incapable of not caring. Once he'd committed to something, he was in. Period. It was stubbornness taken to an insane level. A level most people rightfully never approached, because at that level stubbornness looked a lot more like certain death.

He was simply unable to stop caring about the solution he'd determined was right and proper until he stopped breathing altogether. It was unfortunate, really. Everything in him wanted to leave, to escape this hell and float to the surface before it was too late, but there were two other people who needed help. Everything in him wanted to ignore whatever it was still holding out, but whatever it was that was holding out was stronger than anything his conscious mind could throw at it.

He was resilient, and it was his curse.

The shuttle dropped, deeper and deeper into the abyss. Reggie was pulling his arm, trying to get his attention.

I know, he thought. *I know we're dead.*

Reggie pulled harder, and Ben was about to turn his head and try to see what it was Reggie needed from him that was so damned important right now.

But he couldn't turn away from the glass, from the ocean outside the bubble.

Something in the back of his mind crawled forward, creeping ever closer to his consciousness. Something had captured his attention, though his own mind was keeping it from him. It was either due to the fact that it wasn't worth seeing, it wasn't something his mind was confident enough about, or it was just a fluke.

He dared a glance out the glass into the murky waters. It was darker now, the rays of light no longer penetrating and traveling all the way down to their location. He squinted, knowing he couldn't afford to be focusing on anything other than getting Dr. Lindgren and Reggie out of the Subshuttle.

Still... there was something out there.

He assumed it was Julie, seeing the dark shape floating past, but then realized it was not at all possible that a human could take that form, even considering the strange distortions that might be caused by the glass and the lack of light.

It was something... else.

Another shadow flicked through his vision, just to the right of where he was staring.

What the...

Reggie saw it, too. That must have been why he was tugging at his shirt collar. Ben shrugged it off once again, now focusing fully on the water just outside the shuttle. A deep, intense flicker altered the light around the water, flowing quickly from the left of his sight to the right.

He knew, then. Without a doubt, he knew. It was what Julie had been trying to warn him about.

There was something else in the water.

CHAPTER 50

REGGIE PULLED Ben's shirtsleeve to get his attention. After he'd heard the snap and felt the sudden lurching of the Subshuttle as it began to descend, Reggie was forced to quicken his pace. Two of their team were already safely outside, and they needed to pick up the pace significantly or he, Ben, and Sarah would run out of air long before they made it to the surface.

He had wanted to tell Ben to speed up as well, to move over, to slide to his left so that Dr. Lindgren could launch herself from the opposite side of the shuttle toward the hole and out into the open waters. Ben's shirt was floating up, drifting in front of his face, steadily and gently in the calm waters. The shirt was the only thing feeling calm right now, and it contradicted the true situation Reggie found himself in. While the shirt flickered back and forth in the waters, Reggie and Ben were hard at work, pushing people out of the vessel and up toward the surface. Their heads were completely submerged now, and Reggie was working on readying his body to leave the Subshuttle after he helped Dr. Lindgren out of the shuttle.

Ben looked across at Reggie. *What?* his eyes were asking. And... something else.

Fear?

Why would Ben have been afraid now, of all times? There was plenty of time for freaking out, like right after the idiot had smashed the glass and allowed their only lifeline to sink to the bottom of the ocean.

Reggie searched Ben's face for any sign of what had spooked his friend. Finding nothing useful, he shrugged.

What? he motioned again, hoping Ben could read the expression.

Ben pointed. A long arm and a finger, aimed at the ceiling. Reggie watched the area, but didn't understand.

He shook his head.

He watched, still seeing nothing. He began to shrug, to move his head and try to get Ben to mime what it was he was talking about.

And then he, too, saw it.

The briefest of movements, nothing but a deep shadow that simultaneously matched and contradicted the shadows cast by the deeper hues of the surrounding ocean.

It was like he hadn't seen anything at all, and he did a double-take, still staring at the ceiling where Ben had pointed.

It came again, and went again, just as it had before, but this time it was off to his right, farther in the distance. He was sure of it now: it wasn't just a shadow, an apparition caused by strange dancing light or some other natural phenomenon.

It was an animal.

Some sort of sea creature, huge and menacing, judging by the only part of the animal his peripheral vision had allowed him to glimpse: the tail.

And it was a *monstrously* long tail.

He wanted to open his mouth and gape, but they were out of time. Ben was pulling his arm now. For some reason wanting him to leave. To get out of the shuttle.

But...

He wasn't sure how to tell Ben.

I know what you're talking about now, buddy.

He wanted to tell him. To say, *yeah, I saw it.*

But he also knew what Ben wanted. Ben was motioning with his head and eyes now, screaming even in the silent infinity of the ocean.

The Subshuttle sank.

Deeper, every second deeper. Ben was yelling and saying nothing all at the same time.

Let's go, he was saying.

We have to, but we can't, Reggie was saying back to him.

He ran a mental calculation, checking and estimating his vitals. He didn't have much air left. Possibly enough to get back to the surface, but hardly more than that. And that was assuming he knew where the surface was. It was impossible to tell how fast they were sinking. Hopefully there was still a bit of air left in the ballast, inside the rubberized plastic wall compartments, and other small spaces within the craft. It would slow them down a bit, up until everything was filled with water.

He wasn't sure about Ben, but he knew the man wasn't trained like Reggie was. He was no Navy SEAL, but he was a very capable swimmer, kept himself in peak physical shape, and knew he could hold his breath for nearly three minutes without unnecessary exertion.

There was no way to measure exactly how much exertion he was placing his body under, but it was clear it was more than 'none.' He also hadn't been tracking the time, but he looked at his watch anyway out of habit. *Has it been two minutes? One?* There was no way to be sure. It felt like an eternity had passed, but time had slowed to a crawl ever since Ben had smashed their lifeline and allowed the shuttle to sink.

He tried to push the thought away. It wasn't Ben's fault — if Reggie had thought about it first, he would have done the same thing. The man was trying to avoid a certain death-by-firing-squad, and without being able to control the Subshuttle's motion from inside the boat, it had been their only option.

Reggie knew that, but he felt betrayed that Ben hadn't consulted him first.

Ben pointed. *Up.*

Then he nodded. *Now. Let's go.*

Reggie shook his head. There was still one more member of their team who needed to get out. Dr. Sarah Lindgren had helped Susan and Julie out of the shuttle, and now it was her turn to swim out to safety.

Or into the mouths of whatever the hell those *things are.*

Another one of those 'things' swam eerily close to the glass just behind Dr. Lindgren as Reggie looked over at her. Long, black, slender. It looked like no fish Reggie had ever seen, but it was also fast — too fast to get a good look at it.

She was 'crouching' on the back of a chair on the opposite side of the aisle, her hair floating freely above and around her head. He was about to motion for her to swim over when he saw why she was still halfway across the shuttle in the first place.

Sarah was struggling with her right foot, which had become caught between the glass of that wall of the shuttle and the chair. Apparently when the Subshuttle had detached from the broken cable and shifted, the glass on that side had swelled and swayed, temporarily widening the gap between it and the side of the chair.

Shit.

She was pinned, completely unable to move her foot. It looked painful, judging by the look in her eyes as she frantically worked to free her leg.

Ben pulled at Reggie's shirt, but Reggie brushed his hand away.

Again, Ben yanked at Reggie, this time grabbing his collar. Reggie spun around, shaking his head. He pointed at Sarah. Ben looked, then turned his attention up at Reggie.

He shook his head.

Reggie was stunned. His friend was telling him it was too late; there was nothing they could do for her now.

Reggie exploded into action. He kicked off the back of the chair he had been balancing on, the water holding him straight and steady. It was strong enough of a motion for Ben to lose his grip on him and still carry him through the center of the Subshuttle and across to Sarah's location.

He turned around and quickly looked at Ben. The man's expression was startling: a smorgasbord of fear, confusion, and sadness.

This is it, Reggie thought. *He's trying to say goodbye, but he can't.*

It was hell that they were underwater right now. Whatever Ben was thinking about telling him would have been good.

Reggie nodded. *It's been good, friend.*

There were no smiles. No hugs exchanged, or high fives. It wasn't a happy parting, nor was it as solemn as he would have expected.

Ben was stoic, Reggie was reserved. This was true for both of them, and both were trying to stay true to form, even in this situation. It was understood. Neither would bend, even now. They were who they were, and neither of them was going to change that about the other.

He'd felt this before, long ago.

He was barely a man then, but man enough to have his life's compass set in the direction of his own true north. There was no lying to a compass like that, no fooling the natural order of things. He remembered the moment like it was yesterday, remembered the feeling of betrayal, loss, anticipation, desire for something he would never feel.

He swallowed. His lungs were panicking now, adding to the panic of the rest of his body. He wanted out, to ignore Sarah and just get on with it, but he was committed.

Ben would understand. He saw it on his face.

You save her, he was saying, *but I have to save Julie.*

Reggie understood. He knew it had to be this way. Reggie

couldn't leave an innocent woman to die like this, right in front of his eyes, without even trying.

That, too, was a road he'd been down before.

He thought he had tried then, so long ago, but he knew that was just a lie he tried to tell himself to calm the nerves, to ease the pain.

Sarah's eyes were wide, frantic still. He grabbed her wrist, pulling it up. There was blood, coming from either her ankle or her fingers, either from the tightness and pressure on her leg or from the scratching, desperate clawing to free herself.

She was like an animal in a hunter's trap — she would have done anything to free herself.

He only hoped he'd be able to help. There wasn't enough air in his lungs to do much — either help her or try to get to the surface. *There's a good chance we can't do both,* he thought.

He pulled. One hand, then two. Then she added her hands to the mix, and all four hands pulled up and around and back and tried to dislodge her foot.

It held. Her prison was simple, but effective. Her foot was stuck, and there was nothing they could do to free it with their combined strength, especially underwater.

His lungs were starting to poke outward, the pinpricks of flashing pain alerting him that he was dangerously close to expelling the pent-up carbon dioxide and replacing it with a huge gasp of deadly seawater.

He could tell Sarah was in the same predicament, though she continued to work her hands down and around her foot. He tried pressing on the glass, even kicking it a few times, but it was solid. It barely budged, nothing but a quick reverberation up his leg telling him that he was even making contact.

Ben was gone. He'd left at some point, obviously having decided that it was more prudent for him to check on Julie and the *Ocean-Tech* employee Susan rather than wait around and watch Reggie and Sarah die a horrible death.

Good for him.

Reggie felt no anger, no remorse. They'd made their decisions, and if the situation had been even slightly different he would have made the same decision. Further, he would have forced Ben to make the decision he'd made no matter what. He had more skin in the game than Reggie. Julie was far more important to Ben than Reggie, and Reggie wouldn't have had it any other way.

No, there was nothing Reggie would have changed.

He smiled, even as the shuttle slipped deeper still into the depths, the water turning from blue to black and then to a permanent nothing. The darker shapes melted into just shapes, then disappeared completely. He thought he could feel them swimming circles around them, waiting.

No, he thought. *Not today, boys. We're not coming out of here.*

The lights on the rounded rectangular floor of the shuttle flickered, then died. The darkness was shocking, but Reggie allowed it to overtake him. *Nothing more to do here.*

He grabbed for Sarah's hand. She knew, even though he couldn't see her. She had stopped struggling, waiting for Reggie to notice that it was over.

He smiled into the dark, knowing that it would be light, not darkness, that would finally take him. No matter what, he was going to go out wearing the characteristic grin that he knew defined him. The ocean may be infinite, its bonds unyielding, but he wasn't going to lie back and take its beating. He'd go out knowing that he'd fought, and fought hard.

He'd go out knowing that his best friend was somewhere up there, still fighting the battle he'd pulled him into.

He found Sarah's hand. She grasped his, interlocking their fingers. He squeezed it, wanting to talk to her.

Then again, there was nothing to say. Nothing else to do but wait.

It wouldn't be long now.

CHAPTER 51

"FIND THEM!" Crawford shouted.

His hair was starting to fall, as if it could read his mood, the normally perfect shape of it drooping and sliding over to the side. He pushed a strand of the longer part of it out of his eyes. He was proud of his hair, like he was proud of all of the things regarding his looks people praised him for.

He'd built a career on his looks and charisma just as much as on his brilliance. Equal doses of all of them, and he'd mastered just when to use each one.

Right now, however, he wasn't feeling particularly brilliant. And if his hair was any sign, he wasn't feeling terribly *handsome*, either. This hair was only the outward display of what he was feeling inside.

Turmoil.

He *hated* this feeling. He'd fought against it his entire life, forcing it back into his subconscious, a demon he thought he'd defeated long ago.

Thoughts of his son started working their way upward into his consciousness.

No, he thought. *Stop it.*

Vicente Garza — 'The Hawk,' as his men liked to call him — turned to face him.

"Do you know where they are?" Crawford asked. "I need to find them."

"Adrian, they're —"

"*Sir,*" Crawford corrected.

"Right," Garza said through clenched teeth. "*Sir,* they're somewhere at the bottom of the Atlantic by now."

"How do you know that?"

Crawford stepped up to the first desk he could find. The man seated there rolled backward, not happy about the sudden subversion of his power, but not fighting about it, either. Crawford tried to make sense of what he saw on the screen, but instead of closed-circuit camera feeds and the typical surveillance-style GUI, he saw nothing but spreadsheets, numbers and graphs. Apparently the desk he'd usurped was that of a lower-level Ravenshadow soldier, a man tasked with tracking the day-to-day inputs and outputs of the three rings' energy production.

They were in the control center, or 'command' as the Ravenshadow men called it. The second ring, just beneath the surface in the first sub-level, where the laboratories, crew quarters, and employee offices were housed. It was a far cry from his own office and apartment, at the top of the hotel section in the center ring. This place was like an afterthought — empty and drab, efficient yet stark, as if the entire place was calling out in despair.

He hated it, and it was part of the reason he rarely traveled out here. The bridges and Subshuttle routes were abundant, but he couldn't stand spending time out here with the employees. It made him uncomfortable, and though he could never admit it, it felt beneath him.

But now, in a crisis situation, Adrian Crawford couldn't bear to be away from the action. Garza was capable — that was why he'd hired him and his team in the first place — but Crawford never trusted anyone else, at least not without a bit of oversight. Garza may have been smart, but he wasn't the genius Crawford knew he was.

His entire life had been a roadmap of goals and challenges, with only brief stops along the way: graduation from high school at age 13, undergraduate work at age 15, graduate and post-doc at age 21. He had a brilliant mind, they'd told his parents, and there was nothing that would be able to stop him.

The man running his security, Vicente Garza, was hardly an exception: Crawford had hired him to do a job, and if he failed, he would be removed, like so many of his other employees. He'd found ways to work with the system when needed and against it when no one suspected. There was no government that would be able to halt his progress, and if they finally found some way to do it, it would be too late.

His research was already complete.

Now it was only a matter of testing and perfecting.

Ravenshadow and the CSO, the team it was after, was only slowing down his progress, and he wanted to see the resolution of it as quickly as possible.

Only because of these circumstances had he let his guard down, deciding to travel out to the second ring and watch the progress with his own eyes.

He realized that Garza was talking to him.

"What?" he asked.

"I said, *sir*," Garza said, "we don't know *exactly* where they are because the Subshuttle fell off its cable. It's impossible to tell what exactly happened out there, since —"

"My shuttle *fell off its cable*?"

Garza nodded. "Yes, that's what I said, *sir*."

Crawford was half a foot shorter than the man, and far less intimidating, but he wasn't about to let a subordinate give him attitude. "I respectfully request that you treat me as your superior officer, Mr. Garza."

Garza's nostrils flared.

"I know I'm not up to speed with the specific military lingo you boys all use," Crawford said. "But whatever you call your *top dog* — that's me. Got it?"

Garza sucked in the sides of his lips as though he were about to spit something across the room. "We call that 'general.' Sometimes 'admiral,' depending on where you're from. Or, if you're getting fancy, maybe even 'President.' You heard of that one?"

Crawford's fists balled. He stepped up to Garza. His breathing was faster, and there was nothing he could do to voluntarily slow it. He had never been in the military, and he wasn't much of a fighter. His battles were won by wits, in the courtrooms, boardrooms, and private offices of the richest members of philanthropic society.

Still, he wasn't about to back down. He'd faced off against far larger opponents. Perhaps not those quite as large as Garza, nor as brutal and physically imposing, but nonetheless, Crawford hadn't achieved his successes by backing down. He stepped a foot closer, putting the two men eye to eye.

Garza just smiled. "You got something to tell me, *boss*?"

Crawford was appalled. It was rare someone was so blatantly nonchalant with his authority, and it was even more rare it was someone that worked directly for him.

"I — I want to know what's happening, Garza," Crawford said. "I thought I made that clear."

Garza leaned in, nearly leaning *over* Crawford. "You did. However, I might remind you that our *contractual* agreement allows me and my team to operate in whatever manner as I please, including — as our contract states — 'systems, personnel, operations, and procedures.'"

"What's your point?"

"Simple. Finding your CSO friends now falls completely and ultimately under my list of responsibilities. You are welcome to stand by and observe my process, but I will take any questions, criticisms, and similar remarks as direct threats against my authority. In which case, I might add, will instigate a breach of contract on your part, resulting in your paying my full payment and fee, as well as the additional 'forfeiture of rights' fee as stated in the rider clauses."

Crawford fumed. He was seething, but he knew Garza was right. *He's smart, but nothing I can't handle,* he thought. *I've dealt with worse.*

He knew it was true, too.

Garza was a strong-arm. He had hired Ravenshadow to keep the peace here at the park, and he had given them a hefty bonus for luring and capturing the CSO team as well. At the end of the day, however, the CSO team was the priority. He couldn't operate with a carte-blanche team like theirs running around the world.

Garza was the man who had appeared to be the most qualified, and his men had appeared to be quite the impressive group of soldiers, but Crawford had always maintained a 'slow to hire, quick to fire' mentality. If Garza wasn't going to get the job done, he needed to be working on an alternative.

He was already upset that he had allowed himself to let finding an alternative or two slide, assuming that Garza and Ravenshadow would be able to handle things.

"Listen, Crawford," Garza said. "I understand where you're coming from. You have assets out there, and those assets are under threat of attack right now. But you need to allow me to do what I need to do to rid you of this problem, understand?"

Crawford looked up at Garza.

"Understand?" he asked again.

Crawford was mad, but he nodded. "What does that even mean?"

"It means I'm going to do whatever it takes to get them back. Dead or alive, you'll have them. Got it"

"What does that *mean*, Garza?" Crawford asked.

Garza looked up, staring out the glass window of the sub-level.

He sighed. "You've got millions invested here, and a lot of reasons to keep this thing afloat. But I might need to do things that you wouldn't necessarily approve, under normal circum—"

"*What* are you talking about, Garza?" Crawford asked. "If you so much as *interfere* with the research going on here, I'll —"

"I might need to turn this entire place against them," Garza said. "If there's any way they got out of the shuttle — it's not likely they survived, mind you — but if they come out, swim to the surface... I need to use everything I've got against them. You understand that?"

Crawford took a deep, long breath. He wanted to tell him no, that it certainly *wasn't* okay to put his entire facility and the research here at risk. The research was still the most important facet of *Ocean-Tech's* progress, and there were finely tuned ecosystems that were interdependent. If even *one* of these systems was thrown out of balance, it could completely destroy the integrity of the research.

But they have to be found, Crawford thought. *Above all else, I have to know they are dead.*

Finally, he turned back to the man he'd placed in charge of his security. "You have ten minutes. Find them, and report to me directly. Do whatever it takes. You have the station at your command. You know how to reach me."

Garza looked like he was about to hit him, but both men stood their ground. Finally, in a half-grunting way, Garza spoke. "Fine. Ten minutes."

Crawford turned and started walking toward the door without acknowledging his subordinate's response. As he left, he heard Garza barking orders to his staff and soldiers.

"Fire up the protocols tab," Garza said. "We're temporarily taking over this facility, and I've got an idea."

CHAPTER 52

THE SWIM to the surface was the most intense thing Julie had ever experienced. She'd been in more than one firefight, had more than one person shooting at her at the same time, and had gone to hell and back on more than one occasion.

But swimming straight up from a sinking submersible vehicle with hardly a breath left in her lungs through crocodile-infested waters was by far the most taxing thing she'd ever been through.

And Ben is still down there.

She couldn't think about Reggie and Sarah. There was only room in her mind for the task at hand — getting to the surface — and Ben.

Nothing more, nothing less.

If she had control of her thoughts, she would have tried to push those of Ben out, but it was impossible. She loved him, and there was no ignoring the fact. He was part of her, as much as she knew she was a part of him. She could try to survive, using all of her conscious energy and mind's power to plow up and forward through the water, but she couldn't *not* think of Ben as well.

He'd have protected her. He would have prevented the crocs from getting to her, if he could.

They were swimming around her now, teasing her. Playing. Possibly trying to figure out what it was, exactly, was swimming around in *their* tank.

She shuddered, but she continued forward. Her lungs were about to burst, but she knew she would make it. The problem was, of course, that air wasn't the only challenge she was facing.

The crocs were darting back and forth through her field of vision, closer every time.

She knew nothing about their habits, whether they fought in packs or in singular units. She assumed they were individual, and likely all one gender. They seemed to be fully grown, as the ones swimming circles around her were between eight and fifteen feet long.

Smaller than some of the larger crocs she'd seen, but still...

Eight feet of crocodile was about nine feet too many.

With a final thrust of her arms and a kick with her legs, she burst through and broke the surface.

She gasped for air, filling her lungs. It was only a momentary reprieve.

A long, black shape was swimming directly toward her.

And it was *fast.*

She screamed, seeing Susan in her peripheral vision. The woman was struggling against the side of the tank, trying to pull herself up and over the two-foot tall edge that stuck up above the water. It was the side of the ring they were nearest, and Julie knew it wouldn't take much to pull herself up and to safety.

If only she could get there.

She shoved the water, trying to make it obey an entirely different set of physics laws, and her hands unsurprisingly shot straight up, splashing water up into the air. The croc wasn't deterred. It bore down on her, and she treaded water until the thing was right in her face.

At that moment, she slid sideways, twisting at the same time. She was far smaller than the beast, but their maneuverability was matched. Still, she was a half-second faster than the croc, and her torso slid under the water right as the crocodile flew over her head. It bucked, realizing that it had lost its prey, and Julie felt its powerful claw scrape against her back.

She wanted to scream in pain, but she kept her mouth shut, knowing that to give in was to lose everything.

Where's Ben? she thought.

The croc turned, awkwardly but fast in the water, and she knew she wasn't going to be nearly as lucky this time around. This crocodile had to be at least fifteen feet long, possibly even larger. It was clearly the leader of the pack, and while she was not the least bit interested in fighting off an alpha, it meant the rest of them were, temporarily at least, ignoring her.

The croc made its arc, then pummeled down toward her. She was farther away from the wall than she had been before.

She prepared herself. It would come in teeth-first, knowing its strengths. It was a reptile, so it wouldn't be able to calculate her position or movement much beyond 'it's trying to escape.' That was the only advantage she could think of, but she planned to exploit it as much as possible.

Wait until it's close, then duck out of the way, she thought. *He's just trying to defend his territory now. There's no element of surprise.*

She tread water, facing off against her reptilian attacker.

The croc was ten feet away, gaining speed.

She wanted to close her eyes, get it over with.

The croc opened its jaws. *A display of power, or an anticipation of its meal?*

It was five feet away, and Julie braced herself for the impact. *Would it hurt? Would it just swallow me whole, or would it take its time?*

There *was* no time. She couldn't afford to be thinking about things like that.

She was planning on ducking to the right this time, not that it would trick the stupid beast anyway. It was acting on instinct, solely doing whatever tiny component of its tiny brain that controlled its huge body told it to do.

Three feet.

She prepared to lunge to the right.

The croc's jaws widened, then snapped shut. It darted to its right — Julie's left — then sank beneath the surface of the water. Julie tracked it, seeing its tail whip up and back down, a gigantic splash following.

What the?

The croc rolled, then buckled, nearly in half, as it reacted in surprise. Something had attacked it from below, causing it to panic and roll away from Julie and the sure prize she offered.

The croc splashed again, frantic and still caught off guard, and Julie took the opportunity to begin her swim to shore. She pulled herself along with her arms and legs, grabbing the water by the gallon in her cupped hands and kicking harder than she'd ever kicked. She wasn't much of a swimmer — she could do it, but she'd never trained for 'chased by crocodile' before. Still, she didn't allow herself to look back.

The other crocs, if they were still there, were watching and waiting to see their alpha's success or failure. Julie had a straight shot to the shore, where Susan was just now pulling herself up and out of the water, dripping from every inch of her body.

Keep. Going.

She willed herself to speed up. She could rest on dry land, where the crocs wouldn't be able to reach her.

She hoped.

The alpha was still writhing in the water, unsure of what had attacked it, and how. Apparently it hadn't expected an enemy from below, and Julie watched it out of the corner of her eye as she swam. She reached the shore just as she saw a head pop out of the water.

Ben...

He was alive, and very much pissed at the crocodile that had almost claimed his fiancee's life. He roared in anger, then ducked underwater just as the croc passed over his head.

The croc was heavy, but Julie saw its belly lift up out of the water as Ben punched it from below. It would do nothing but anger the crocodile, but she was happy to see it nonetheless. The croc writhed and tumbled, off-balance for a moment.

Ben took advantage of that moment and swam a few paces away from the alpha male.

He reported the threat, raising his arms up and over his head to call the croc toward him.

Julie pulled herself out of the water, then turned around to watch the display out in the water. There was nothing she could do for him from up here. Ben was writhing around, making the same motions Julie had been, trying to dodge the massive croc's attacks. The crocodile was taking a long, wide arc around to prepare for the next attack, giving Ben time to swim a bit closer to the wall. He went slowly, however, so as not to give the other crocs any reason to attack.

Ben was the designated meal of the alpha croc, and the others weren't going to touch him until their leader had finished. Julie only hoped the leader was playing with him and would allow Ben enough time to get away before he decided it was time for a snack.

Please, Ben, Julie thought. *Hurry.*

They were standing on a makeshift pier, a long, narrow section of concrete that extended out into the larger tank. And from this vantage point, Julie could tell that it was, indeed, a tank.

The shuttle had stopped in the middle of the tank, Ben had broken the glass, and they had found themselves swimming up through crocodile-infested waters.

This can't get any worse, Julie thought. There was nothing out here to use as a weapon against man or reptile, and there was no rope or ladder to throw toward Ben.

To top it off, she hadn't seen Reggie or Sarah surface. She knew there was no possible way they could hold their breath this long, and since the crocodile tank was a closed structure, there was no way they'd found another way out. The entire pool was about a hundred feet square, and there was nothing else to hide behind, meaning she would have seen them surface by now.

Unless this just got worse.

Just then a loud klaxon sounded from behind her. She turned and saw a pole with loudspeakers pointing down and out on opposite sides barking the siren toward her and Susan.

She instinctively reached up and covered her ears. "What the hell is that?" she yelled at Susan.

Susan's face was sheet-white. She, too, had been watching Ben's progress as he faced off against the saltwater croc, but now she turned and stared at Julie.

"It's... it's an alarm. Telling the staff that someone's initiated an unscheduled command."

"An *unscheduled* command?" Julie asked.

Susan nodded. "Most of the animal facilities are automated as much as possible, to save on overhead costs. This one included."

"Okay," Julie said. "What does *this* unscheduled command mean?"

Susan's face didn't change. It hung there, hopeless and down. "It means someone called the order to start their feeding time."

Julie closed her eyes and forced herself to breathe. The sirens seemed to only be growing louder in her ears.

CHAPTER 53

THE CROC HAD FINISHED its arc and was about to turn and make its final lap down the long straightaway between it and Ben's location. Ben was watching it out of the corner of his eye, focusing on the rest of the herd in his peripheral vision, and simultaneously making for the edge of the pier where Susan and Julie were standing.

He was going to have to dodge the croc's attack at least one more time, but the croc wasn't going to attack the same way again. It had learned that its prey was smarter than expected, so it would attempt to strike when Ben was least expecting it.

Which meant Ben put his odds of survival somewhere between 'swallowed whole' and 'bloody mess.' He preferred the first, but he still focused on the task at hand.

Get out of the water.

He'd never wanted to be on dry land more than right now. He'd trekked through the Amazon, splashed through shallow piranha-infested river beds, and had brief encounters with anaconda and black caiman, but this was something else entirely.

He was *not* interested in playing cat-and-mouse with a prehistoric apex predator any longer than absolutely necessary.

The other crocs' heads were floating, their eyes and snouts

poking above the surface of the water. Cold, evil eyes. Ancient eyes. Whatever it was Crawford needed them for, the two seemed a good fit for one another. Saltwater crocodiles and their reptilian leader, Adrian Crawford. A soulless, cold-blooded lizard.

The croc started in on him. *What's the plan, Ben?* he thought. *Dodge left? Straight down?* He couldn't win an underwater battle, and he was never going to out-swim the beast, so his only plausible chance was to dodge one way or the other and hope he'd guessed correctly.

The croc sped up, and Ben could see the water spraying up from behind it as it cut through the water.

A klaxon sounded from somewhere up in the distance, the noise ripping through the air and reaching Ben's ears as his head rose and fell in the lapping waves. It was a strange sensation to hear the sound waves from above and below the surface of the water, and it only added to the confusion and chaos.

The hell does that mean?

He looked around, and noticed that the crocs were stirring. Their steady, completely still bodies were now sliding left and right, bumping into one another. He dared a glance back over his shoulder to see how far the alpha had before it was on him.

It had stopped.

Ben squinted, taking his hand out of the water to rub the ocean out of his eyes, and looked again.

It wasn't moving. It was staring at Ben, glaring with those cold, evil eyes, and then it shifted and looked away.

Suddenly it flashed into motion, rolling to the side and swimming to the left. Ben watched it, then realized the others were following.

A crane had appeared above the water, swinging out slowly from behind a wall farther out. Ben watched the crane and saw that it held something in its claw.

A seal.

The seal was alive, kicking its fins and bleating like some kind of terrified goat. The claw reached out toward Ben, the crocs all watching with distinct anticipation.

Oh, crap.

Ben suddenly knew what the klaxon meant, and what was about to happen.

He felt a bump as one of the crocs pushed against him. The crane pushed the seal out farther, now right above Ben.

And then it dropped.

"Ben!" Julie shouted. "Get out of the —"

Ben didn't wait to hear the rest of her sentence. He felt the panic rise in his chest, the adrenaline coursing through his veins as they tightened and every muscle in his body screamed in pain as he surged forward.

He didn't watch the seal, but he saw a crocodile leap out of the water, fly *over* him, and then splash back down behind him, the croc's heavy tail landing just to the right of Ben's head. The force of the water's impact with his head pushed him a foot to the side, and he almost took in a mouthful of water.

He heard another splash behind him — the seal, probably — and then immediately the sound of thousands of pounds of instinctually driven flesh tearing at one another to get to the meal.

Ben swam faster than he knew possible. His arms stung, his legs kicked, every foot agony, but he wouldn't stop. He felt two more crocs bumping against him, and when he put his head below the water he made the mistake of opening his eyes.

The alpha was there, swimming straight up at him from the depths.

His heart caught in his throat, but he refused to hesitate. He squeezed his eyes shut once again and threw his arms out, pushing with his right and pulling with his left, the water making everything a struggle. He turned, rolling to the side just in time.

He hoped.

The croc's massive body came halfway out of the water, one of its thick, scaly legs striking Ben below the chin. It was an accidental uppercut, but it was extremely effective. Ben saw stars, but he gritted his teeth, refusing to black out.

Get... to... the... dock...

The words repeated in his mind. Over and over again. The croc fell, the tidal wave it created pushing Ben faster away from it, and he plowed on.

There was a hand there, then another. They pulled him, yanked him.

He couldn't move. He was already dead, unsure of whether it was his mind playing tricks on him or if this was some sort of extended hell he'd fallen into.

The hands grabbed at his shirt, his legs, one holding onto his hair. It hurt, but not really. He could feel it, but he wasn't truly experiencing it.

Sounds of thrashing and tearing from behind him. And somehow squeals from the still-dying seal.

The water was frothy, foaming and white with the chaos, as if the ocean was now playing along with the sick game happening all around him. It had become a character here, a guide in Ben's personal version of Dante's hell, and it was laughing at him.

You can't escape.

There were voices now — the ocean was trying to mock him? The crocs themselves?

More pulling, tearing, his hair hurt but it felt far better than the rest of him. He waited, squeezed his eyes shut, probably for good.

More voices. The seal? Begging for help?

No, these were womens' voices. Gentle voices. Soothing, pulling him back out of it.

He was alive. It was hot, sunny.

He wanted to open his eyes, but the sun was there, too bright and menacing. He kept them closed.

He tried to breathe, then felt the water. It was still inside him.

He coughed, twice, then again a third and fourth time. It hurt, coming back out. It splashed around, making his wet clothes feel wetter, the humidity and sunlight and heat and cold all hitting him at the same time.

He groaned, then rolled over and threw up.

"Ben," the voice said. "Ben, are you there?"

What kind of question is that? Where is 'there?'

He threw up again, coughing bile and seawater.

"Ben, come back," the voice said.

Finally, after deciding it was worth the risk, he opened his eyes.

Julie was there, kneeling, sobbing, holding him. He breathed, finally feeling like his body was able to provide the involuntary action without causing more pain.

"Ju — Jules," he whispered.

She nodded.

"I'm here."

"I know."

She leaned down farther and held his head up, then kissed him.

He was about to enjoy the kiss, but suddenly a shadow fell over the sun, blocking it out.

The Hawk was there, along with two of his men.

CHAPTER 54

"GET TO THE SECOND RING, *NOW!*" Crawford yelled into the phone.

"Sir, we have a team there already. Our own office is right below, and Garza is already —"

"I don't *care* where the office is! I want *every Ravenshadow soldier* on that ring in thirty seconds."

The kid on the other end of the line hesitated. "Sir, I don't think that's a —"

Crawford hung up. He didn't need to hear the kid's particular flavor of insubordination. *'Sir, I don't think that's a good idea,'* or *'Sir, I don't think that's possible.'* Neither was an appropriate answer.

He was too upset to think. Too upset to plan a strategic attack on the CSO group. He had hired Garza for that job, and so far all Garza had done was upset the crocodiles in the research tank. He'd watched the crane being swung out from its hoist, watched the live feeding take place from his office above the hotel, watched Harvey Bennett get pulled out of the tank by the two women, Juliette and one of his own employees.

A useless waste, he thought. Changing the crocs' diets would force his team to restart an important — and expensive — line of testing.

The insulin levels in their blood would have massively spiked, not too mention thrown off every other carefully calibrated reading they were trying to collect.

It would take a week to normalize the crocs' behavior enough to get a satisfactory blood sample.

He'd slammed his fist onto the top of his desk after seeing the charade of garish power his security contractor had displayed. He made sure to use his left hand. That was the hand he could no longer feel.

He reached for the bottle of pills he kept inside the top drawer of his desk. Opening the lid, he slid two of the capsules into his hand, then into his mouth.

I'm feeling too much, he thought. *Calm down, just relax.*

The pill was something the lab had been testing. He was impatient by nature, and having gotten so close to his ultimate goal — developing the ability to grow back limbs — only made him more zealous for victory.

He'd ignored the warnings given to him by Dr. Joseph Lin and the rest of the medical staff; that the medication was still far from understood. He didn't care if his doctors didn't understand the nuances and the intricacies of the new drug — he understood it.

It worked. So far, at least.

That was all he'd needed to know.

The drug had only one known detrimental side effect, but Dr. Lin had been assigned the task of eliminating that effect altogether. He'd failed, but he'd gotten close.

Crawford needed to get out to the second ring, but he pulled up the video of his laboratory that he'd saved to the desktop of his computer. He'd watched it a hundred times, even before Dr. Lin had wiped everything useful and tried to destroy the evidence. Crawford had saved the video long before the server hard drives beneath the lab had been erased.

It was all backed up anyway, and Crawford had ensured that the bulk of the data he would need to move forward was stored elsewhere, on an offsite server.

This video, however, he'd made sure to keep close. It was *special*.

It was *proof*.

He felt the effects of the medication hit him as he pressed play, then he sat down in his chair, leaned back, and watched the security footage.

Dr. Lin stepped up to the man's enclosure — the chief of the tribe they'd captured in the rainforest, now called *thirty-one dash three*. He reached for the syringe and carefully administered the dosage, then his face saw 31-3's face behind the glass.

The smile.

The chief of this tribe, smiling back at his captor. His eyes, clearly and cleverly masking the pain he felt.

It should have been impossible.

31-3 was exhibiting symptoms of 'emotional resonance,' or, in layman's terms, he was 'able to feel emotion.' The drug was supposed to be able to fully suppress that emotion, to allow for the subject to be placed under severe stress and experience vast amounts of pain without feeling — or at least without reacting.

31-3, up to that point, had taken the drug and exhibited no emotional resonance whatsoever. He had simply sat still, allowed the medication to pass through his system, allowed Lin's team to document the physical changes to his body, and allowed life to pass him by, just as every other subject had.

Until the drug stopped working.

The man smiled at Dr. Lin, a sign of emotional resonance they had thought was beyond impossible while on the medication.

But Crawford knew it was not impossible.

He knew, because he was personally aware of the drug's side effect.

Crawford's laboratory-assigned number was not on any record, and Dr. Lin's petty actions in destroying the laboratory data would be the perfect scapegoat for why that was. Crawford had ensured that his record was nowhere in the research, that his name or assigned subject value did not exist in the system.

But Crawford knew.

He was the number *31-0.*

'Patient zero,' he liked to say.

Dr. Lin's previous assistant hadn't been removed because of an infraction, or because she had deviated from some protocol.

No, the reason was much simpler than that. The woman had been removed because she *knew*. She knew about Crawford, because she had been the one administering his dosages.

His daily trips to the laboratory, to 'check in on his team,' were driven by a far more important objective: he needed the medication.

And he knew the medication worked well, with one *minor* side effect.

It allowed the patient to *feel*.

He shut down the computer, grabbed the bottle of pills, and marched out of his office.

It was time to put an end to all of this.

CHAPTER 55

THERE WAS no way to remove the tank from its mount and take it with them, and it was probably too large anyhow, so he was now worried they wouldn't have enough air to get from the seabed to the surface.

Reggie had realized the answer to his problem when it was nearly too late. The oxygen tank was stored beneath the Subshuttle, piped in through vents in the floor, the access hatch and control panel hidden behind the plastic cupboard Ben had found.

He was lucky: there was a plastic hose stretching from the tank to the control panel, where the oxygen level was measured and reported on the LCD screen. He only had to rip open the rest of the wall panels to trace the hose, then pull the end of the hose itself up and out of the floor of the shuttle. He was able to rip the end of the hose from the vent system, then backtrack and pull the hose through the cupboards and out into the open. The air bubbles violently streaming from the end of the hose told him everything he needed to know.

There was oxygen — and pressure — still in the tank.

He allowed his chest to collapse, relieving his lungs of the depleted oxygen, then he placed his lips over the end of the hose and took a deep breath. The air tasted tinny, metallic, but in that moment it was fresher than any of the mountain air he had ever breathed.

He pulled the hose over to Dr. Lindgren, who reached for it and took a hit of the precious oxygen. They swapped once again, each taking another deep breath, smiling at one another the whole time.

We might just make it out of here, he thought.

He got to work on her foot, pausing every few seconds to take a breath from the hose Sarah held out to him. It took finding the makeshift wrench Ben had fashioned from the end of the broom handle and using it as a lever to work her foot and ankle out of the space it had been crammed into.

She pulled it away quickly the moment it was free, rubbing it with her hands. He passed her the oxygen hose and allowed her to take a breath, then he attempted to mime their plan.

Swim. Up.

It was a pretty simple plan, so she nodded in agreement and they each took a final hit from the air hose.

He sucked in as much of the air as his lungs would hold, then he pushed off the floor of the Subshuttle and out the hole in its side.

The water outside felt cooler, an effect of the vastness of the open space they were now in, but he didn't stop to look around or ponder any of that. Sarah was right behind him, having followed him out immediately after. He waited for her to reach him, then he grabbed her hand. She squeezed onto it, allowing him to guide them upward.

He turned his face to the lighter water above him, noticing the dark, long shapes splashing and swimming up there. Whatever they were, they were occupied. They didn't notice the two humans swimming up to greet them, and he didn't plan on changing that.

Reggie changed course a bit, away from the creatures, hoping they would have enough air to go diagonally upward instead of straight up. Sarah was still there, holding tight but kicking with her legs to hurry them along. They were making good time, swimming fast, and it seemed as though the ocean's floor was only forty or fifty feet beneath the surface.

As long as they didn't run into trouble, Reggie knew that was an easy swim, considering their own buoyancy was on their side.

They didn't run into trouble, but they ran into something else.

Something Reggie hadn't at all expected.

Chunks of flesh began to appear.

Blood, thick swirls of it.

All of it raining down slowly, as if they were in a slow-motion storm. The water was holding it in place, a macabre scene of suspended-animation gore.

A bone, still attached to some hunk of skin and muscle, floated directly in front of his face.

He kicked harder, not daring to look back at Sarah. He already felt like he was going to throw up.

He tried to talk his mind into focusing on the lightening waters above, about getting out of the water and *then* processing whatever the hell happened. But he couldn't shake the thought, it kept sliding out into the front of his conscious mind, unprovoked.

Is this what's left of my friends?

CHAPTER 56

"GET UP," Crawford said. He had walked up a few moments later, after Vicente Garza and his men had arrived.

Ben was laying on the concrete, the warm sun now a friend, no longer a foe beating down on him. It was nice, save for the hard ground. But hard or not, *anything* was better than the water.

The saltwater crocodiles plowed through the remains of the seal, fighting each other for the scraps. The alpha had disappeared, probably sulking from the loss of his own prize.

Ben looked up at Crawford.

He sat up.

"*All* the way up," Crawford said.

"Adrian, buddy," Ben said. "It's over. You tried to have your creatures in there eat us, but it didn't work."

Crawford fumed, but his eyes remained rigidly fixed on Ben's. His dimple was nowhere to be found. One of his arms hung by his side, lifeless, while his other was in a pocket.

The Hawk was suddenly there. "Get up, Harvey. We need to finish this."

Ben was surprised, but he obeyed. Julie and Susan had been taken by two of Garza's men, but there was no one else on the dock.

He stood, eye-to-eye with the soldier. Crawford stepped to the side, allowing The Hawk to take his place.

"You going to throw me back in there?" Ben asked. "I already fought off your big one, I'm sure I can do it again."

"No," The Hawk said. "That would be too complicated. What if they're not hungry anymore? What if you're not to their liking?" he smiled. "While I would *love* to see you get ripped apart by crocodiles, I need this to be very simple. One shot, through the temple. Ends it quickly, unfortunately for me, but I wasn't hired for my creativity."

Ben swallowed.

The Hawk held up a pistol. 45 calibre, a monstrous thing. "This baby is a favorite of mine. Makes a hell of a racket, and it's a bit showy, but *damn* if it doesn't get the job done."

He held it up to Ben's head. "Turn around."

"You're going to shoot a man with his back turned."

"There's nothing poetic about dying face-to-face with a man, Ben. I don't care if it's a bullet to the head or a knife through the back. It's all the same, as long as the heart stops beating."

"In that case, get it over with."

Ben was tired. He didn't want to die, but he couldn't fight. There was no point. Reggie was dead, Julie was as good as dead.

If there was an obvious thing to do, it didn't come to him. He couldn't fight his way out of this one. Even without his army, The Hawk had him surrounded.

"Find Gareth Red, and the doctor," The Hawk spoke into his wrist mic. "Sarah Lindgren can't be allowed to leave either."

Crawford watched them. "Are you sure they weren't on the shuttle?" he asked. "Some of your men say they saw them get on with the others."

"If they did, they're already dead," The Hawk said. "They either drowned or were torn apart by the crocs. We need every man we can spare searching the ring, all levels. They won't stop until they're found. *Dead*, preferably."

Crawford nodded. He didn't look happy.

Ben closed his eyes. *They wouldn't find his friend and Sarah Lindgren in the labs.* Ben knew *exactly* where they were when he'd left them.

He dropped his head. "Get it over with, Garza."

Garza paused. "No, I'm not going to make it *that* easy for you, Ben."

Ben frowned.

"I kill people who get in my way. But people who *annoy* me, consistently, and *take* something from me, they get my full wrath."

"Sounds scary," Ben said. "Can we dispense with the pleasantries. I've been in this situation before, man. Just pull the trigger and get it over —"

"No, Ben," The Hawk said. "I don't think you understand. I'm going to make you *watch*."

Ben turned his head, but Garza shook him, hard. He straightened up again, staring out at the white-capped water as the crocs fought.

"Push her in," The Hawk said.

Ben struggled against The Hawk's grip, but his muscles were sore. He wrenched an arm free, but then Garza's huge pistol came down and found a spot just above Ben's spine on the back of his neck. He went down to his knees, dazed.

Susan fell into the water, pushed by one of The Hawk's men.

Julie screamed.

Ben couldn't believe what he'd just seen, but he wasn't going to watch, either.

Three of the crocs immediately turned and swam over to the spot where the woman had entered the water. She surfaced quickly, her arms flailing above her head, her mouth and eyes opening and closing rapidly. She screamed.

And the first croc pulled her under.

Ben shut his eyes.

The Hawk pressed the gun into his temple, pushing his head

sideways. "Open your eyes, Ben," he said. "This is *your* fault. *You* did this, you understand?"

Ben clenched his jaw. He kept his eyes closed. He tried not to hear the sounds of the reptiles eating.

"If you weren't going to die here, today, you would have to live with that knowledge. I hate that you won't, but I want you to *feel* that, at least for a minute. Got it?"

Ben felt his captor turn to address Crawford. "When does the chopper arrive, Crawford?"

"The investors leave within an hour. Bahamas, then back to the mainland on a commercial air—"

"I don't care about their travel plans, Crawford. I'm commandeering that chopper."

"You can't do that!" Crawford shouted. "It's not yours to —"

"I need to perform a surveillance sweep of the area, and I can provide support best if I'm in the air."

He turned back to Ben and pressed the gun against his head once more. Apparently the conversation was over.

"Jacobsen," The Hawk barked. "Get her ready to go in. Ben, you watching?"

Ben felt his heart rising into his throat. He swallowed it back down, blinked twice. *Is this real?*

He waited.

"Okay, Jacobsen," The Hawk said. "Throw her in."

CHAPTER 57

SHE WATCHED Susan's body torn to shreds by the crocodiles, unable to look away. It was horrifying, but Julie was in shock. She was numb to the reality of it, the pain gnawing at her insides but still not quite hurting.

The blood darkened the water, spreading outward and yet still somehow just as deeply crimson as it had been after it spilled out of its owner's body.

"Okay, Jacobsen," The Hawk said. "Throw her in."

Julie wasn't sure who he was talking about. *Is it me?*

Ben was going to die. Susan had already died, and Reggie and Sarah had already died. They were all going to die.

There was no denying that fact now, and while she wasn't necessarily welcoming her own death, she wasn't sure she was against it, either.

Ben seemed to be resigned to his fate as well, and she felt as though she were looking out of her eyes through a filter, as if her eyes weren't her own but someone else's. It was surreal.

It was *unreal*.

She felt the Ravenshadow man, Jacobsen, pushing her over. She felt his arm, but it wasn't hers. She felt her body sliding sideways, giving in, but it wasn't hers. She stepped with him, allowing him, *welcoming* him.

What is happening?

Ben turned and looked at her.

Suddenly, in that moment, in those eyes, she saw everything. Her past, her future, and — of course — her present.

Right now.

She knew where she was. What was happening.

She was on a pier. Standing precariously close to a crocodile-infested tank of saltwater, on a secluded artificial island called *Paradisum*.

She was here with her fiancé, and that was all that mattered.

And she had had enough. Everything fell back into place, her reality no longer tainted by the life-sucking filter she had been viewing it all through.

She was done. She wanted out.

She ducked, spun around, caught the back of the man's knee with her foot. She wasn't as strong as he was, but he wasn't expecting the retaliation. Reggie had trained her in hand-to-hand combat, and she was getting better every week. The blow brought the man down, but he recovered and compensated by falling onto his other knee.

He brought his subcompact machine gun out from around his shoulder and tried to get it into position to fire on her.

That's a mistake, she thought. She was in the worse position, the lower ground, standing on the edge of the tank.

She capitalized on the man's mistake by punching him, her fist long and tight with her first knuckles pointed, catching him right in the Adam's apple. He coughed, choking, and she threw her body around but slung the nook of her elbow around his neck and used his own body weight against him.

He fell backwards, but she wasn't even close to done. He tried to roll, but she was still attached to him. His gun fell from his shoulder, and he brushed it away. Julie heard it skidding against the concrete.

She caught movement out of the corner of her eye and saw Ben reacting as well, trying to get a grip on the end of The Hawk's pistol. Both men were locked in a struggle, each dancing back and forth and changing positions dangling over the edge of the croc tank.

Her man writhed around again, trying to shake her loose. She wasn't going to be able to choke him to death, or even hold him forever, so she came up with a different plan.

Time to shift gears a bit, she thought. *Make him think he's winning.*

She screamed in pain, then released him. She popped up onto her feet in a crouched position, making sure she was out of arm's reach. Her bet was that the man would be in close combat mode, either forgetting about his weapon or choosing to ignore it in favor of beating this far-smaller woman without extra help from propelled munitions.

She was only half-right.

He lunged forward, an impossibly large Bowie knife in his hand. He held it well, like Reggie had taught her and Ben. She sidestepped, swiveled, then turned to face him again.

He was now standing on the edge. Right where she had been standing a moment earlier.

She kicked, her foot low and straight, her leg no higher than the man's waist. *No sense trying to be a ninja,* Reggie would have said. *Just get in, get out, get both feet on the ground again.* Fast, efficient, effective.

And it was.

The man let out a sharp cry of pain as Julie's low kick hit him right in the groin, doubling over.

He tried to recover, but Julie was already there. Right in front of his face.

Pushing him.

He started rotating his arms as he felt the weightlessness of gravity taking over, but it was too late. There was nothing left to grab onto, as Julie had anticipated the man's action and backpedaled a step, simply watching him fall backwards into the water.

The first croc was already waiting for him, mouth open.

She turned away at that moment.

Ben and The Hawk were still locked in battle, neither man appearing to have the upper hand, but Julie knew better. Ben was stubborn as hell and wouldn't back down, but he was tired. Beaten, worn, and shaken to his core, he wasn't going to make it much longer.

Julie started running.

Get to Ben, she thought. *Get to Ben, and then fight. That's it.*

There was nothing else to do.

She had defeated one foe, she and Ben together could defeat a second.

Especially someone like The Hawk, who had a permanent place in her mind as a man who needed to die.

But she was intercepted halfway there.

Crawford had stepped in front of her, blocking her route. She tried to barrel through him, but the man held out an arm, a football-type move that would have worked on any pro NFL team. His straight-arm hit hard, and she fell backwards to the concrete floor of the pier.

"Game's over, Juliette," Crawford said.

There was a gunshot, and Crawford spun around. She caught sight of a little blood spurting from his arm.

She turned, saw Reggie standing there, soaking wet and somehow alive, Dr. Sarah Lindgren by his side. He had the Raven-shadow man's subcompact in his hands, and he was taking aim at Adrian Crawford.

"No," Reggie said. "*Now* it's over."

CHAPTER 58

A FEW THINGS happened at once. Reggie heard the rotor wash of the chopper as it flew into view from behind the hotel in the central ring, the noise increasing as it drew near to land and pick up the hotel's other guests.

He wondered how much they had seen — they had mostly kept to themselves in the hotel, and he hadn't seen them since they'd first arrived. Still, a steady barrage of gunfire and fighting would likely not have gone unnoticed.

He also saw The Hawk release his grip on Ben, turn to face Reggie, and then stumble backwards. Ben swiped at him but missed, and Garza began running across the bridge connecting the pier and second ring to the main central ring.

I should go after him, Reggie thought. *He's the reason we're here.*

But a third thing happened as well. Crawford and Julie both turned to look at him. Crawford was smiling, an eerie grin that felt completely out of place. It threw him off, and he faltered.

Crawford was quick, especially considering the bullet wound in his shoulder. He grabbed Julie from behind, then pushed her out and over the water, holding onto her neck.

It seemed impossible, a man as physically average as Crawford, to be able to hold the woman out and over the edge without leaning or anchoring himself on something.

Ben rushed over.

"*Don't*, Harvey," Crawford said. His voice was a growl. "Take a step back."

Ben did.

"Reggie, go ahead and put that weapon down."

Reggie considered it. He could make the shot with just about anything other than the small subcompact, but there wasn't enough accuracy in the weapon, and he hadn't had enough practice with it, for him to feel comfortable from this distance. A shot wide to the left would strike Julie, and a shot that strayed too far right could hit Ben.

He put the gun down.

"Now," Crawford said. "Garza is on his way to get his men. They will return, and they will kill you."

Reggie sneered.

"I've given them the *order* to kill you all, and they're quite good at following orders. So we have less than a minute, I would guess, before he tells his men that you and Dr. Lindgren are up here with the rest of us."

"What's the point, Crawford?"

"The *point* is that you all could have been part of something grand — a vision for the future that the board and I have developed over the course of years. Something the world has never seen."

"Growing back human limbs?" Reggie asked. "You're years away from production. There's nothing here but torture chambers and tanks full of your little science experiments."

Crawford seemed offended, but he recovered and smiled once again. Then, reaching out with his other hand, he unbuttoned the shirtsleeve on the arm that was holding Julie and pulled it up.

Reggie couldn't help himself. He took a step forward, trying to get a better view.

The arm was gray, oddly bulbous and strange-looking. The hand around Julie's neck seemed normal, but the arm itself looked like something that had washed up on a beach after months of floating dead at sea.

"What the…"

"That's right," Crawford said. "I was patient 31-0. The same medication that has been helping those subjects down in the lab maintain their emotionless state has been coursing through my veins for weeks now."

Crawford looked at his arm, examining it like a coroner would examine a cadaver. Clinical, emotionless.

"You — you're one of them?" Dr. Lindgren asked.

"Let Julie go," Reggie said.

Crawford ignored Reggie.

"The picture in your office," Ben muttered. "It was you."

"I had my arm amputated at age eight," he said. "It's the reason I founded *OceanTech*. *Paradisum* has always been a dream of mine. I truly wanted to build something spectacular; a modern-day Disney. A medical breakthrough that would change the world."

"Disney didn't kidnap tribes of natives and rip their arms off," Reggie said.

"Greatness comes at a cost, Gareth."

Suddenly Julie pulled herself upward, using Crawford's arm as a support. She twisted and threw her legs over and around the man's head, pulling him down to his knees. She maintained the fluid motion, ending up on the ground behind him, his own arm pulled tight to his chest as she held it.

It was a brilliantly executed move, one he had taught her, and Reggie was both proud and surprised.

She jumped backwards, pushing herself away from the man. Crawford struggled to get up, but one of his legs rolled off the edge of the pier and fell into the water. He reacted quickly and the crocodiles missed him by inches.

Reggie sprang into action. Crawford was laying on the pier, face-down, about to push himself up. Julie was safely away from the action, and Ben was out of range.

He fired two shots, both into the man's back.

Crawford coughed, blood spilling from his mouth, then he rolled over onto his back. His breathing was staggered, uneven. He had a fury and confusion in his eyes as he stared up at Reggie.

"I — I can't... it wasn't done," he finally said. "*I* wasn't done."

The CSO team, plus Dr. Sarah Lindgren, gathered around the dying man.

"You *are* done," Reggie said. "All of this is done. Everything here will be gone. We will make sure of it."

A bullet zinged past, impacting in a cloud of white dust with the concrete pier. The sound of two more gunshots followed, both rounds landing in the water nearby.

"Time to go, Reggie," Ben said. "Finish this."

Reggie nodded once, then fired a final shot. He lifted the weapon up and aimed it at the group of advancing Ravenshadow men making their way toward them over the bridge.

Too far for an accurate shot from either side.

And he knew they needed to keep it that way.

The sound of the helicopter made it to the forefront of Reggie's mind, and he looked over his shoulder. It was there on the helipad, waiting. A line of three people was running toward it, covering their heads.

I guess they know about the fighting, he thought.

Another sound reached his ears. Motors, higher-pitched than the chopper, and closer.

Boats.

He saw three of them arcing out around the waters between the central and second rings, appearing from somewhere on the other side of the hotel. He knew it was Ravenshadow, as the men on each were armed, all but the drivers staring down their sights at them.

A door opened at the base of the hotel, the spot they'd entered only a day before. Two huge palm trees floated up on either side of the doors, a thatch-roofed bar standing sentinel right next to the doors.

A six-man team of Ravenshadow men spilled out from the doors. *Time to go.*

It was a straight shot to the helicopter, but it would be a tight fit inside. He wasn't sure if the chopper would have enough fuel to power through having all of them aboard, but it didn't matter now.

Ben saw it, too. "To the helicopter!" he yelled, running with Julie's hand in his.

Reggie waited for him to pass, then pushed Sarah along behind them. "Get inside! I'll cover you from here as best I can!"

The group ran back over the pier, toward the advancing teams of men and boats, then took a hard left toward the bridge that connected the second and third rings. They ran full-tilt over the bridge, aiming for the spot where the helicopter was loading the last of the group of investors and park guests inside.

Reggie turned and fired at one of the boats, which had pulled up alongside the bridge just inside the second ring. He missed, but it bought them a few extra seconds as the soldiers all ducked for cover.

Julie reached the chopper first, nearly diving inside. The chopper lifted off, but she began yelling something Reggie couldn't hear. Ben made it, then Sarah. He caught a glimpse of one of the investors inside, a fat man wearing a suit, a shocked expression on his face.

He ran harder, ignoring the onslaught from behind him at the moment. He dove at the chopper's skid, grabbed it with one hand, and felt the aircraft lifting up from the pad. His feet left the ground, and Ben and Julie reached out to help him aboard.

Bullets pinged at the paneling around him. *They're* seriously *firing at us?* he thought. Either they didn't realized the chopper was filled with innocent civilians, or — more likely — The Hawk had ordered the attack.

He pulled himself up and into the belly of the chopper, then climbed over people to get to the pilot. He was alone in the cockpit, and Reggie could tell he was struggling with the controls.

"They're shooting at us!" the pilot yelled.

"They're shooting at *me*," he said. "Just get up as fast as we can, and get us out of range."

The pilot nodded, but Reggie could see him checking the instrument panel. "We're over capacity," he yelled. "Not sure we can make it to —"

"Just get us *up*," Reggie said. "Then land on whatever can hold us. Forget about getting all the way to your destination."

The pilot nodded again, then muttered something under his breath.

He turned to the group of scared investors sitting in the chopper's cabin seats facing each other in two rows, his own team scattered about on the floor between their legs.

Julie's eyes were closed and she was leaning on Ben's knees. He caught Sarah's gaze. She was smiling at him, breathing heavily.

He turned to the fat man he had nearly stepped on when entering the helicopter. The man looked beyond angry.

"You want to tell me what this is about?" he barked. It was nearly impossible to hear him over the sound of the straining chopper.

"Not really," Reggie said. "But I do know that your investment here isn't going to pan out."

He squeezed into the space between the fat man's gut and the woman in the chair next to him. Her face was white with fear, but she moved over a few inches to allow him more room. It was uncomfortable, too tight and he could feel the man's fat leeching out of his own space and into Reggie's, and it was hot.

But we aren't getting shot at, he realized.

He leaned his head back against the hard, metal wall panel that separated the cockpit from the cabin, and fell asleep, smiling.

CHAPTER 59

THE FLIGHT to the Bahamas was a smooth, half-hour flight. Most of it was uneventful, with the exception of when the pilot ordered them to discard the civilians' luggage into the sea. The fat man and another man in the group of investors rose to argue, but Reggie's subcompact machine gun and Ben's glare sat them right back down.

Finally under the weight limit, the pilot was able to get them moving well. They landed at Grand Bahamas' West End Airport, right on the tarmac of the single runway, as there was no helicopter pad. The small cluster of five buildings, surrounded on all sides by palm trees, was the entirety of the 'airport.' A lone employee ran out to greet them, surprised by their sudden appearance on his runway although the pilot had attempted to hail his UNICOM frequency numerous times.

Reggie jumped out first, offered help to the investors, and finally helped Ben, Julie, and Dr. Lindgren off the chopper.

He turned to greet the pilot and shake his hand as he exited the cockpit, and finally Reggie turned and followed the procession into the first of the buildings next to the runway.

There the employee offered them warm sodas and cold beer. There was a water jug upended in a pouring station in the small lobby, but it looked as though it had been there since the airport's facilities had been installed.

Reggie, Sarah, and Ben opted for a beer, and Julie grabbed a soda. The investors sat in folding chairs against the wall, Reggie's weapon still providing all the motivation they needed to stay in one place. Until he was sure they were innocent, he wasn't about to let them leave.

"What now?" Ben asked.

"We wait."

"For what?"

"For me," a voice said.

They turned, and Reggie saw the framed silhouette of a large body in the doorway. Tall and muscular, short-cropped hair, it could have been any Marine or Army grunt he'd served with.

But it was no Marine.

"Mrs. E," Reggie said. "Welcome."

"Glad I caught you," the woman said in her thick accent. She looked around the room, her eyes falling on each of the investors and glaring at them individually as if she had already decided they were guilty. "I was getting tired of sitting around working on my husband's research projects." She smiled, shaking each of their hands. Dr. Sarah Lindgren was introduced to their benefactor, one of the founding members and representatives of the CSO.

"You got here fast," Ben said. "You must have been nearby."

She nodded. "I have been in The Bahamas since yesterday, anticipating a retrieval operation, although I am glad to see you all made it out safely. We were monitoring the UNICOM and ATC channels. I heard your pilot trying to hail the West End airport, announcing a 'heavy load incoming.' Matched up the coordinates and decided it was impossible for a chopper to make it that far from the mainland. It had to be you."

"And it was. Thanks for coming, E," Reggie said. "What's going to happen to *Paradisum?* And *Ocean Tech?*"

"We are preparing a statement that will be delivered to the United Nations, as well as all countries the company has a footprint in. Four in total that we have found, though I suspect there are many more. I am sure these people behind you will be more than happy to help with that. And *Paradisum* is in the process of being requisitioned by the Bahamian authorities, and some US Coast Guard personnel will be there by tomorrow morning to clear out any remaining staff and escort the Ravenshadow teams from the premises."

"If they're even still there," Reggie muttered.

"We predict that they will be long gone." Mrs. E sighed. "You might be giving yourself a tough time, Gareth, in that you failed to bring in Vicente Garza, but your team succeeded in discovering a major medical and pharmaceutical coverup. That will not go unnoticed."

Reggie hung his head. "Still — I feel like we were too late. Make a note that there is a group of people, captives, on the lower level beneath the second ring of *Paradisum.* They'll need to be treated and examined, but I want to know that they'll get back to wherever they came from, safely."

She nodded. "Of course. And Mr. E is interested in debriefing as soon as you are ready."

Reggie sighed. "Right. I figured he would be. Listen, E, we could use some shut-eye." He held up his half-empty beer. "And about four more of these."

She smiled. "I told him the debrief would take place no earlier than tomorrow, but only on one condition.

Reggie raised an eyebrow. "Yeah?"

"I told him you would need a week here afterward to rest and catch up. All expenses paid, courtesy of the Civilian Special Operations."

"And?"

"He agreed. He is working on your accommodations as we speak."

"Great," Reggie said. "I can stand a few more days in The Bahamas, I guess."

He looked over at Ben and Julie. Ben's arm was over his fiancee's shoulder, and she was leaning heavily on him. He stood straight, completely stoic and silent.

"I'm sure they could use a vacation from their vacation, as well," he added.

Ben nodded, and Julie smiled.

"My husband has a room for you two," she said. "And one for you, Gareth. Two rooms total, but we can make it three if you would like. We were not sure if you would be staying or not, Dr. Lindgren. But we are happy to extend our offer to you as well."

She grinned, then winked at Reggie. "I'd be happy to stay. But two rooms is fine."

The greatest mystery of all time is about to be solved...
And it's going to kill a lot of people.

The grand opening of a new exhibit in a museum in Athens garners attention from the elites of high society. It's an elegant affair — and no expense is spared. But the night quickly devolves into disaster and terror.

Click here to read the next in the bestselling *Harvey Bennett Thrillers* series, *The Atlantean Artifact.*

AFTERWORD

If you liked this book (or even if you hated it...) write a review or rate it. You might not think it makes a difference, but it does.

Besides *actual* currency (money), the currency of today's writing world is *reviews*. Reviews, good or bad, tell other people that an author is worth reading.

As an "indie" author, I need all the help I can get. I'm hoping that since you made it this far into my book, you have some sort of opinion on it.

Would you mind sharing that opinion? It only takes a second.

Nick Thacker

ABOUT THE AUTHOR

Nick Thacker is a thriller author from Texas who lives in Hawaii. In his free time, he enjoys reading in a hammock on the beach, skiing, drinking whiskey, and hanging out with his beautiful wife, two dogs, and two daughters.

For more information and a list of Nick's other work, visit Nick online:
www.nickthacker.com

 facebook.com/AuthorNickThacker
 twitter.com/NickThacker
 instagram.com/TheNickThacker

BOOKS BY NICK THACKER

Jake Parker Thrillers

Containment (Book 1)

The Patriot (Book 2)

False Allegiance (Book 3)

Six Assassins Thrillers

Primary Target (Book 1)

Subtle Target (Book 2)

Unstable Target (Book 3)

Captive Target (Book 4)

Vendetta Target (Book 5)

Final Target (Book 6)

Mason Dixon Thrillers

Mark for Blood (Book 1)

Death Mark (Book 2)

Mark My Words (Book 3)

Harvey Bennett Mysteries

The Enigma Strain (Book 1)

The Amazon Code (Book 2)

The Ice Chasm (Book 3)

The Jefferson Legacy (Book 4)

The Paradise Key (Book 5)

The Atlantean Artifact (Book 6)

The Book of Bones (Book 7)

The Cain Conspiracy (Book 8)

The Mendel Paradox (Book 9)

The Minoan Manifest (Book 10)

The Napoleon Job (Book 11)

Harvey Bennett Mysteries - Books 1-3

Harvey Bennett Mysteries - Books 4-6

Harvey Bennett Mysteries - Books 7-9

Jo Bennett Mysteries

Temple of the Snake (written with David Berens)

Tomb of the Queen (written with Kristi Belcamino)

Harvey Bennett Prequels

The Icarus Effect (written with MP MacDougall)

The Severed Pines (written with Jim Heskett)

The Lethal Bones (written with Jim Heskett)

Gareth Red Thrillers

Seeing Red

Chasing Red (written with Kevin Ikenberry)

The Lucid

The Lucid: Episode One (written with Kevin Tumlinson)

The Lucid: Episode Two (written with Kevin Tumlinson)

The Lucid: Episode Three (written with Kevin Tumlinson

Standalone Thrillers

The Atlantis Stone

The Depths

Relics: A Post-Apocalyptic Technothriller

Killer Thrillers (3-Book Box Set)

Short Stories

I, Sergeant

Instinct

The Gray Picture of Dorian

Uncanny Divide (written with Kevin Tumlinson and Will Flora)